MOURNING WOOD

USA TODAY BESTSELLING AUTHOR
HEATHER M. ORGERON

Mourning Wood
Copyright © 2021 by Heather M. Orgeron

All rights reserved. Without limiting the rights under copyright reserved above, no part of this publication may be reproduced, stored in or introduced into retrieval system, or transmitted, in any form, or by any means (electronic, mechanical, photocopying, recording, or otherwise) without the prior written permission of both the copyright owner and the above publisher of this book.

This is a work of fiction. Names, characters, places, brands, media, and incidents are either the products of the author's imagination or are used fictitiously. The author acknowledges the trademarked status and trademark owners of various products referenced in this work of fiction, which have been used without permission. The publication/use of these trademarks is not authorized, associated with, or sponsored by the trademark owners.

Photographer Michelle Lancaster
Model Mason Kreidt
Designer Kate Farlow with Y'all that graphic
Formatting by Champagne Book Design
Editor Kiezha Ferrell

For Erin.
Thank you for humoring an old friend.
Your assistance was invaluable.

MOURNING WOOD

CHAPTER ONE

Whitney

I'M JAMMING OUT TO SOME OLD SCHOOL 90S R&B WHILE painting the final touch of rose onto Mrs. Thibodaux's lips when Prissy barges into the prep room, her mouth running a mile a minute—the way it tends to when she's overexcited.

My little girl drops her black Jansport bag near the door before dragging a stool over to the table and climbing up beside me. The metal screeches as it scrapes along the cement, making my shoulders tense and my teeth clench tight. "Before you look in my folder," she announces, reaching to brush an errant strand of hair from the cheek of the old woman, "lemme tell you what happened."

Oh, Lord. Here we go… "Well hello there, daughter of mine." I plant a kiss to the apple of her cheek, noting the actual rat's nest that sits atop her own head. I swear she's presentable when she leaves the house. What happens after that is beyond me. "I can't wait to hear what havoc you've wreaked on your fellow first-graders today."

She gives me a heavy dose of side eye. "It wasn't me. It was Jenny Boudreaux." Her lips pucker like the poor girl's name tastes sour on her tongue.

I nod. *Of course, it was.*

"Which one?" I hold the pallet of nude eye shadows out for her to choose.

She points to the one in the middle—beige with a hint of gold. "That one." Her blue eyes wander to the outfit hanging from the hook across the room. "It'll look nice with her dress."

She's right. The gold will be gorgeous paired with the deep plum hue. My little girl possesses all the attributes to make a great mortician someday. Her attention to detail is astonishing for a six-year-old, and her comfort around the deceased is borderline scary, but crucial in our line of work.

After coating the brush with color, I urge her on. "Well, what did Jenny do to make *you* move *your* clip?"

"Can you believe she asked me who's funeral I was going to?" Her little finger points straight up and wags as she cocks her head. "Just because I was wearing my black pants and my new boots." Which also happen to be black, and of the combat variety—along with her charcoal T-shirt and black leather jacket.

Long gone are the days when I could dress her up in pinks, lavenders, and ruffles… I miss it.

"Uh-huh." I lean in closer to the body to get a good look, making sure the application is even on both eyes. "And what did you say?"

"I said"—I have to bite down on my lips to keep from laughing when her head whips side to side—"I don't *know* yet… and then I looked at her like this…" Her strawberry blonde brows dart toward the ceiling and she widens her eyes. "And then she sucked in some air really loud and I told her it might be a good idea to get her affairs in order."

"Priscilla Louise Daigle!"

"What?" Her little button nose scrunches, and it has nothing to do with the stench of formaldehyde lingering in the air.

"Dammit, child! You're gonna get yourself kicked outta that school before long."

She shrugs. "She's so dumb, Momma. Jenny didn't even know what that meant. Only Mrs. Bourque heard what I said, and she made me move my clip."

I'm gearing up for a nice long rant when the door once again flies open, nearly popping off its hinges—only this time the body filling the doorway is that of my mother. The sound of the metal knob slamming into the wall forewarns that she ain't happy. "They're gone!" she shrieks, grabbing two fists full of her auburn bob and tugging. "Just took the money and ran."

My heart starts beating double-time. The makeup falls from my hand, clanking against the metal tray. "Wh—who's gone?" I ask, afraid I already know the answer.

"Those con artists you hired to renovate the chapel!"

A bitter taste forms in my mouth. "Ma…I'm sure they just had something come up. I'll try to get in tou—"

"They. Are. Gone." Her tone is one that bodes no argument as she begins pacing back and forth in the small room.

"Oh, shit," Prissy hisses, wanting no part of the epic blowup about to ensue. "I'm going find Paw-Paw." She snatches up her school bag and runs out before I can swat her little bottom for cursing.

It's a good thing that our clients are mostly dead, because my family can be downright embarrassing. Oh, we can turn on the charm and professionalism when needed, but one look at this crazy clan behind the scenes would send our customers running for the hills.

Suddenly feeling lightheaded, I take the seat my child just vacated. "You're sure?"

"Cashed the check three days ago and they haven't been back since." Mom's hand goes to her chest, rising and falling with her labored breaths. "I tried Phillip's cell phone and it's no longer in service. Went by the hotel they was stayin' at and they're gone. Just gone, Whitney!"

"Fuck." I smooth a thumb over the vein pulsating in the center of my forehead.

"Fuck is right," the tiny, explosive woman shouts. "I knew. I knew that deal you struck with them people was just too damn good to be true. Now they done hauled off with our money and we got ourselves a mess, Whitney Jean. Just a big ol' mess!" She's gonna work herself into a coronary one of these days.

"I'll fix it," I promise, without a single clue how the hell I'll manage such a feat. "Don't worry."

"That's easy for you to say," she shouts back. "It's only our livelihoods at stake."

"Nothing about this is easy!" I counter, leaping to my feet. I'm a perfectionist by nature—having to admit I screwed up is about the hardest thing in the world for me, and she knows it. "Just give me a few minutes to figure out how to make this right before you start jumping down my throat."

She sends me a hard look as she heads back toward the door, muttering a string of profanity along the way before slamming it behind her.

With no clue where to even begin, I do what I always do and call my bestie, Kate. She's the most level-headed person in my life. Surely she'll know where to start.

"Hey," she answers on the second ring. The sound of my goddaughter Lucy babbling brings a brief smile to my face. "What's up, Morticia?"

"I fucked up." Vomit climbs in the back of my throat.

"Wait," she says, before hollering at her husband Beau

to lower the music. "Can you say that for me one more time? I thought I just heard you say—"

"Cut the shit." My voice cracks. "I'm in real trouble this time."

"I'm listenin,'" she drawls.

"Okay, so you know those guys I hired to redo the chapel a few weeks ago?"

"Uh-huh… The ones I warned you not to pay until the job was complete?" I hear her pass the baby off to her husband. "Those ones?"

"Yeah… *those ones.*"

"*Uh-huh.* What about 'em?"

I gulp hard. "They uh—they finished the demo a couple days ago, and I gave them the final payment."

"Made out to cash, right?" she inquires. Her condescending tone has me feeling even more ridiculous.

A lone tear trickles out from the corner of my eye, scorching a path of shame along my cheek. "They said it had to be cash for the cash price…so they didn't have to claim it on their taxes." *It sounded totally reasonable at the time.*

I can practically see the "I told ya so" fighting to escape her lips through the phone. "Well…what are you gonna do?"

"I don't know," I cry. "Why do you think I called you? It's a complete disaster. All the old woodwork is in pieces in the back yard. We only have the one tiny makeshift chapel set up in the smaller viewing area. This is gonna kill our business." I don't have to tell her that the upcoming holiday season is always our busiest. It's a sad reality that suicides and car accidents spike this time of year, and she's been in my life since kindergarten—long enough to know the ins and outs.

"Wait a second…" she muses, an idea already taking shape. Kate is a problem solver and has saved my ass more times than I can count. "You remember Beau's cousin, Wyatt?"

"From your wedding?" I ask—as if there's any way I could forget him fucking me up against a dumpster in an alley on Bourbon Street the night of her and Beau's joint bachelor/bachelorette party.

"Mmmhmm," she singsongs. "That's the one. Well, he's actually just moved to town and is lookin' to get his construction business started here. I bet he'd be willing to—"

"No," I blurt, cutting her off. "Absolutely not."

"Oh, come on, Whit, that was years ago. He probably doesn't even remember you."

"Good! And we're gonna keep it that way." My cheeks radiate enough heat to melt the makeup I just applied to poor Mrs. Thibodaux's face. I've been so careful not to introduce any of the guys I've hooked up with to my daughter. It's bad enough her father chose not to be a part of her life. She deserves better than a revolving door of men. The last thing I need is one lurking around for heaven knows how long.

"But—"

"No buts," I argue. "There has to be another solution."

Any other solution.

CHAPTER TWO

Wyatt

"Home sweet home, Rufus." I throw my old, beat-up Chevy into park beneath a limb of the sprawling oak that drapes over the front of the fixer-upper I snagged for a steal in Moss Pointe, Louisiana. The mature trees and property alone are well worth every penny I paid. This little slice of heaven was my present to myself two months ago, on my twenty-fifth birthday, when I finally gained access to the trust my parents set up before they died.

The eighty-pound puppy follows me out through the driver's side door, immediately popping a squat.

"You piss like a bitch," I grumble, shaking my head at the sight while hauling my luggage and essentials to the porch.

I laugh when I catch myself looking around to be sure no one is watching the shameful act. All that surrounds us are acres of unkempt land that'll keep me busy for months on end. Such a welcome change from the apartment life we left behind with my maternal grandparents in Dallas.

The spotted Dane looks up at me with his head cocked to one side. He's a good listener, even if he seldom understands a word I say.

"Come on."

Rufus is right on my ass as I ascend the drooping steps, leaning every bit of his weight against my thigh while I wiggle the key into the lock. We're welcomed by the musty scent of mildew and rot. "She doesn't look like much right now, boy, but her foundation is strong." I slap my palm against his ribs, giving his coat a nice rub. His back leg lifts, vibrating with delight. "They don't make cypress frames like this anymore."

His tail wags, slapping me behind the knee a few times.

After transferring my belongings inside, I head right to the sink to fill Rufus's water bowl. The sound of a vehicle approaching steals my attention. I move the yellowed curtain aside and peer through the window above the sink to find my cousin Beau's Jeep rumbling to a stop.

Dropping the water bowl on the worn linoleum, I hear, "Wyatt, my man!" Beau comes charging in and moves his briefcase to the other hand so he can hit me with an enthusiastic one-armed hug. The genuine smile splitting his face reaffirms that this was the right decision. "How was the drive?"

"Long." I yawn, stretching my arms up, my fingertips easily meeting with the low ceiling. "But it's good to be back."

I've spent every summer since the accident in Moss Pointe, bouncing between our Maw-Maw and Paw-Paw's house, God rest their souls, and Beau's parents'—Uncle Curtis and Aunt Sue.

To see the two of us together, him in his three-piece suit and short tapered cut and me in my worn jeans, dingy tee and my unruly hair that's always in need of a trim—well, you wouldn't imagine our fathers were brothers, or that despite our differences we could be as tight as we are. But even growing up hundreds of miles apart, in completely different states, we've managed to remain thick as thieves.

"How's your Mimi doing with all this?" he asks, referencing my big move to the country.

I roll my eyes. "Ten times worse than whatever you're imagining," I answer, smiling to myself at her theatrics. "You'd swear I was moving to another continent."

"Ah," he waves me off. "She loves you."

"I know it." I shut the door behind him to block out the chill. "Was just about to take a walk through and check out the furniture I had delivered last week." I motion with my head for him to follow.

Rufus needs no encouragement to join us. I'm forever tripping over the big galoot.

The rich brown leather sectional looks out of place, surrounded by scuffed wood floors and the wall of cracked bricks that's crumbling around the old fireplace. This living room is in desperate need of some TLC. But that's what I love about construction—where most would see nothing but headache, I see endless possibilities.

"Lotta work to do," Beau says, whistling as he runs a hand over the mantle. With a frown, he walks into my space and wipes the layer of dust he just picked up right across the front of my T-shirt. *Pretty boy.*

"Yup. Dig out your work boots. I'm gonna need all the manpower I can get."

He snorts. The mere suggestion that he owns anything besides loafers and brand-name tennis shoes is hilarious.

"I actually came by to talk to you about something." He's still grimacing as he peers into each of the doors, one after the other.

"Oh?" I peek my head into the master at the king-sized bed that's beckoning me, dying a little inside as I walk away.

"Yeah." He follows me back into the kitchen, taking a seat at the little wood breakfast table. "I know you're literally just pulling into town, but Kate's got a friend in a bit of a bind."

I retrieve two beers from the box on the top shelf of the ancient fridge, literally the only thing besides dog food I bothered to pick up on my way in. After sliding one over to Beau, I whip out the chair across from his and straddle it. "She need a date to Christmas dinner or something?"

He laughs. "Not that kinda bind. Do you ever stop thinking with your dick for even a few minutes?"

"Not if I can help it." I wink, popping the tab on my Bud Light. "What'cha got?"

"All right, so her friend hired this crew to update their family's chapel… She paid cash." His head shakes with disappointment. Pretty sure I already know where this is going. "They ran out on her halfway through the job."

I hiss. "That's tough…but what's it got to do with me?" I hope he doesn't think I'm about to restore a whole fucking church as a favor to his wife, no matter how much I like Kate.

"Well, the Daigles are a pretty influential family in this town. It would be a great contract to land for your first local project." He drums his fingers, worrying his lip between his teeth.

Contract. Now we're talkin'. My interest is piqued now that I know it's a *paid* job. "What's the catch?"

His victorious smile seems a little premature, taking into consideration I haven't agreed to anything yet. "I actually took the liberty of stopping by and hashing out the details with Hank, the owner."

What the hell? He better not have already volunteered me for anything. "You did what?"

"I didn't want anyone else snagging the position ahead of you." His blasé shrug proves he's not the least bit sorry.

"Oh yeah, I'm sure people are just lined up to take over a half-cocked job at some broke church."

Beau slings his briefcase up onto the table and opens it, completely disregarding my tirade. "This lays everything out in black and white." He slaps a stack of legal papers in front of me, open to the last page. "Basically, they'd need you to self-finance, allowing them to make monthly payments on the labor portion for two years. In exchange you could brand every pew with a metal plate with your information. Leave your business cards at the front desk. Stuff like that."

I take the paper, glancing over the terms. I don't bother with reading the whole thing. If Beau drew them up, I know they're legit.

"Look, this place gets tons of traffic," he urges. "It'll be a great jump start for your business here."

I nod, tapping the pen rapidly. It's not like I'm hurting for money. I still have a good chunk sitting in the bank. If it'll get my name out, and help a friend of Kate… "You know these people, right?" I quirk a brow. "Cuz I'm not looking to get chained to a bunch of whack jobs."

"Extremely well," he assures me. "Great people."

I take in the light bead of sweat on his forehead and slight shake in his voice. "Then why do I get the feeling there's something you're not telling me?"

He shrugs, popping the top on his beer and taking a long swig. "No clue. You know I'd never suggest anything that wasn't in your best interest."

I'm positive he's up to something, but I also know that if anyone on earth would be looking out for me and mine, it's this man right here. So, despite the niggling worry in the back of my mind, I throw caution to the wind, and sign on the dotted line.

It's not yet six in the morning when I roll to a stop at the address Beau scribbled down on a fast-food napkin for me before leaving in an Uber late last night. His drunken scrawl ain't easy to read.

I place a booted foot on the ground, shielding my eyes from the sun to make out the sign posted in front of the Victorian style mansion. *Daigle Family Funeral Services. Don't be caught dead any place else.*

I look back down at the napkin, comparing the address again 2222 Main Street. This is what the motherfucker was hiding. *It's a goddamn funeral home.*

Fuming, I wrench my phone from my back pocket. "You're an asshole," I growl before he has a chance to greet me.

His answering groan is one part dread, two parts laughter. "Mornin.'"

"Are you serious with this shit?" I slam the truck door harder than necessary. "This is a joke, right?"

"'Fraid no—"

After a series of garbled noises, the voice on the other end of the line changes to one a little more cheery and decidedly feminine. "Hey, Wyatt!" Kate pipes.

"I can't—" I start, my breathing escalating at the mere thought of spending my days surrounded by a bunch of dead people.

"You can," she counters. "Please? Please, please, please..." she drags that last one out for effect. "The Daigles are like family, and they really need the help. Plus, it'll be good for you too. Please say you'll do it... *for me?*"

I don't answer right away, too focused on the pit of dread unfurling throughout my chest. I don't think I *can* respond without losing my breakfast right here on the sidewalk.

"Anyway, you owe me for getting my husband piss drunk," she continues. "I had to wake up with your niece four times last night all on my own."

The bitter taste of bile fills my mouth. "I don't think you understand—"

"You listen to me, Wyatt Landry. You're being hired to put up walls and build fucking pews, not embalm bodies. You don't even have to see any dead people…unless you want to," she adds.

"I don't."

"Great. Then you won't. Don't be a pussy."

"Gotta go," I mumble when a vision in heels and a form-fitting black skirt walks out the front door. My cousin-in-law's still gabbing when I drop the phone unceremoniously through the passenger window onto the front seat.

"Mr. Landry?" the blonde Barbie calls, making her way down the cobblestone path, her hips swaying side to side with a confidence few women possess. It's incredibly sexy. As she approaches, her features become clear—ice blue eyes, pillowy lips, dimples for days… She extends a manicured hand in my direction. "I'm Whit—"

"Whitney," I rasp, before clearing the sudden frog from my throat. I can feel my own eyes practically bugging out of my head.

Talk about a blast from the past.

"Wyatt?" I swear I see flames shoot out of her eyes and smoke billowing from her ears. I'm scrambling to clear my head and think straight, because I can't recall having done anything deserving of such ire. "There's been a mistake," she blurts out, yanking her hand from mine. I swear I hear her mumble something about *murder* and *new best friend* beneath her breath. "I'm sorry. I was actually just coming out to tell you that the job has already been filled." With that she spins on her toes, fully intending to take off with a hasty retreat.

Before I think better of it, I reach for her wrist. "I don't think so."

What am I doing? Isn't this what I wanted…a chance to get out of this shady-ass deal?

"Excuse me?"

I retrieve the folded paperwork from my back pocket and hold out the fully executed document for her examination. It's already been signed by a Mr. Hank Daigle. Now, I don't know if he's her husband or father, but a quick glance at her left hand shows no ring, so I'm feeling pretty damn hopeful—and suddenly desperate for this job. My ego won't stand for being so easily dismissed—self-preservation be damned. "I've been contracted to restore the chapel. I'm sorry if that's awkward for you, but I'm a man of his word and have every intention to make good on my promise." I glance back down at the paper. "To…Hank."

"Awkward for me?" she asks, incredulous, closing the distance between us. "What about you? Pretty sure you were there too."

I don't even attempt to fight the crooked smile tugging at my lips. "And where might you be referring?"

Her blue eyes dart around the street. Dear God, she's beautiful when she's angry. I've only ever seen the woman tipsy and horny. And, well…embarrassed. She wouldn't even spare me a glance the day of the wedding, a brush-off that still stings, to this day. "You *know* where," she mutters.

"The dumpster?" I decide to just throw it out there—the elephant. I've never been one for beating around the bush.

"Shh," she hisses, balling her fists at her sides. I swear if she purses those little lips any tighter, she's gonna have smoker lines she'll never be able to get rid of. I almost tell her as much but decide I shouldn't poke the bear…not yet, anyway.

"Listen," I say, backtracking to try to smooth things over. "I had no idea that it was your family who owned this place, but I've already agreed to the job. For whatever reason, Beau and Kate went through a whole lotta trouble to make this happen. I'm sure their motivation wasn't entirely innocent, but from what I can see, you're not exactly drowning in options. I'm certain we can both be adult enough to put one night of hot se—"

"Stop!" she snaps, her slender index finger landing at my lips. "That's enough." Frazzled, she smooths down the front of her skirt and takes a step back. "I guess you can keep the job…just—" Her perky tits rise and fall with a deep breath, and I try not to stare. "Just don't bring up that…*situation*…ever again. Mmmkay?"

I shift myself, trying to hide the growing *situation* in my pants. "I'll do my best."

"What's that supposed to mean?"

"Just that my…*situation*…sometimes has a mind of its own." I shrug and try to look innocent.

Even she isn't able to resist a quick grin at my clever retort.

"Whatever," she sighs, sticking out her hand for a shake. "Try and behave yourself, yeah?"

An unexpected thrill jolts through me at the brief contact of her silky-smooth hand in mine. "Like I said," I rasp, already losing the battle, "I'll do my best."

CHAPTER THREE

Whitney

I GIVE MYSELF A FINAL ONCE-OVER, TOUCHING UP MY PALE pink lipstick and passing a brush through my long strawberry blonde locks before heading back downstairs. With an appointment in ten minutes I still need to prepare for, I have little choice but to come out of hiding.

I can do this. I can totally put my humiliation aside and work with this man, if it means saving my parents' business. And my own job. I really don't have a choice, seeing how I'm the one who put them in this predicament to begin with.

So what if he's hotter than sin?

Who cares that his syrupy drawl sends all of the blood in my body rushing to my lady bits?

I live right upstairs. I can sneak away for panty changes throughout the day as needed. Hell, I'll just stuff an extra pair into my front pocket right now to be safe.

Yup, I think to myself, running my hand along the oak

banister as I navigate the ornate staircase down to the business floor. *Whitney, girl—you've got this—*

"Hey, Whit!" Sin wrapped in a cotton tee and light wash denim greets me with a grin that sends me tripping over my own feet, right into his arms—his massive, masculine arms.

I so don't got this! My grip tightens around his bicep. Solid—not overly muscled. He isn't one of those gymheads, but an honest to goodness, hard-working virile male.

I take a deep inhale before removing myself from his hold. He smells of wood and leather, and my pheromones like it—a lot.

"I'm fine," I insist, righting myself. *Jesus, did it just get hot in here?*

He takes a step back, palms out. "Just trying to help."

"And I appreciate it," I snap tartly, fully aware that I'm sounding like a complete shrew but seemingly unable to help my reaction to this man—inward or outward.

"You look beautiful," he offers as he observes me fiddling with my clothes and hair in the framed mirror behind him.

"Don't." I even out my breathing to the best of my ability and fan my face to alleviate some of the flush from my cheeks.

"What have I done to offend you now?" he asks, still doing a shit job at hiding his amusement. "Was it that I dared to save you from falling on your ass? Or my complimenting the appearance you're fussing over needlessly?"

I shut my eyes and take a deep breath, swallowing some of my pride. "Why do you find this so funny?"

"Because it's been over two years and you're being ridiculous."

I grit my teeth. "What the hell does it matter how long it's been?" The memory is still as fresh as if it was yesterday. *The cool metal of the bin pressing into my back while he thrusts mercilessly...*

"Just let the memory play. Get it all out of your system, *mon chérie.*"

I stand up straighter. *Did he just call me his dear?* He has a lot of freaking nerve. Damn if I don't want to slap that cocky smirk off his ruggedly handsome face. To feel that scruff between my thi… No. No, Whitney. Stop this shit right now. "I don't want to talk about it; and just to be clear, I'm not *your* anything."

"I think we need to"—he brushes a lock of hair off my shoulder, his gentle fingers trailing along the nape of my neck—"clear the air."

A shiver reverberates through me, and I fight the urge to purr. I'm a mess…a wanton hussy.

"You're a beautiful woman, Whitney." His tongue darts out to wet his lips, and I find myself mimicking the act. "I won't lie and say I'm not crazy attracted to you, but I'm a professional. I'm here to do a job."

"As am I."

He nods, brushing a thumb over his lower lip. *Is every move this guy makes just naturally arousing, or is he screwing with me?* "No need to be ashamed of the chemistry lingering between us. We fucked." He shrugs. "It happens."

Definitely screwing with me.

He moves closer, but I'm too shocked to back away. "We were two consenting adults. It's not like I plan to maul you against a *casket.*"

Is that a shudder? A break in his confident demeanor? I shake out of my stupor enough to regain some of my wits. If he's going to play, then so can I.

"No?" I ask, running a hand over his chest. "Suddenly you have standards?"

He shrugs, playing it off, but I know what I saw just now.

A crack in his armor. I latch onto that weakness like my dignity depends on it. "I have respect for the dead."

"Just not for me?" I whisper, keeping my voice low and purposefully wobbly. *Way to be strong!*

He hangs his head. "Look, we were both drunk and horny, and while the location may not have been *ideal*—"

"It was a *dumpster*."

"You will never convince me you weren't thoroughly satisfied."

He's right. And that's a huge part of the problem. I'm ashamed of myself. Ashamed that I wasn't responsible enough to have learned from my past mistakes. That at the age of twenty I was still as reckless as the sixteen-year-old who let her hormones lead and wound up with a baby before finishing high school. *Not anymore.* I've grown a lot over the past two years. I will not be brought down so easily. "I just… I don't do things like that." *Anymore.* "I have a reputation…" *I'm still trying to restore.*

"And I'm not here to ruin it." He grips my chin in his thumb and forefinger, and I melt at his touch. I'm stunned by his audacity to—after so much time has passed—take such liberties with me. "What'd'ya say we start over? Pretend it never happened?"

"You can forget we *slept together?*" I shriek. "Just like that?" I snap my fingers.

What the hell is wrong with me? Now I'm appalled at the notion of being forgotten… I don't even recognize myself right now.

"Well, no… I'm just trying to help you get past this."

I snort. How very ladylike of me. I clap a hand over my mouth before hearing a distinctive grunt behind me.

No. No, no, no, no, no…

"Dad," I say brightly, as I turn around, pulling out the remains of my acting skills. Watching the color draining from

Wyatt's face is almost worth the sheer mortification I'm suffering at his mere presence. "What can I do for you?"

"I was coming by to tell you the Andersons are here to meet with you." His eyes bounce between the two of us. "In the main parlor."

"Well," I say, dipping from between the wall and the man my father's attention is now laser focused on. "I won't keep them waiting."

CHAPTER FOUR

Wyatt

Never have I ever wanted to disappear the way I want to right fucking now.

"Did I hear what I think I just heard?" The intimidating boar of a man rests his broad shoulder against the wall beneath the banister. Gone is the jovial guy I just spent over an hour chatting construction with—along with every ounce of oxygen from this room.

"Sir?" I ask, not wanting to volunteer any more than absolutely necessary. I have no clue how much he heard, and right now, I'm having a hard time even remembering exactly what was said.

Did someone turn the thermostat up?

"Don't play dumb with me, son. You just said you had relations with my daughter."

I roll my head shoulder to shoulder to alleviate the sudden strain while sweat beads my brow. "It was a few years ago." *Now*

would be a great time for the floor to split open and swallow me up.
"I—I'm real sorry."

Hank holds out a hand, silencing me. "Don't apologize. My daughter is of age to make her own decisions about who she allows into her life and her…her…" The big burly man is suddenly at a loss for words.

"Her *affairs?*" I offer.

He nods, his weight shifting uncomfortably. "Exactly."

"What happened between us won't affect the work I do for you," I assure him, my palms beginning to feel clammy.

"That's good, but I still got a few things to say. Wanna be sure we fully understand each other."

"Okay." I take a step away, which he follows with two forward. My back is literally against the wall. He's so close I can smell his breath. It takes all my effort not to pull a face.

"While she might be just another notch on your bedpost, Whitney is the love of my life."

I must be seeing things, because I swear the old man's eyes start to water.

"She's been hurt." He clears his throat, and it takes everything in me not to recoil from the spittle that lands on my cheek. "Let's just say, I wasn't a fan of it… Whatever you two do on your own time is between you and her and the Lord. But mark my words—the minute you make my baby girl cry, it'll become about you and me. Got it?"

"Yes, sir. I wo—"

"I'm not looking for empty promises." He finally backs a few paces away, allowing me to draw in a huge breath of clean air. "I saw the way you two looked at one another." He shakes his head as if an eventual fallout is imminent. "Just remember, you knock that girl up, it's a two-for-one deal."

"Huh?" It's probably the most immature response I could

come back with, but the only one I can seem to conjure at the moment.

"She didn't tell you about little Prissy, did she?" He shakes his head. "I'm not surprised. Got a six-year-old daughter, me and her momma been helpin' raise. That little girl's daddy ain't worth a shit." He mutters something nonsensical beneath his breath. "Look…just don't start nuthin' with my girls you ain't plannin' on finishin', and we'll get along fine."

"No sir," I answer, not having the slightest clue how the mention of one little hookup evolved into a lecture on relationships and children. But I'm not a dad, and I haven't had one since I was four years old. So, while the man scares the shit out of me, it's also heartwarming to witness him champion his daughter this way.

"All right then." He claps a hand on my shoulder and squeezes affectionately. "I got a body to take care of… I'll see you in the chapel tomorrow morning at seven." And just like that, he's back to smiling and agreeable.

"I'll be here."

I wait for him to disappear down the hall before I start for the door. A little wad of black fabric on the floor of the last step catches my eye.

"Well, that isn't safe," I mutter to no one at all, nudging it with my boot. *Hmmm*. What have we here?

Panties.

Whitney must've dropped them when she tripped.

Why the heck was she carrying around lingerie?

Ever curious, I scoop them up and head in the direction of her office.

My timing could not be more perfect; I arrive just in time to see her walking out the elderly couple she was meeting with.

She waits until the door shuts behind them to give me her

attention. "Well, you're still standing." Her eyes make a slow perusal of my form. "That's good." She shrugs. "Or bad, depending who's asking."

I wave a hand through the air as if it was no big thing. Like I wasn't just practically shitting my drawers. "Went well," I lie. "He gives us his blessing."

Her cocky smile slowly morphs into a scowl. "His what?"

"Relax," I say slipping past her into the office. "Don't get your *panties* in a wad. I'm just fucking with you."

With a loud huff she follows me inside, kicking the door shut behind her. "You don't know shit about my panties."

Swear to all that is holy, I couldn't have planned for a better opening if I'd tried. "Oh, I know a little."

"A lot can change in two years, Wyatt, including a woman's taste in lingerie…" She looks at me pointedly. "Also in men."

Ouch.

I punch a hand to my chest, recoiling dramatically from the blow before reaching into my pocket to retrieve the scrap of fabric that's burning a hole in my thigh. With deliberate slowness, I shake them loose then drape the skimpy elastic over the tip of my index finger.

Her mouth falls open. "Where did you—?" She pats the front of her skirt, feeling for the lump that's no longer there. Just as I suspected…*definitely hers.*

"Black," I say, beginning to tick off all the things I just so happen to know about her lingerie of choice. I give my finger a twitch, so they sway just slightly. "Lace." I nod my approval. "Thongs."

"Give me those!" Red-faced, she practically jumps at me, trying to snatch them away, but at 6'3, I'm much taller, and easily lift them out of her reach before balling them up in my fist and stuffing them back into my own pocket.

"Come get them." I lift my arms, folding them behind my head to give her clear access.

She blows out a long breath. "You that desperate to have a girl touch your junk?"

"Just desperate for one."

"One touch?"

"One *girl*," I tease, giving her a solid eye fucking.

Her hands rest at her hips, and she taps one heeled foot while giving me her best momma stare. "You're hilarious," she says, rolling her eyes. "Just give me my underwear."

"Finders keepers."

"What happened to being professional? Gave up on that fast, didn't you?"

I shrug, thoroughly enjoying seeing her so flustered. "I don't officially start the job until tomorrow."

"You make a habit of stealing girl's panties?"

"Do you make a habit of walking around with thongs in your pocket?"

I didn't think it was possible, but the red in her cheeks deepens.

"Tell you what… you explain to me why you're carrying these around in your pocket, and I'll give them to you."

She chews the inside of her cheek, clearly cooking up a response. "Not that it's any of your business, but I'm on my period. They're emergency backups."

"Nice try."

She throws her hands out. "What?"

"You think just because I'm a guy that I don't know about 'period panties?' These sexy little thongs ain't no period panties." I run my lower lip through my teeth while slowly roving my eyes over her form. "Try again."

She growls. "Incontinence."

"In—*what?*"

If looks could kill, I'd be vapor. "I have weak bladder control, okay?" she mutters, looking adorably embarrassed at her knee-jerk response.

That does it. I'm shaking with laughter.

"You're making fun of me? Seriously? What are you, like five?"

"Not five, but not an idiot either."

"'Scuse me?"

"Not buying it." I move toward the door. "Think I'll hold on to these for a while longer. If you're willing to lie and say you carry around extra panties in case you *tee-tee* on yourself… the real reason will be worth the wait."

CHAPTER FIVE

Whitney

"YOU ARE DEAD TO ME," I GROWL, STORMING through the back door of my former best friend's house without knocking, Priscilla in tow.

"You're welcome, you ungrateful twit." She doesn't skip a beat—just continues scraping the skin off a huge russet potato into the trash, all the while looking like she belongs in a freaking magazine.

Kate Landry brings to life the term *domestic goddess*. I don't know another housewife who gets up every morning and curls her hair and puts on a full face of makeup just to chase a baby around all day. But you can rest assured, without fail, the girl is always put together. She says the least she can do is give her man something to look forward to coming home to at the end of the workday.

She *says* it's for him, but I know it makes her feel better about herself, and there's certainly nothing wrong with that.

"Pissy he-ya. Pissy he-ya," my goddaughter chimes, wobble-running on those stubby little tree trunks of hers.

My daughter grips two fists full of my blouse and presses herself against my back trying to hide from the tot.

"Hey there, Lulu muffin." I scoop her up, smothering her chunky cheeks with kisses while she wriggles around trying to free herself from my hold. "One day you're gonna realize how awesome Nanny-Whit is," I tease setting her to her feet.

"Thanks a lot, Mom," Prissy groans when I move aside, letting the toddler attack. "Luciferrrr!" she growls, wiping a dollop of drool from her lips. "You're so disgusting."

Kate and I share a laugh when Prissy takes off sprinting down the hall with Lucy toddling behind.

"Now, where were we?" the smug brunette inquires, drying her hands off on the front of her apron. Yes, an *apron*. "Ah, yes, you were about to thank me profusely for saving your ass." She cups a hand around her ear. "Come on…don't keep me waiting."

"How could you do this to me?" Just speaking of the man in question has my heart racing out of control and heat pooling between my legs.

"He's a good man." She grabs a stock pot from the cabinet, fills it with water, and sets it on the stove. "You're just embarrassed and taking it out on the poor guy."

She's probably right. She usually is, but I don't even care because having him in my space is stressing me out! "I can't work under these conditions."

"What conditions, exactly?"

I start pacing the kitchen, worrying my fingers. "Well, for starters, I can't look at him without turning into a fucking tomato… Also, my father heard us talking about the dumpster." I make air quotes around that last word to sum up all the details of a night I wish like hell I could forget.

Kate spit laughs. "Shut up." She dumps the bowl of peeled potatoes into the boiling water before lifting the lid on the gumbo pot and giving it a good stir. "I was only kidding…" she says when I clamp my lips together. "Tell me more."

"I'm so glad you're enjoying this."

"Mmmhmm," she nods, taking a swig from her bottle of water before rotating her hand in circles toward me. "Go on…"

"He stole my panties!" I hiss.

"Hey now!" Her big brown eyes widen like saucers. "How, pray tell, did he get his hands on your underwear?"

"They fell out of my pocket."

She stares after me, waiting for more.

"Just forget it. It's not even important. What *is* important is that it's only his first freaking day and he's already ruining my life."

"You say ruining," Kate singsongs, "but sounds to me like he's bringing some much-needed excitement to your mundane existence."

I halt my stride and gawk. "Why are we even friends?"

She winks. "Quit your bitchin' and make yourself useful. Put on a pot of rice, and let's get this potato salad finished. Gumbo's almost done."

My ire cools mildly while I busy myself with rinsing the grains until the water runs clear. Once it's clean, I fill it to the first line on my index finger the way my Granny taught me, add a splash of vinegar, sprinkle a little salt, and drop it in the cooker. As soon as I flip the toggle to cook, the back door opens and all hell breaks loose.

"Hey there, Roofy," Kate coos, slapping her hands on her thighs.

The biggest dog I've ever seen comes charging into the house, nearly knocking me on my ass for the second time today.

His incessant bark is deep and deafening. And don't even get me started on the drool hanging from his jowls.

"You got a dog?" I'm shouting, twirling in circles trying to dodge his wet nose that for some reason he's hell bent on getting up under my skirt.

"He's mine."

You've got to fucking be kidding me.

"Wyatt," I say, forcing a smile. "Didn't know you were coming," I add, my teeth clenched and eyes narrowed and homed in on Kate.

I shouldn't be surprised to learn that the wild beast belongs to him. Let's be honest, *this* rotten apple didn't fall very far from *that* tree.

"Down!" he yells at the mangy mutt. "Down, boy."

"A puppy!" my child squeals, rushing toward the gray and black-speckled brute. "You didn't tell me y'all got a dog," she says to Kate, giggling while he licks her from chin to forehead.

"He's mine," Wyatt offers again.

Prissy's brows dip inward. "And *who* are *you?*"

"Prissy, this is Mr. Wyatt… Paw-Paw just hired him today to clean up the mess Phillip and his crew made of the chapel."

Her eyes narrow as she sizes him up, still running her hands over the dog. "You better not piss my Maw-Maw off like those other guys," she warns.

"Prissy!" I shout, slapping a hand to my forehead.

"I have no intention of doing anything of the sort," he assures her, grinning ear to ear.

"Then we should get on just fine." She nods.

This is what happens when your parents treat their grandchild like a whole grown-ass adult whose opinion actually counts for anything: you get a frequent urge to crawl under the nearest piece of furniture.

"Why don't you take Rufus out into the back yard before your momma has a heart attack?" Kate suggests to my kiddo, ushering her through the door with Lucy and the giant dog not far behind. "And quit that cussin'. You get my baby talking like a sailor and I'll be the one tanning your hide!" she shouts.

"So, how was your first day?" Kate asks, after the commotion has died down—a lame attempt at breaking up what has become a painfully awkward silence.

"It was good," Wyatt says, beaming. "I think my new boss really likes me, and his secretary is fine as hell."

I gasp, ignoring his hooded gaze, and correct his erroneous assumption. "Funeral Director."

Kate smothers a laugh while he stares on in confusion.

I clarify. "I'm not a secretary. I'm the funeral director and makeup artist." I toss my hair, vexed at his minimalization of my extremely important position.

"My apologies," he says in an annoyingly sincere tone as he pulls out a stool behind the bar-height counter and straddles it. "So, you actually meet with the bereaved?"

"I do."

"That's awesome. I—I didn't realize…" He shakes his head to himself. "Sorry, that's got to be an extremely difficult job. I just thought because the Andersons weren't in any way upset…"

"Preplanning."

He nods, but I can tell he doesn't get it.

"We have a lot of people who come in to make their own arrangements ahead of time, so that when they die, it's something their children aren't left to deal with."

"Gotcha." He drums his fingers on the granite. "And you like…put makeup on dead bodies?"

"They don't bite," I assure him.

He visibly shivers. "That doesn't creep you out just a little?"

"Not a bit. It's an honor that their loved ones trust me to prepare them for their final gathering." A prideful smile stretches my cheeks. "Anyway, it's like my daddy always told me, 'It's not the dead folks you gotta watch out for…it's the living ones that'll getcha in trouble.'"

"Guess I never really thought of it like that."

Another agonizing silence descends upon us. And once again, it's Kate who breaks it. "Why don't you go find Beau in the man cave? He's out there watching Sports Center."

He tips his ball cap farewell, all but jumping at the chance to escape.

"What's his deal?" I ask when he's out of earshot.

"What do you mean?" Kate passes me a bowl of boiled eggs to peel and starts dicing up the potatoes.

"I don't know…he just seems really weirded out by death…I mean, more than most people."

My friend walks over, bringing her lips close to my ear. "Poor thing lost his whole family in a car accident when he was just four."

My heart squeezes, and chill bumps coat my skin as she continues.

"He's the only one who made it. Mom, Dad, and his baby sister…well, they weren't so lucky."

A hollow ache steals my breath as Wyatt Landry suddenly becomes *more*.

More than an old fling.

More than a test of my wills.

His time with Daigle Family Funeral Services just became more than a job, and he doesn't even know it yet. Because I've just decided to make it my mission to heal this broken man—to gift him with a whole new outlook on life and death.

Lucky, she says. Such an ironic word so often used to describe those left behind.

CHAPTER SIX

Wyatt

"Did you know one in every five work-related fatalities occurs in construction?"

I power off the circular saw and lift my safety goggles, once the blade comes to a stop. "Well, hello there. It's Prissy, right?" I ask, turning to greet the tyke.

She nods, letting her backpack fall to the floor.

Guess she's planning on hanging around a while.

"That's some awful big knowledge for someone so young."

"I'm little," she says, rolling her eyes. "Not stupid."

I choke on my saliva. "Noted."

She nods. "I'm gonna run this place someday. Paw-Paw said so. Cuz Momma…she's too squeamish to drain and embalm the corpses…but I'm not." She crosses her arms over her chest, standing tall and proud in her little combat boots. "I wanna do it all!"

"Oh, yeah?" I rock back on my heels from my crouched position, dropping to seat myself on the dusty plywood floor.

"It's so cool. I bet he'd let you come watch if you wanna. We're embalming Mr. Rick tonight after dinner…"

Jesus Christ. "I'll pass," I say, trying to hide the horror from my expression.

"It's okay. Not everyone has the balls for it."

What the— "You're something else, you know that?"

She grins, taking my observation for a compliment. "Thanks."

"Priscilla Louise," Hank calls with a dopey grin on his face—one that shows just how much he adores the little heathen. "You aren't out here bothering Mr. Wyatt while he's tryin' to work?"

"Who, me?" Her little hand flies to her chest. "Never! Just tellin' him to be careful. I'd hate to see him on the table one of these nights."

The little shit turns back in my direction and winks.

"Cute kid," I say, pushing my palms on the ground to get up to a standing position. "I'm glad you're here. I was about to come find you. Had an idea for those windows on the outer wall."

"I'm listenin'." He scrubs a hand over his clean-shaven chin.

"Well," I say, excited by the prospect, "What if we take them out? Replace them with some stained glass?"

His lips purse and he nods, but not in a permissive way, more like he's mulling it over. "I like it," he finally announces. "But you'll have to run it by the boss."

"Whitney?" I lose a little steam with the question, positive she'll shut the idea down for no other reason than my being the one to come up with it.

"He means me," the modern-day Wednesday Addams announces. "I just told you, he's groomin' me to run the place." Her head shakes. "Don't you listen?"

Of course, the six-year-old is in charge.

I look to the man who's signing my checks, waiting for his nod of approval before posing the question once again. "Well, what'd'ya say, Miss Priss?"

"Let's do it." She pumps her little fist into the air.

"Really?" Well, that was easy enough.

"As long as," she adds, "no biblical scenes are depicted."

"*Okay…*" I drawl, half shocked by the child's vocabulary. "I think we can make that happen."

"I mean, I got nothin' against Jesus and the Bible, being Catholic myself, but we get people from all walks of life, you know? Jews and even some atheists." She looks to her Paw-Paw for his consent.

"That's very nice of you to consider everyone's feelings, my girl. Paw's proud of ya."

She beams, obviously very pleased with his praise. "A funeral is not the time to have anyone feelin' judged or like they don't belong."

"All right then," Hank says, scruffing the top of Prissy's ponytail. "Abstract it is…now get your little tail upstairs with Maw-Maw and get that homework done. I'm gonna need my favorite assistant in a couple hours."

Once they've both departed, I decide to wrap up for the day and start fresh in the morning. I've just coiled the last of my extension cords when I hear a commotion on the other end of the wall I share with Whitney's office.

"What the hell are you talkin' about, Nelly?" an enraged old man shouts. "We agreed on side-by-side drawers, now yer just changin' shit up without discussin' it with me first?"

"It's *my* body, and therefore *my* choice," a woman snaps back.

"Mr. Neal," Whitney calls, her voice a soothing balm. "Why don't we just hear her out before working ourselves up for no good reason?"

He groans with such force that it vibrates the ear I have plastered to the unfinished drywall.

"Now, Mrs. Nelly…go on ahead and explain your wishes."

"Well, I'd love to if that old…*son of a gun* would just shut up for two damn minutes."

What's happening in that room puts any reality TV I've seen to shame. Forget following around the younger generation. Geriatric reality shows are the way of the future. This shit right here's an untapped goldmine.

"I need a damn cigarette," he growls.

"Well, as you both know, I've recently been diagnosed with bladder cancer. And while I'm doing the treatments and in all likelihood will be more than fine for a while yet, it just got me thinking that I could go first…and what I'd want should that happen."

"Damn it all to hell." The pain he's masking behind his sour demeaner is palpable—I feel the ache bone deep.

"You said you was gonna let me speak. For God's sake, stop being so dramatic… I ain't planning on going tomorrow. *Anyway…* in light of our new circumstances, I'd like to be cremated—"

"No way in hell I'm lettin' 'em burn you," he interjects.

"I'd like to be cremated," she says a little louder, "and placed in the most gaudy, ornate urn available."

"What about the second coming of Christ, Nell? How you gonna rise with no damn body?"

"I understand your concerns, Mr. Neal." There Whitney goes again, controlling the chaos with expert skill and the patience of a saint.

"Listen, priorities change when you're facing your own mortality, and that's just not my biggest concern at the moment."

"What could be more concerning than makin' sure you're right with the Lord?"

"I'm getting to it if you'll let me speak…"

"This is a buncha cockamamie bullshit, that's what it is." The sound of a chair screeching on tile has me jerking back with a start. I can just imagine him leaping to his feet and throwing it back in his frustration.

"My wish is to be placed dead center of the mantle…where his next lover will have to pick me up and dust me. My wish is not to be forgotten."

It's so quiet in that room you could hear a pin drop. I'm literally holding my breath.

"You're so stupid. God love ya, woman. There won't be nobody else. I'd end up carrying ya around with me, lookin' like a total fool the rest of my life. That's what'd happen."

"A man has needs, Neal. I ain't stupid enough to believe you won't be finding someone to soothe 'em."

"Hell woman, I got needs now you haven't tended in going on five years!"

"Let me take you to dinner," I say, startling Whitney clean out of her shoes when I approach just as she finishes locking up her office for the day.

"Uhh," she says, looking around. "You talkin' to me?"

"Don't see anyone else."

"Thanks, but I'll pass."

I brace a hand on the wall above her head, to keep her from running off. "Why not?"

She takes her time, worrying her lips like she's wrestling with some internal demons. "I just don't want to." Nothing about the energy she's giving off agrees with that statement.

I hang my head and give it a little shake. "You really were just using me?"

"What?" Her muffled laughter is almost as sexy as that smile she's fighting so hard to hide.

"For my body."

She gives my chest a little shove, moving me out of her way. "Have you lost your mind?"

"One date?" I press.

"Listen," she says, using the same tone she used with that irate man less than an hour ago, "it's not you."

"Ohh," I groan, grabbing at my chest. "And the hits just keep on coming."

"I have a daughter."

"I'm aware."

"I have responsibilities you wouldn't understand."

"It's one date. You don't even have to tell her if you don't want to."

"And one date'll turn into two and maybe even three. Then come the awkward glances."

"Pretty sure we've already mastered that part," I interrupt.

She sighs. "Eventually you'll get over the whole single mom gig and start seeing someone else, and break my child's heart in the process, because she already thinks you walk on water all thanks to that damn dog of yours."

"I don't see how her liking me is a bad thing. I mean, I would think that should be a requirement."

"It's a bad thing because I'm not going to give her even an inkling of hope to cling to that anything will happen between us."

"Fair enough." I can tell by the depth of her conviction that she believes every word of what she's saying, and I'm not about to pressure the woman. "See you tomorrow," I offer, retrieving my ballcap from my back pocket and slipping it on my head as I make for the door.

"Friends?" she calls after me.

"For now," I say, before shooting her a wink on my way out.

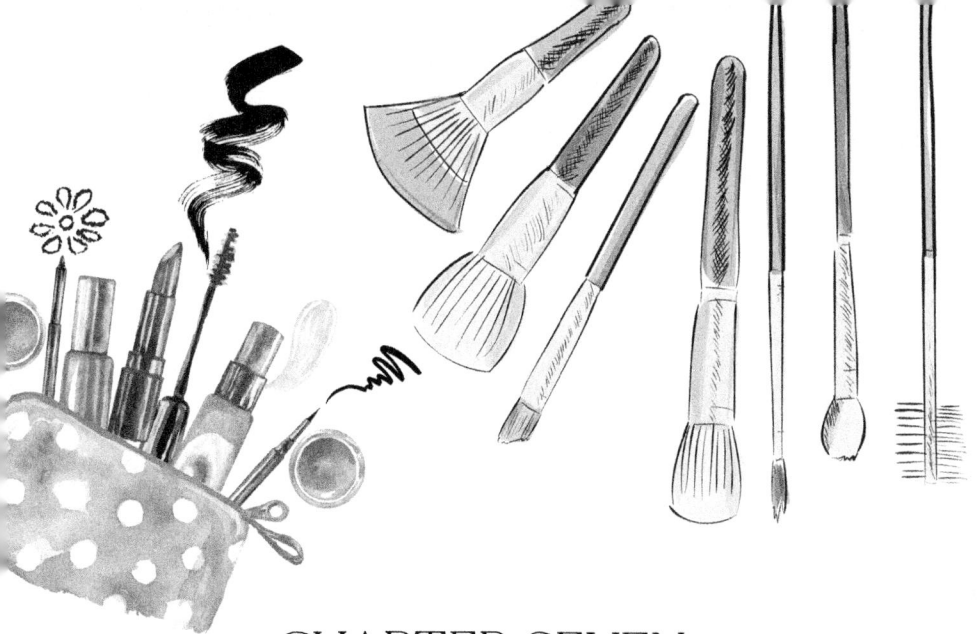

CHAPTER SEVEN

Whitney

With only a few days left until Thanksgiving, we're all running around like chickens with our heads cut off, trying to get things taken care of so we might be able to share a turkey day meal together.

Bodies are being embalmed, services held, and others planned around the holiday. There's still no guarantee we won't be interrupted by a death, but we do what we can to have what little normalcy we're able to manage around here. I don't think people outside this industry realize just how demanding it is. Unfortunately, death doesn't adhere to our schedules. We have to be ready at a moment's notice to go out and scoop up those bodies. There's no telling Betty she'll just have to throw a sheet over Bill till tomorrow, 'cause we're taking a day off. In our line of work, there's no such thing as a day off.

"Whit?" Momma peeks her head into my office, and just from her tone, I can tell something isn't right.

"Ma'am?"

"We got us a situation."

God bless my mother and her flair for the dramatics. I look up from the papers I'm sorting, giving her my full attention. "Well, what is it?"

"Got a body to pick up, and Rusty just called…said he done tested positive for the flu and won't be in all week."

Wonderful.

"Well, I'm meeting with poor Elly Joe in an hour to make arrangements for her Gramps…I can't go," I say, nibbling on the end of my pen. "What about Daddy?"

Her head shakes. "He's in the middle of an embalming."

It's times like these I wish we had another person on payroll, but we just can't justify the expense of more than one apprentice. We don't usually run into issues unless one of us falls ill—like right now. There's no way Momma can move a body on her own. She just isn't strong enough.

"You think, maybe…you might ask Wyatt to help out?" She flutters her lashes at me, gnawing on her thumbnail. If there was any doubt as to whether my father filled her in on our sordid past, there isn't anymore. That's the look of a meddlesome mother if I've ever seen it.

"I mean…*you* can ask him," I say, looking back down at my papers, but I can still feel her looming presence.

Annoyed, I jerk my head back up. "Something else?"

"Well," she says, plopping her butt down in the chair across from mine. *God help me.* "As the funeral director, making sure all the business is tended to really is your job…seeing how I'm retired and all."

My eyes bulge. I look around at all the work sitting on my desk and throw my hands out in her direction. "You serious right now, Momma?"

"Yeah." She sighs deeply. "I'm afraid I am." Her right leg

crosses over her left slowly and she leans back, making herself nice and comfy.

"Ugh," I groan, shoving back from my desk. "Sure, I'll just stop all what I'm working on to go ask the contractor to accompany you on a body removal."

"Atta girl," the irksome woman says, slapping her hands twice on the wooden arms of her chair. "Good luck."

It's an effort not to flip her off as I walk past while she's staring at me with that mischievous smirk of hers. Always up to no good, that one. She thinks she's playing matchmaker, and she needs to just stop and mind her own dang affairs.

The clomp of my heels seems to echo louder than usual as I make my way to the chapel. I can feel my heartbeat pounding in my ears. My nerves are at an all-time high, and not for the reasons my momma's thinking. She has no clue of his past—of just how much we're gonna be asking of this poor man.

"Wy—" My voice gets lodged in my throat when I round the corner to find him bent over a table saw, his white tee tucked haphazardly into his back pocket and little bits of sawdust stuck to his glistening back as he guides a plank of wood through the machine. It takes me a minute to regain my senses and knock on the open door. I don't know why I even bother. "Wyatt," I call, but he doesn't hear that either.

Carefully, I cross the room in my stilettos and yank the extension cord until it comes unplugged from the wall. *That* gets his attention.

He does a double take when he finds me standing there. I can't blame him seeing as I rarely make my way over to this end of the building. "Too loud?" he asks, swiping the sweat from his upper lip with the back of his hand.

"N—no. I—can I talk to you for a minute?"

"Sure," he answers, ripping his thick plastic goggles over his head. The little red indentation they leave around his eyes and over his nose are sickeningly adorable. "What's up?"

I bite my lip, trying to figure out the best way to pose the question. "Dammit," I growl. "This is hard."

Wyatt looks down at his crotch, pointedly. "Oh, that? That's barely a bump."

"Ugh," I groan, fighting back a smile. "I'm trying to be serious here!"

"Just spit it out. Whatever it is, can't be that bad."

I take a deep inhale and go for it. "We're kinda in a bind and were hoping you might be willing to help?"

He gulps down half a bottle of water before nodding. "Sure."

There's that word again. "Ummm, you might wanna hear the rest before you agree."

"Whitney, just ask me already."

"Okay, so…Rusty. Remember you met him last week?" Gosh has he really only been working here less than two weeks? It seems so much longer. Sexual tension has a way of transforming minutes to hours and hours to days. Days to weeks and weeks to years, and now I'm just stalling because I'm the worst person on earth for asking this man to do this. I know it, and I'm gonna ask anyway, and that makes me the worst of the worst. *Deplorable.*

"What about him?" Damn, but his smile is beautiful. Shame I'm about to wipe it clean off his face.

"Well, he's usually the one to accompany Momma on body retrievals, only he came down with the flu, and I have a meeting with a family and Daddy's in the middle of an embalming."

His answering laugh lacks its usual warmth. "You're lucky you're cute," he groans.

"So, you'll go?" I can't keep the surprise from my voice.

He takes his time, retrieving his shirt from his pocket and shaking off all the dust before pulling it over his head. "On one condition."

"Name it," I rush out.

"I was hoping you'd say that." He clucks his tongue. "I'll pick you up at seven."

"Huh?"

"I'm 'bout to go earn me a date," he says, grinning like the cat that ate the canary.

CHAPTER EIGHT

Wyatt

WHY ON EARTH DID I AGREE TO DO THIS?

I'm beginning to question my own sanity while I follow Mrs. Marie's instructions and pull around to the rear entrance of Moss Pointe Retirement Community.

"Just back the van up to those doors."

"You got it." A cool sweat breaks out over my forehead and the nape of my neck as I maneuver the white stalker van under the covered parking and the reality of what I'm doing here begins to sink in.

"I really appreciate you helping us out like this, Wyatt." Her smile conveys her gratitude while her eyes hold the sincerest of apologies.

"No problem." And it's not—so long as I ignore the fact that my esophagus is collapsing in on itself and I'm beginning to feel a bit woozy.

I meet up with her at the double doors at the rear of the van, where she's already sliding the gurney out of its slot. "Come with me," she says heading for the entrance. When the automatic doors slide open, I'm hit with the scent of antiseptic and coffee, a smell that triggers memories of late-night emergency room visits with Mimi and Pop as a child.

It's my first time in a retirement home, and I find myself stunned by how clinical of an environment it is. I guess I expected that since it serves as a residence, it would be a little homier—warm and inviting. This place is neither of those, although I'm sure my purpose for being here is clouding my judgment.

We're met inside by a few staff members who are obviously quite familiar with Marie Daigle. She talks in hushed tones with the head doctor while they lead us back to the patient's room. We're told he died peacefully in his sleep. The family has already come and said their goodbyes, and they've been instructed to contact the funeral home to make the arrangements. The body has been cleaned and prepared for transport.

"These are the easy ones. Sometimes," she whispers as she lowers the cot, positioning it beside the bed, "we have to bag 'em ourselves."

It takes me a second to realize she's referring to the dead body that's already nicely zipped for us. "Can't imagine that's very pleasant." I shudder at the thought.

"Oh, darlin', nothing about this profession ever is."

"Then why do you do it?" I ask, stationing myself at the foot of the bed while she takes the head.

"You know, oftentimes I ask myself that same question, and it always boils down to, if not us, who?" She shrugs her shoulders, and that's the end of that. "Make sure you get a good grip on his ankles, and when I count to three, we're gonna lift and move him over to the gurney."

Somehow, despite feeling like I'm going to hurl, I muster the wherewithal to follow her orders.

"You done good," she says, brushing a tuft of hair from in front of her face with the same hand she just used to move a dead body.

"Thanks," I rasp, internally cringing while rushing to the sink at the far end of the room. I rip my gloves off and fling them into the bin before scrubbing my skin raw.

"You had gloves on," she huffs, shaking her head while busying herself with fastening the straps. I'm amazed by how comfortable she seems—how this is all second nature to her, while I have never been more freaked out in my life.

"You 'bout done?"

"Almost," I say, passing my hand under the automatic sanitizer dispenser a few times and slathering it all the way up to my elbows.

Her eyes widen.

"I'm good," I say, waving my hands through the air to dry them off.

"You sure?" Marie chuckles. "Cuz there's a shower behind that door." She dips her head to the right. "I'll wait…"

How can she have a sense of humor at a time like this? "Let's just get this over with," I say, my voice flat. I'm too disturbed to even smile at her attempt to lighten the mood.

In what feels like slow motion we wheel him out the way we came, while I try desperately not to make eye contact with the patients lingering along our path. I can't help but assume they're all wondering how much longer until they're the ones under the sheet, making their final procession through these sterile halls.

Once outside, we hoist the cot up and slide it into the slot. When those twin doors slam shut, I fold in half, resting my hands on my knees and drawing in a few deep cleansing breaths.

I did it.

"That was a whole lot to put yourself through just for a date," Marie muses, patting me on the back.

"Ah," I say, shrugging my shoulders. "I'd have helped y'all out, regardless. I just saw my opening and took it."

"My Whitney-girl's a tough egg to crack…be patient. I promise, she's worth it." With that she leaves me to collect myself.

As soon as I start the van, Marie reaches for the radio dial, switching it off out of respect for our passenger. She's not so chatty on the ride back, I'd imagine for the same reason. There's a somber cloud that seems to have fallen over us—a quiet that's giving me way too much time to reflect on what just happened.

I'm so preoccupied that I hit a pothole straight on, giving us a good jolt. "Sorry."

"No worries," she replies, right as a loud *brrrt* fills the cab.

I side-eye the petite spitfire of a woman next to me, but I'm too much of a gentleman to comment on the fact that she just passed gas. Noticing my gaze, she sucks in her lips, trying not to laugh.

A polite *pardon you* is on the tip of my tongue, but then it happens again and, call me crazy, but I swear to the Lord it's coming from behind me.

I sneak another glance at the woman beside me, who's trying like heck not to burst into hysterics.

Maybe it was her? It had to have been. Surely the dead guy ain't back there lettin' 'em rip.

It's all I can do to keep a straight face once the stench reaches my nose. I try holding my breath, but the odor doesn't fade. I'm starting to think this sweet, Southern grandma might've gone off and shit herself.

I'm so focused on maintaining my composure that I drive

us right into another pothole—this one the size of a damn crater. And that's when I hear it, the groaning coming from behind my head.

"Holy fuck!" I shout, jerking the wheel to the right. "He's *alive*! Why? How?"

Before Marie can reply, I plow us right into a neat row of mailboxes.

CHAPTER NINE

Whitney

WYATT INSISTS ON PICKING ME UP AND DRIVING, not buying into my argument that it would save him time and hassle if I went in my own car and took myself home after dinner.

I think he knows I'm just trying to put an added barrier in place, and he's not having it. That boy is determined to get the most out of this sham of a date.

He rushes ahead of me to open my door and helps me up into the cab, every bit the gentleman. When he reaches across my body to fasten my seatbelt, my heart takes off at a canter. His attentiveness doesn't go unnoticed and neither does my attraction, if that cocky grin of his is anything to go by.

"Have I mentioned how beautiful you look tonight?" *Wow.* Isn't he just laying it on extra thick? The guy's a real charmer, I'll give him that.

I clear my throat, giving my head a little shake to break the heat in my gaze and do my best not to swoon when his hand brushes my thigh. "Three times now." Dear God, he smells heavenly. A mix of sandalwood and *yum*. "Thank you…*again*." My breathing is shallow, and my cheeks warm with want. I'm nothing but a ball of sensation, and if this is indicative of how the night'll go, I'm in bigger trouble than I originally thought.

"Don't mention it." Careful not to smash any limbs, he shuts my door before rushing around and climbing up into the driver's seat.

He looks so natural behind that wheel… a true country boy made to travel these wooded back roads. "I can't even picture you in the city," I say, staring at his profile.

He laughs. "I was a fish outta water, no doubt."

"But you lived here before, right?" My voice fades out, the uncertainty over whether I should even bring up his past fueling a bout of instant regret. "Kate told me…" I give an apologetic shrug. "The other night when we were at her house."

"Yeah," he says, casting a brief glance my way. "After the accident, I went to live with my mom's parents. There was no will or anything. They were just better suited financially to raise a kid." He pauses briefly, rubbing a hand over the back of his neck. "I owe them so much."

His love for the people who raised him comes shining through his every word. "I'm glad you had them to help you to deal with that loss." *Why can't I just shut up?* I promised the man a date, not a session with a grief counselor.

"It's fine," he says, sensing my reluctance to continue. "It all happened so long ago."

"I'm sorry. I just get chatty when I'm nervous." *Way to out yourself, idiot.* "I mean, not that you make me nervous, or anything…" Hot lava bubbles in my tummy.

"Of course not." He rolls his tongue over his lips, biting back a smile, and his grip tightens on the wheel, flexing and unflexing with manly pride. "How else are we gonna get to know one another?"

"Is that the goal here?" I ask, starting to backpedal. How could I allow myself to get sucked into his orbit so easily?

"Isn't it?" He grants me another brief look before turning his attention back to the winding road.

"I'm just here to repay a debt." I'm trying to keep it real, but one look at the disappointment on his face has me wishing I could take it back.

"Right," he says, his jaw suddenly tense. He doesn't say another word for the remainder of the short drive to Clotille's Riverside Restaurant.

I'm stewing in a mixture of relief and regret, sure I've just ruined the entire night, when we pull into the gravel lot. But I shouldn't be surprised to find that Wyatt is extremely forgiving—at least where jaded females such as myself are concerned.

"Get your fingers off that handle," he orders when I reach to open my own door. "My Mimi didn't raise no millennial."

His comment has me choking on a laugh. "What, no Fortnite and Tinder for you?"

He scoffs. "One of the benefits of being raised by old people who didn't know the first thing about *interwebs* and those *playboxes*." The way he mimics their language with such fondness is priceless.

"You'll be glad to know you're dodging a bullet here," I say, referring to myself.

"Why do you say that?" He takes my hand, helping me down from the cab.

Once standing, I rise up to my toes and lean in close, pressing my lips against his ear. "I might have had a YouTube channel in high school."

He gasps. "Say it ain't so."

"I'm not proud of it…it was a dark time in my life."

"You go through a goth phase or something?" He laces his fingers with mine, leading me up the wraparound porch of the quaint eatery.

"Quite the opposite." I chew the inside of my cheeks, hesitant to expose myself. "A cheerleader."

"Table for two under Wyatt Landry," he says to the hostess, who grabs two menus and instructs us to follow.

"That actually doesn't surprise me at all," he says, guiding me along the uneven floors with his hand at the small of my back.

"Really?"

"You look the type." He shrugs. "Gorgeous, leggy, blonde, with a bangin' body." He makes a show of looking me over head to foot. "I could see you on the arm of a quarterback, easily."

"Yeah, well, I'll never make that mistake again."

The hostess seats us at a table in the courtyard, leaving us with menus and a promise that our server will be with us shortly. It's a beautiful evening, nice clear skies granting us the perfect view of the stars that are just peeking out to make their nightly appearance. The temperature is perfect, too—cool enough that we aren't being eaten alive by mosquitos but not so cold we have to bundle up.

I stupidly think I won't have to elaborate on my earlier comment, but Wyatt doesn't skip a beat, picking up right where we left off.

"Bad experience?"

I groan, hoping to convey just how much I'm not wanting to have this particular conversation. "Prissy's father was the star running back of our rival team. We dated for a bit…until I popped up pregnant. The rest, as they say, is history."

"What a dick."

I shrug, trying not to dredge up old hurts. "He was a teenager, and a baby didn't exactly fit into his plans."

"So were you." He reaches across the table laying a comforting hand over mine. And although I know that I shouldn't, I let him. "I'm sorry you had to go through all of that on your own…" He shakes his head with a timid smile. "Fucking millennials, man. No sense of responsibility."

"I haven't really been on my own, though. My parents didn't bat an eye, just stepped in, and they've been by my side every step of the way."

"Your folks are good people."

I smile at his assessment. "I can only hope someday to be half as decent as they are."

I'm grateful for the interruption when our waitress finally arrives to take our orders, gulping down half the glass of water she sets in front of me without stopping for a breath.

We order two of their famous hurricanes to sip on while waiting for our food, making small talk about the weather and the house he purchased on the river. His passion for what he does is infectious. He's so animated when he speaks about the big plans he has for the renovations.

"I can't wait to see it all when it's completed," I say while scrolling through the before pictures on his phone, shocked by how much I mean it.

"I'll look forward to showing it to ya."

By the time the server delivers our meals, an easy friendship is already forming between us. I'm truly taken by how witty and intelligent he is.

Charming, sure, that I expected. I mean, he charmed the panties right off of me the night we met. But he's also fun and thoughtful and so much more. It's a shame we can't just erase the past and have a do-over. If it weren't for that unfortunate hookup,

I might be inclined to explore this crazy attraction… but who the hell starts their happily ever after with a quickie in a public alley? *Not this girl.*

I wait until we're a few drinks deep and almost done with our meals to bring up what went down earlier in the day. It's killed me to hold off this long. I've been itching to interrogate him since Mom filled me in.

"So, you actually thought my mom pooped her pants, huh?" I am snickering over my plate of shrimp alfredo, just imagining the way it all went down.

His face turns beet red. "I knew it wasn't me… I assumed there was only one other option."

"When a person dies, their muscles relax," I explain, sucking my tongue to my front teeth. "*All* the muscles."

"Disgusting."

"It's no bed of roses, that's for sure… Sometimes they leak so much that Daddy has to pack 'em with cotton."

His eyes get big and round. "Their butts?"

I nod. "Uh-huh."

His face starts to look a little green as he stares down at what's left of his ribeye smothered in crawfish etouffee.

"How 'bout a change in subject," I offer, starting to feel bad for ruining his dinner.

"I'm good," he assures me, pushing his plate away. "I'll just take the rest of this to go."

"Oh, come on, if you're gonna be hanging around the Daigles, you're gonna need a stronger stomach." I twirl my fork in my plate, loading it with pasta, and pop it into my mouth, before shielding my lips with a hand to speak. "Besides, we haven't even gotten to the part where you took out three mailboxes."

"Didn't say I was ready to go." He sets his utensils down, ready to indulge my antics. "You really should have warned me."

I finish chewing and swallow before shrugging a shoulder. "Didn't dawn on me. We're all so used to it."

"Well, next time you send a guy out to fetch a body, I suggest mentioning the deceased have a tendency to groan and gurgle." He outwardly cringes. "Pretty sure you're responsible for shaving ten years off my life."

"Oh, my God. I wish I could have been a fly on that windshield."

He dips his head into his hand, giving it a good shake. "I'm never gonna live this down, am I?"

"Not a chance."

We order another round of drinks and continue chatting. Wash, rinse, repeat, and before I know it, we're closing the place down.

I haven't laughed this hard in ages. It was totally worth having to suffer through a date with Mr. Hot Stuff over here to have a night of normalcy. To feel like an actual person—like a woman—not just a mom.

And by *suffer*, I'm being a total drama queen. I don't think a better view exists than Wyatt Landry in a baby blue button down, cuffed at the elbows, and thigh hugging blue jeans. And that smile of his. Good Lord Almighty. It sends my hormones into overdrive.

I'm still giggling when he pulls up to the house to drop me off.

"Thanks for tonight," he says, reaching across the bench seat to squeeze my hand. "It was fun."

"Yeah," I agree, shocking myself. "Surprisingly, I had a really great time."

"Ah-ah," he reprimands when I reach for the door handle. "We're gonna end this night right."

Nervous energy starts bubbling in my chest as I try to

decipher what exactly he means by that comment. I'm admittedly a bit trigger shy and will be devastated if he ruins what by my estimation was the perfect night, by taking things too far.

When the door swings open, my throat squeezes. I hope he can't see the hearts in my eyes when I look at him, because if he makes a move, I'm already too far gone to refuse it. The last thing I need is to wake up with more regret. Lord knows I've got enough of that to last a lifetime.

"Come on," he says, taking my hand, and once again helping me down from his truck. This time I'm just buzzed enough that I think I actually *need* the assistance.

He walks me all the way to the door and waits for me to unlock it before tipping my chin with his finger.

This is it, I think. Butterflies flutter in my tummy and I run my tongue over my lips, preparing myself for the wreckage.

"Thank you," he says, placing a kiss to my forehead.

He withdraws his hand, and I'm filled with… *disappointment?* This can't be right.

He gives me one final look before turning for his truck and calling back, "See you tomorrow!"

CHAPTER TEN

Wyatt

"How's it going, Wyatt?"

Prissy's loud greeting echoes throughout the empty chapel, nearly knocking me off the ladder where I'm applying the first coat of paint to the new crown moldings I installed yesterday. "Hey," I say, after regaining my balance. "It's Monday. Shouldn't you be at school?"

"Thanksgiving break."

I glance to the date on my watch. "So it is."

She places a hand on the third rung of the ladder to hold it steady. "Did you know over 300 people die each year from falling off ladders in the United States alone?"

This kid here… "No, Miss Priss, I sure didn't."

"Now ya do." She beams, like she's just offered me lifesaving information.

"I guess I do… You always so morbid?" I ask, climbing the rest of the way down.

She shrugs. "Just curious. I researched construction death stats when we started the renovations on the chapel a few months ago. Paw-Paw says I'm like a sponge for useless information."

"Is that right?"

She nods, fiddling with something in the pocket of her hoodie. "You need something, or just stopping by to say hi and put the fear of death into me?"

"Momma told me I had to go find something to do with myself cuz there's a wake today and I'm being too loud."

Poor kid looks bored out of her mind.

"That's why I'm stuck painting. She told me I can't use my power tools." I hang my lip to the floor in a sign of solidarity.

"Think I could hang out in here with you?"

"Sure." I give my shoulders a shrug. Misery loves company, right? "Whatcha got in there?"

"Thought you'd never ask." With a shit grin, she retrieves something small and furry from her pocket. "Name's Squishy." She lifts the little fuzzball to her face, placing a kiss on the top of its head. "He's a flying squirrel, and he's top-secret, so don't tell Momma."

"You have a pet squirrel your mother knows nothing about?"

Prissy nods, stroking its back with a finger. "She says the funeral home is not the place for animals, so I can't have any pets." She follows that statement with a drawn-out sigh. "But Paw-Paw says what she doesn't know can't hurt, and he lets me keep him in a birdcage in the climate-controlled shed where he stores his embalming stuff. Momma never goes in there."

"I'm not sure I wanna be in on this secret, Priss. I'm already walking on thin ice with your mother."

She waves me off. "No worries. I won't tell. Wanna hold him?"

Knowing about this classified rodent is one thing…coddling

it feels like a whole other level of deceit I want no part of. Plausible deniability is important. "Nah," I say. "I'm good. Why don't you go put him in his cage before you get us both into trouble? Then you can come back and help me paint those moldings on the floor over there."

"Fine," she grumbles. "Be right back."

"I'll be here."

The kid isn't gone five minutes before I start hearing one hell of a commotion coming from the area of the viewing. My stomach sinks to my toes, and I close my eyes and pray to Jesus that it isn't what I think it is.

Mrs. Marie pops into the chapel, red-faced and breathing like she's just run a marathon. "We got us a situation."

"What's going on?"

"There's a—a *squirrel* flying all around the visitation room." Tears drip down her cheeks. "We ain't never had nothin' like this happen before." She clutches my sleeve, tugging me toward the door. "Will you come help?"

"Of course." Not that she's affording me much chance to say no.

"*Stop it! Don't! You're gonna hurt him.*"

Upon entering the parlor, I find Prissy screaming while yanking on the shirt of a teenaged boy, who's chasing after her pet, wielding a broom like a sword.

There are guests laughing, others crying, some hiding behind chairs and a couple others who've made it their mission in life to catch the damn thing.

"It's okay," I say, trying to get some kind of control over the situation. "He's friendly." I snatch the broom from the kid's hand, passing it off to Whitney, who is presently breathing fire in my direction. I half expect her to come after me with it. If we weren't surrounded by mourners, I'm positive she would.

It's painful to watch all the progress I thought I made with the woman last night burst into flames. But I'll have to save that problem for another day, seeing as I can only focus on one crisis at a time.

"Come here, Priss." I hold my arms out for the distraught child. "I'm gonna lift you up, and you grab him."

She nods, sniffling into her sleeve.

"Everyone else, stay calm, and try not to spook him."

Stay calm, I repeat in my head, while making my way toward the casket. I hoist the little girl up higher, dangling her over the body of an old man—an old *dead* man, so she can retrieve her frightened pet from the top of the casket lid.

I don't breathe until she's back on the floor and I've moved away from the corpse.

That's when I look up to find nearly every pair of eyes in that room glaring in my direction. "What?" I say to no one in particular.

"What the hell, Wyatt?" Whitney grabs my wrist, dragging me from the room like I'm the one to blame for that epic shit-show. "We'll be lucky if we don't get sued for that."

"It's not mine," I say, once we're closed up in her office.

"No? Then how'd you know it was tame?" Her hands land on her hips.

I sigh, not wanting to break Prissy's trust but also not willing to take the fall for something I truly had nothing to do with. "If I tell you, you have to promise not to get mad."

"Too late," she growls.

"You're pretty when you're angry."

"Not now, Wyatt." The woman looks truly defeated.

"It's your dad's." A little white lie never hurt anyone. I hate doing it, but it's the only explanation I can think of to save Priss from her mother's wrath. I'm positive Hank won't mind, being he's the one that's been aiding and abetting this situation.

"You expect me to believe Daddy has a pet squirrel?"

"I don't care what you believe," I snap back. "It's the truth. He showed it to me this morning."

She shakes her head in disbelief, pinching the bridge of her nose like she's trying to ward off a migraine.

"I don't appreciate being treated like the enemy, either, considering I just saved your asses in there."

Before Whitney can think up a response, her office door flies open, and Hank and Marie come charging in.

The fire-breathing blonde whirls on her father. "Is it true?"

He crinkles his nose. "Is what true?"

"That rodent belong to you?"

I'm nodding behind her head, widening my eyes and praying he'll catch my meaning.

"Yeah," he says. "So, what? Last I checked, this was my house. I pay the bills, and I can do what I damn well please."

"Well good then," she snaps, stepping into his personal space. Her hand flies out, her finger pointing in the direction of the chaos we all just fled. "Then you can go deal with that man's children, cuz I am done with this entire situation."

Marie and I stand in silence, watching the father-daughter duo argue over which one's gonna handle the fallout. I don't say it, but my money's on Hank. Whitney is a force to be reckoned with when she's not angry—I wouldn't dare going toe-to-toe with her right now.

"Well, while y'all figure this out, I'm just gonna take my *uninvolved* self back to the chapel." I throw up a peace sign while making my way for the door.

"Wait!" Whit says, following me out into the lobby.

"Yeah?"

"I'm sorry for assuming that was your fault." She sucks her lower lip between her teeth. "I don't handle stress well."

"It's fine." I try rushing off again, afraid she'll be able to sense my guilt and I'll have no choice but to come clean about the real owner of that squirrel. But when she reaches out for my hand, stopping me in my tracks, I can focus on nothing else but the fireworks exploding inside my chest.

"It's not fine. I was wrong, and I really am sorry."

"Apology accepted." I tuck a loose strand of hair behind her ear, any excuse to keep some form of contact between us.

"I don't really have a lot of time right now." She gestures with her head toward the viewing room. "But I know you're off the rest of the week after today, and I don't know what you're doing on Thanksgiving, but we're planning a little lunch…nothing big. It's just us. Momma told me to make sure I invite you."

"Your momma told you?"

Her cheeks flush. "She did…but I'd also really like you to be there…as a friend," she adds, almost as an afterthought.

I dip my head in agreement. "Well, all right then. Guess I'll be seein' ya Thursday, friend."

CHAPTER ELEVEN

Whitney

While Mom and I are elbows deep in turkey and mashed potatoes, a call comes in for us to pick up a body at a private residence. To make matters worse, the decedent is a friend of my father. The two played high school ball together and have remained close ever since. He's been on hospice care for a few months, so everyone knew it was coming. Nevertheless, losing a loved one is always difficult, particularly so during the holidays.

"Y'all just stick around and finish up here. I can manage this one on my own." Daddy kisses Mom on the cheek and Prissy on the top of her head. "I'll try to be back in time for lunch, but if I'm taking too long, just go ahead without me."

"As if," I say, rolling my eyes. "You take as long as you need. We'll keep the food warm til you get back." When he leans in to kiss my forehead, I wrap my arms around my daddy's neck, giving him a tight squeeze. Momma and Prissy join, cocooning the grizzly old man in an unsolicited group hug.

"Love ya, Paw-Paw."

When he scruffs the top of his granddaughter's head on his way out, I have to catch my breath at the rare gleam of tears shimmering in his eyes.

It's difficult to see my seldom-ruffled father in so much pain. Today's situation is a harsh reminder that no matter that this is a job and can become routine—that we can at times seem detached—none of us are free from basic human emotion. Not even Hank Daigle, the town undertaker himself.

He isn't gone long when there's a heavy knock on the door.

"I'll get it," Prissy sings, sprinting for the entryway. She's really taken to our new employee in a way I haven't seen from her before. She's been on pins and needles awaiting his arrival since she rolled out of bed this morning.

"Happy turkey day, Miss Priss." After not having seen Wyatt in nearly three days, the mere sound of his voice brings a smile to my face and a tingle of excitement zinging through me.

"Don't think I didn't just see that, Whitney Jean," Momma taunts while stuffing the green bean casserole into the oven.

"What're you goin' on about?"

"I saw that lovesick smile of yours. You ain't foolin' nobody."

"You hush." I swat her on the bottom with the dish towel in my hand. "You saw no such thing."

"How goes it, ladies?" tall, blond, and sexy asks, stumbling in with a stack of baked goods boxes in his hands and my child dangling from his left leg.

"Prissy! Get off that man!" My mother proceeds to peel my little pain in the ass off of him.

"Ah, she's fine," he insists, while I relieve him of the mountain of sweets he's carting. "I picked up a few pies and cookies and apple fritters at Dana's Bakery last night. Hope that's okay."

"Duh," Prissy says. "Desserts are always okay."

He looks around the small living area like he's lost something. "Where's Hank?"

"Mr. Wiltz finally dropped dead this mornin' and Paw went to scoop him up."

Wyatt visibly shudders at the reminder of his recent experience with body retrieval.

"He might be a while." I offer an apologetic shrug. "I told him we'd wait to eat…hope that's okay."

"It's no problem at all. Y'all need some help in the kitchen? I ain't much of a cook," he confesses rolling up the sleeves of his button down, "but I can wash dishes like a boss."

"Leave the ladies to the cookin'." Prissy tugs on his arm. "Since Paw took off there ain't nobody to hang out with me." My child has puppy dog eyes down to an art form. That shameless begging of hers has me wanting to crawl under the table.

"Go on," Momma shoos him away. "We got this."

"There's a game on," Wyatt says, raising his brows at his biggest fan. "You like football?"

"Eww!" The little drama queen shoves a finger into the back of her throat, forcing herself to gag. "I got a much better idea. Come on," she says, taking him by the hand. "I wanna show you something in my room."

Wyatt glances over his shoulder back toward me and Momma to make sure it's okay. "Go 'head," I say, trying not to let the laughter I'm stifling explode, because there's only one thing she'd be this excited to show the man, and his reaction is one I don't want to miss.

As soon as they turn the corner into her room, I scurry over, posting up beside the door to listen in.

"You collect anything?" Prissy asks.

"Not really. Not unless you count the collection of beer cans in my garbage." He laughs, but ever solemn, my daughter doesn't react in kind. *Tough crowd.*

"You a big drinker?" Where the hell does she get off with that judgmental tone of hers? Girl thinks she's grown.

I'm unable to hear his response but imagine it was either a nod or noncommittal shrug by her reaction. "Remind me to go over some alcohol death stats with you later."

"Sure thing." He huffs out a laugh, and I find myself picturing the easy smile of his that would accompany it. "Why's everything so dark in here?" he asks. "I thought little girls liked pink and unicorns and rainbows?" His pitch suggests he's messing with her. Anyone who knows my daughter wouldn't expect anything less than exactly what they find in that dungeon of hers.

She grunts. "I'm not your average six-year-old."

"No kidding?"

I'm biting my lips with anticipation when I hear her begin riffling around in the drawer. "Here it is," she says, her voice brimming with pride.

I hear the case meet the wood of her desk and the snick of the clasps being unlatched, and my own heart accelerates. "Are you ready for this?" she asks.

Drama—all about the drama.

"As long as a dead body ain't about to pop outta that little briefcase, I'm all good."

Prissy snickers. "Okay," she drawls, "here it comes…I present to you, Gramma Agnes's *eyeballs!*"

"Holy, cow!" he says. From the crack in his voice, I can tell he's feigning excitement for her benefit, but she'd never know the difference. "Are these real?"

"Uh-huh. My momma's Gramma Agnes got her eye poked out. So, she got to have a really cool glass one."

"Why do I see three rolling around in here?" By this point, he sounds less shocked and genuinely curious.

I hear the clanking of the globes in her hands. "Because she used to like to switch 'em out. Sometimes she had two blue eyes, sometimes a blue and a green, but my favorite was at Halloween time, when she would wear this purple one."

I peer around the door frame to witness his reaction as she passes him the little glass eyeball. Prissy gets in real close, pointing out the webbing. "See how this one has spider webs instead of veins in the white part?"

He runs his thumb over it, really inspecting each and every detail. "This is quite possibly the neatest thing I've ever seen, Priss."

And with that I slip away to the bathroom to dry the sudden and unwelcome tears trickling down my cheeks. I followed them back here fully anticipating a really good chuckle over his horrified reaction to a little girl collecting glass eyeballs. Never in a million years did I expect to bear witness to him embracing my *unique* child and all her weirdness with such grace. Or that it would affect me so deeply.

They say the quickest route into or out of the heart of a single mother is through her child. That beautiful man has no idea of the way he just latched onto mine. I'm beginning to fear it may require the Jaws of Life to extract him.

Keeping myself in check around Wyatt Landry will be harder now than ever before.

"Who's ready to eat?" Daddy comes barreling through the door at a quarter after two with a smile on his face that does little to hide the pain lingering in his red-rimmed eyes.

The men and Prissy rush to take their places around the table we've had set for over two hours now. Momma and I bring out the feast of turkey, ham, rice dressing, mashed potatoes, green bean casserole, and homemade rolls.

"It all looks delicious," Wyatt says, practically drooling over his plate. "Thanks again for having me over."

Daddy says grace, blessing our family and friends, the food we're about to eat, and those less fortunate. We end with a moment of silence for our own reflections, and a sign of the cross.

If I had to guess, by the look of discomfort on his face as he mimics the rest of us touching two fingers first to his forehead, then to his chest, left shoulder, and finally the right, I'd say Wyatt wasn't raised Catholic. It probably isn't something most would take note of, but you could count on one hand the people in Moss Pointe who aren't. It's just one more thing that sets him apart from the rest. I find him utterly adorable.

"Amen," we all say in unison, and just like that, the signature confidence that oozes from Wyatt's every pore has returned.

Dad immediately strikes up conversation with our guest, making plans for the placement of the new pews and altar while we scarf down an obscene amount of food. Having to smell all the delicious aromas on empty stomachs apparently made us all ravenous.

It was Momma who set the table, so it's not surprising in the least that Wyatt is seated to my right. My mother just happens to be directly across from us. Her interfering brow darts for the ceiling every time she catches me staring at his profile.

"Hey, Priss," I say, jerking my attention from the man beside me when I'm once again busted ogling him like a piece of meat. "What's this I hear about a father-daughter dance the Friday before Christmas break?"

She drops her half-eaten roll back onto her plate, eyes wide, and brings her shoulders to her ears.

"The email Principal Wyler sent out said we had to buy tickets by this coming Monday. You haven't so much as mentioned it."

My dad preens. "Sounds like we got us a date, little missy." He sits up taller, adjusting his signature black tie in a manner that suggests he considers himself to be the luckiest man alive. The way he dotes on my kid is more than I could have ever hoped for. While she may not have a father of her own, she's certainly not lacking for love or attention.

"I'm not going," Prissy announces, slouching in her seat as she braces for my attack.

"Don't be silly," I say, my voice wobbling. "Of course you are."

"Serious as a heart attack," she assures me. "I'm really not."

"Oh, but you have to go," I practically beg, dropping my fork with a jarring clank. My mind goes straight to the junior and senior homecomings and proms I missed out on myself. I know she's just in first grade, and I'm likely being ridiculous, but I don't want her to forego anything life has to offer, especially at the hand of that dickwad who walked out on her before she was even born.

"Ugh..." The force of her groan is one that would top the Richter Scale. "Fine. I'll go."

"You will?" I eye her skeptically. My stubborn as hell daughter is never this easy to sway.

"Yep." She beams. "I'll go, as long as *Wyatt* takes me."

CHAPTER TWELVE

Wyatt

WHEN I ACCEPTED AN INVITATION TO Thanksgiving dinner, the last thing I expected was to be put on the spot like this.

As my mouth opens and closes, searching for breath, I'm realizing the true value of what it means to become speechless. While everyone around me is sputtering as they try to find a way to let the child down easy, I can't seem to formulate a single sound.

"This is a family event, Prissy." Hank is tripping all over himself in his attempt to make this right without crushing the little one's spirit. "You know Paw-Paw loves going to these things with you."

The little girl folds her arms on the tabletop and looks the old guy dead on. "No offense, Paw, but you're kinda...*old*."

His mouth falls open in mock horror.

"Priss. It's fine. You don't have to go if you don't want to,"

Whitney rushes out, blushed to the roots of her blonde hair. "You can't ask that of Mr. Wy—"

"I'll do it." I don't know who's more surprised by my outburst, Whitney or me.

"You will?" Whit's head jerks back with surprise at the same time that a huge smile covers Prissy's face.

A lifetime of feeling out of place over my own lack of parents pushes me to make what's probably a very rash decision. But I know what it's like always being the odd man out. I understand her desire to fit in, to not be the one on the arm of the old guy for once.

"I'd be honored." I dab at my mouth with the cloth napkin in my lap and clear my throat. "I mean..." I turn to my left, locking eyes with the fidgeting woman beside me. "As long as it's okay with you, of course."

"Say, yes, Momma," Prissy begs when the cat seems to catch hold of Whitney's tongue. "I'll even wear a dress!"

"I don't know..." She looks to her parents for guidance, both of whom just shrug their shoulders and smile.

"Makeup!" Prissy shouts, pulling out the big guns to bribe her mother to allow it. "You can put on my makeup." She laces her little hands in front of her face, fanning those baby blues like a pro.

I locate Whitney's hand beneath the table, giving it a reassuring squeeze. "She's so excited," I murmur. "Let me do this for her."

"Fine," the flustered woman says. "But I *will* be taking you up on that makeover, Priscilla Louise."

"Fine!" Echoing her mother, she pumps her fist into the air a few times. "I'm gonna have the hottest dad at the dance."

I won't even lie; my chest swells with that comment.

Whitney's head falls into her hand with a loud groan. "He's a friend of the family, Prissy, not a dad...yours or anyone else's."

"Potato—tomato," she says, waving her mom off. The kid is bouncing around like a little jumping bean, suddenly unable to keep her bottom in her seat. It feels good knowing I'm the one responsible for her excitement.

"You're not, right?" Whit turns to me and asks, her voice laden with unease.

"Not what? Hot? I'm offended."

"*A dad!* This is crazy, I don't even know enough about you to answer that with confidence."

I choke on a sip of Coke. "I have no children."

"But you're open to it, right?" The question comes from the busybody sitting across the table.

"Momma!" Whitney's forehead lands on my shoulder. "I am so sorry," she groans.

"Yeah," I say, biting back a laugh. "Eventually, with the right woman, sure."

"Hear that, Whit?" she gloats. "Said, he's open to it."

"I'd be open to being put up for adoption right about now."

"Well," Hank interrupts. "I hate to be the one to put an end to this titillating conversation, but I have a body waiting to be embalmed downstairs." His chair screeches when he scoots back from the table. "Priss, you comin'?" He hooks a thumb toward the door.

"Can I, Momma?"

"Please," she answers, instantly deflating with relief. "Go on and give us all a little peace."

Once they've left, Marie starts gathering soiled plates in her arms. "I'm gonna go start on these here dishes, if you two wanna go find a movie or something in the living room…or Whit's room. There's a TV in there too," the shameless woman volunteers. "We uh…got a dumpster 'round back as well." Whitney's eyes widen then narrow, and I would not be surprised to see actual laser beams shoot out of them.

"Actually," I say, putting myself between Whitney and her mother before there's a brawl, "I was just about to ask your lovely daughter if she would accompany me for a nightcap. Beau texted me a few minutes ago to see if we wanted to stop by for a Friendsgiving game of poker."

"I don't know," Whitney hedges. "This was a lot." She waves a hand over the table, darting a glare at her mother. "Maybe we should just quit while we're ahead…call it a night."

"Pretty sure I just earned myself another date." I rub a hand over my chest, puffing it out with pride.

"You what?" She leaps to her feet. "No way. That wasn't specified beforehand."

I steeple my hands beneath my chin. "Come on. Don't make me be the third wheel. Beau and Kate are disgustingly in love. It's torture."

She shuts her eyes, slowly shaking her head. "Nothing's changed, Wyatt. This is…*so much*. We're not even together."

Not yet. I don't say it, but I damn sure think it. The more I'm around her the surer I am that I'm gonna make her mine, whatever and however long it takes. "You're makin' a mountain outta a mole hill."

"A what?" she says drawing back with a grin.

"Somethin' my Mimi used to say. Means you're reading too much into this…looking for trouble where you'll find none."

"Am I?"

"We're friends, right?"

"Mmmhmm."

"Then come with me to Beau and Kate's…as my friend."

CHAPTER THIRTEEN

Whitney

I'M SORTING THROUGH END OF THE MONTH FINANCIALS for November when Momma peeks her head into my office. "Eleanor Breaux is here to go over William's arrangements."

A thick lump of emotion becomes wedged in my throat as I set down my pen, and nod. "You can send her in."

I haven't seen Elly since high school, and we weren't really the best of friends back then, but still, it's painful to even imagine what she's going through, losing her husband so young. And to a brain tumor, of all things. Word around town is they just found out she's pregnant a month ago, making their circumstances even more tragic. Death is always wretched, but young people add an extra layer of despair. The tragedy of a life cut short—those are always the hardest to come to grips with.

"Hey, Whitney." The red-faced, puffy-cheeked widow pokes her head into the room, and I wave her inside.

"How are you?" I walk around the desk to greet her with a

hug. "I'm so sorry about William," I say, smoothing a hand over her back.

"Thank you." She sniffles into a wad of crumbling tissue in her palm, and my heart aches. She looks like hell, in a pair of ratty sweats that swallow her thin frame. Her hair is matted with tears, and her eyes sunken in. It's the face of grief, and one I'm all too familiar with.

"Have a seat." I motion to the armchair in front of my desk.

Once she's settled, I pass her a box of Kleenex, and hold the waste bin out for her to dispose of the soiled wad still clutched in her hand.

"Thanks."

I nod. "So, Daddy tells me William wanted to be cremated, with no viewing?" I get right down to business, trying to avoid a breakdown if at all possible. I'll be a shoulder if needed, but she's got family to fall apart with. It's my job to be sympathetic, while also keeping a level head. To think of all the minor details, she's likely too upset to consider.

"That's right," she says, her hand moving to cup her still flat stomach.

A pulsing ache invades my chest. "You're pregnant?"

"Just made ten weeks."

"Do you have plans to have something made for the baby with some of William's cremains?"

"I hadn't really thought about it, to be honest."

"That's what I'm here for." I open my drawer, retrieving a few sample products and line them up on the edge of my desk. "I think this one would be perfect," I say, placing the glass orb in her palm. The glass can be swirled with the color of your choosing, but the dragonfly at the top…"

"It's made of ash," she says, eyes wide as she brushes a thumb over the art. "This is beautiful. It's perfect. Thank you."

"No problem." I offer her a sympathetic smile. "Do you want to go take a look at the show room and pick out an urn?"

"Actually," she says, reaching into her satchel. "I had something custom made."

Her cheeks redden.

"Oh," I say, rolling my chair back under the desk. "Don't be embarrassed. You don't have to buy something from here. People bring their own keepsakes all the time."

She huffs a nervous laugh. "This one's a bit…*unusual*."

"Girl, I have seen it all," I assure her. "Lay it on me."

That's when she whips out an eight-inch circumcised dildo. It's so lifelike—flesh toned, complete with veins.

"Oh," I say, trying my hardest to keep a straight face. "I've heard of these. Never actually filled one yet, but there's a first time for everything, right?"

She grins. "I found it on a handmade site, online…it's actually made from a cast of William's penis."

"That is…*amazing*," I say, at a loss for how to respond. "You know you're still gonna need an urn. Even with the dragonfly and…*receptacle*, you'll have a lot of cremains left."

"Oh, okay," she says, shoving it back into her bag. "Lead the way."

We spend almost an hour in the show room before she finally decides on a large black marble urn with a matching miniature for William's parents. After selections have been made, we go back to my office to finalize details and sign papers and then I get up to see her out.

"Wait," she says, when we reach my office door. "I almost forgot to give this back to you. She whips out William's penis for the second time, and it's still just as shocking.

"Oh, you can just hold on to that and take a little of the cremains from the urn when you pick it up to fill it."

We've managed to get through over two hours together without more than a few tears during what has to be the hardest day of this woman's life, *until now*. Heaving sobs wrack her fragile form.

I shut the door, guiding her back to the chair. "Oh, honey, I'm so sorry."

"It's not you," she says, her lower lip quivering while she snivels into her sleeve. "I—I'm too afraid to—to touch the ummm… the…"

"The ashes?" I offer, realizing what I'm going to have to do. There's not much we aren't willing to accommodate in order to ease the pain of our clients. And it's starting to look like this will be no different.

She nods.

"Hand it over," I say, with as much dignity as I can muster.

She spits a laugh through her tears. "I know I'm ridiculous… God, this is so embarrassing. I promise, it hasn't been used."

Even with years of experience keeping my wits in the most asinine situations, I cannot contain the loud cackle that bursts from my chest. "I really should have thought to ask that question before grabbing it with my bare hands, huh?"

We're both rolling by the time she gets up again to leave. "You have no idea how much I appreciate this, Whitney."

"Don't mention it," I say, walking her to the front door. "Your husband's penis is in good hands with me."

CHAPTER FOURTEEN

Wyatt

Just one…more…screw… I bend until my cheek is almost meeting the floor, twisting my wrist to get the drill beneath the pew and attach the custom kneeler. My back and shoulders are on fire from being in this crouched position for so long. Sweet mercy is finally within reach… *lunch break!*

"Nice plumber crack ya got goin' there."

Thunk! "Ouch! Son of a—"

"Oh my God, I'm so sorry."

I come up, holding the throbbing lump already protruding from the crown of my head. It's more than possible I exaggerate the pain just a smidge when Whitney crouches beside me to inspect the damage. "Fuck. That hurt."

"I didn't mean to scare you," she offers, biting back a grin. "Does it hurt really bad?"

"You think this is funny?" I growl, wincing for affect.

She shakes her head, letting a snort slip through as she

reaches around moving my hands out of the way to feel for herself. "It's not." She sucks in her cheeks. "It's not funny…"

Dear Lord, but it amuses me how hard she's working to keep a straight face. "You trying to convince me? Or yourself?"

"I just can't help it." She snickers. "I have this awful habit of laughing when people hurt themselves." With the gentlest touch, she rubs the pads of her fingers over the knot. "I mean, I like to think if anyone were ever seriously injured in my presence, I would react appropriately."

I grip the back of the pew, cracking my knees when I push up to standing, then reach for her hand to help her back up. "Well, at least we know you ended up in the right career." I take a brief moment to appreciate how beautiful she looks today with her hair pinned up in a bun and a blouse that's cut just high enough to pass for decent while still offering a hint of mouthwatering cleavage. That milky expanse of skin along her neck is just begging for my lips. My pulse speeds up, and I'm feeling hot beneath the collar.

"Why do you say that? Because they're dead?"

Her question draws me from my stupor. I clear my throat. "Precisely."

"I really would be a disaster in the medical field." She cracks a huge grin. "Or, could you imagine…me as a teacher?"

"A lawsuit waiting to happen," I agree.

She shrugs. "What can I say? Gotta have gumption to work here."

"Gumption…" I hold out one hand. "Balls," I say, holding out the other while tipping them side to side like a teeter totter.

"Huh?"

I can't help but chuckle at the recent memory. "A very wise beyond her years six-year-old once told me that not everyone has the balls to work in a funeral home."

Her jaw drops. "She didn't?"

I wave away her mortification. "She was really trying to be sweet."

Her eyes roll. "Sounds like it."

"She was attempting to sooth my ego when I declined her invitation to assist in an embalming."

"She did *not!*"

"Oh, yeah."

"I joke about it all the time, but I really should enroll that child in etiquette classes."

"Don't you dare." I shudder at the thought. "She's perfect."

Her lip quirks with uncertainty. "Thanks for saying that." But she doesn't look at all like she believes I'm serious.

"I mean it." I move to my workstation to put away some of my tools. "Anyway… What can I do for ya?" My hand involuntary moves back to the egg-sized lump. "Or did you just drop by to enjoy the view of my backside?" I glance over my own shoulder, toward the ass in question.

"I did actually come by to ask for a little favor…" She fans her long lashes up at me while pinching two fingers together, leaving only the teensiest sliver of space. "That," she says, following my line of sight to my ass, "was just a bonus."

To say I'm shocked by her flirty demeanor would be putting it mildly. "What's that?" I ask, cupping a hand around my ear. "Did I just hear you say you stopped by to arrange another date?"

"Tell you what," she says, taking my hand and starting for the door, "you help me with this chore, and I'll owe you two."

I should probably be more concerned with the nature of the task at hand, especially since she's readily offering up an extra date, but I've lost the ability to think rationally. My head is suspended in the clouds as I allow her to lead me out back across the yard to the crematorium, only stopping to question her when we're a few feet from the door and deep-seated fear starts to outweigh the looming reward. "You're not gonna ask me to burn a body, right? Cuz you could literally strip down and offer yourself on a silver platter as a bribe, and as much as it'd kill me, I'd have to respectfully decline."

She drops my hand to cover the laugh that bursts forth from her chest. "You have to have a license to cremate people." She's looking at me like I'm positively ridiculous.

"Right…"

"Come on, scaredy cat." She jerks my arm, but my feet stay rooted to the soil. My heart is beating out of control, my earlier excitement quickly being overtaken by panic.

"I'd prefer to know what this task entails first." The prospect of what lies on the other side of that door has me breaking out in a sweat.

"Prissy was right," she taunts. Her sapphire eyes drop briefly to my crotch before lifting to meet my gaze.

"Ouch," I say, "Low blow."

She shrugs, and when I don't budge, blows out a long breath. "A customer requested some of her husband's cremains be placed in an *odd-shaped container*." Her voice wavers. There's a whole lot she isn't saying…*intentionally*. And I'm not sure I want to find out what that something is. "It won't stand on its own… I just need you to hold it so I can fill it. Easy peasy." She twists a key in the lock and pushes the door open.

Immediately I'm hit with an odor I won't soon forget—like a pig roasting over an open flame, combined with burned leather and an acrid, sweet scent so strong I can practically taste it. The worst part is knowing exactly what that smell sitting on the tip of my tongue is.

"You coming?" she asks, staring back at me like I've lost my marbles. "There's nothing in here but ash, I promise." She crosses a finger over her heart. "I wouldn't trick you like that."

"Fine," I say, lifting the neck of my T-shirt to cover my nose and mouth. "Let's make it quick." I follow her inside the dimly lit building, noting the walls covered in black soot stains.

"That's the furnace." Whitney points, drawing my attention to a huge metal contraption. "It's where the magic happens," she says with a smile. She crosses the room, to a steel table. "And this here," she adds, nodding toward what looks like some sort of kitchen appliance, "is the grinder."

A visual of Jeffrey Dahmer turning human body parts into ground meat and sausages comes to mind and I blanch. "I'm afraid to ask…"

"Whatever doesn't burn, mostly bones, gets ground into a fine powder and mixed with the ashes."

"That's only slightly less creepy than what I was imagining."

"I don't find it the least bit unnerving." She looks around the space fondly, like it's just another room in her house, and I guess as far as she's concerned, it is. "Death is an inevitable part of life…a ritual…a rite of passage."

"I couldn't do it."

"Well," she says, "I can't bring myself to deal with them before they're embalmed, mostly because the blood and *other* bodily fluids gross me out."

"That's nothing to be embarrassed about," I say, reading her expression. "And while I appreciate your intent, can we just get this over with, without the grand tour?"

A devilish grin curves her rosy lips, and there's trouble written all over that pretty face of hers when she reaches into the bag dangling from her shoulder and slaps a rubber penis into my palm.

I jump back like it's a snake about to attack, holding it out as far from my person as possible. "This some kind of sick joke?"

"Deathly serious," she offers. I don't think I've ever seen her quite so pleased with herself. "That's no run of the mill willy you have there."

"No?"

"You, *my friend*, are holding an exact replica of William's penis. His widow special-ordered it and would like it filled with some of his *essence*."

Just when I think a day in the life of working in a funeral home can't possibly get any weirder.

"Don't worry, she assures me that it hasn't been used…yet."

"Thought hadn't even crossed my mind."

"Really?" she asks, widening those baby blues.

"I haven't moved past the fact that I have a dead guy's dick in my hand…and that it feels eerily real." I shudder.

She moves to the covered box on the table, smothering a laugh. "I just need you to hold it a moment longer while I get these ashes inside."

"I think this calls for a bit more than two dates." I close the space between us, advancing until she's backed against the table, her palms resting on the surface.

She tilts her face up toward mine. Mischief dances in her eyes. "What'd you have in mind?"

"A kiss."

She pulls her lower lip between her teeth, giving my proposition obvious thought before bobbing her head. "One kiss… when you walk me to the door after our next date." She ticks off her conditions on her fingers, adding one more before I have the chance to counter. "No tongue."

"One kiss," I agree, wrapping my free hand around her slender waist and pulling her close. "No service till payment is rendered."

"What?" She glances around the cramped space, her chest beginning to rise and fall rapidly with the acceleration of her breaths. "Here?"

I nod, bending forward to breathe in her scent, letting jasmine and vanilla drown out the stench of the room. I trail my nose along her collar bone and up the bend of her neck. "Right here," I whisper against her ear. "Right now."

Her gulp echoes in the stillness.

"With tongue," I add.

Her trembling hands flatten against my chest, her little finger stroking absentmindedly over my nipple, driving me positively mad with desire. "O—only a little."

"A lot," I counter, taking hold of her chin and smashing my mouth to hers with a feral groan. Without a second's hesitation, her hands are fisted in my hair. The only fight is for control as our tongues war with each other, desperately seeking to fill the ache we spend every moment in one another's presence denying.

"Wyatt," she mumbles against my lips.

"So good," I say, reaching around to cup her ass before spitting a laugh right in her face when I'm cock-blocked…in the most literal sense.

She backs away, wiping at her face, offended and still panting from our kiss. "What the hell is wrong with you?"

"Sorry," I say, hardly able to catch my breath. "I can't."

Her eyes narrow to slits. "Can't what? Kiss me? It was *your* idea."

I hold the massive penis out in the space between us. "I can't kiss you with another man's dick in my hand."

CHAPTER FIFTEEN

Whitney

It's been three days...

For three whole days, I've been able to do little else but ruminate over that *kiss*. When I close my eyes, I feel warmth of his tongue flicking against the roof of my mouth, and the hairs on the nape of my neck stand on end. I can still taste the coffee on his lips. And the smell of his cologne is seared so deeply into my subconscious that it scents my every inhale with sandalwood and man.

Desire heats my blood whenever I recall the way he dominated the situation, commanding complete control. And my God, did it feel good to shut my mind off for those brief seconds and relinquish it—to react on instinct—to exist wholly in that moment...a luxury I'm realizing I seldom allow myself anymore.

Now here I am, seated less than two feet away from he who occupies my every thought, in the cab of his pickup. We're headed out to join Kate and Beau for some line dancing—*my idea*—and I can't focus enough to hold a simple conversation.

My game is so off…

Yeah, right, what game? More like nonexistent.

"You all right, Whit?"

"Huh?" I turn from where I've been absently staring out the window. He's looking like some kind of model in his signature ass-hugging Levis and a brown leather jacket. Beneath it he dons a crisp white tee that would make anyone else look underdressed. But he wears it better than most men wear a three-piece suit.

Truth be told, Wyatt isn't what I'd normally go for. I prefer my guys a little more…*clean cut*. But the way those unruly blond whisps curl over his ears has me pressing my thighs together thinking about all the dirty things I'd like him to do to me. I steal a glance at him gripping the wheel and suddenly feel those work-roughened hands scraping along my smooth skin, sending tingles down my spine. "Yeah. Why do you ask?" I give my head a shake, tossing my hair back and away from my face.

One broad shoulder rises and falls before he runs his fingers through his locks, offering me a hesitant smile. "You just seem far away."

If he only knew.

"Sorry." I scrub my palms over my thighs, drying the sweat on my jeans. "Just thinking about work."

He nods, turning back to the road, whistling along to some old rock song playing on the radio. I've been so distracted that I hadn't even realized the music was on. It dawns on me he might've resorted to listening to it as a result of my stellar company, and I really start to feel bad. I mean, the man *earned* this date, and even let me choose the venue. The least I can do is be present.

From that point, I give a concentrated effort to at least appear that I'm paying attention while he makes small talk about the construction going on over at his place.

It's not that I'm disinterested, per se. I'm just far too preoccupied by the overwhelming attraction I'm harboring for the man—an attraction that's beginning to feel like a living, breathing entity between us, making it difficult to focus on anything but reigning in my reaction to it, lest I make a complete fool of myself.

"Great, so, tomorrow then?" His thumbs thump against the steering wheel to the beat of the music, jarring me from my thoughts. His boyish smile is warm enough to melt butter…and soak my panties.

"Tomorrow what?" All the agreeing I've been doing has apparently just backfired on me, as I have no idea what I've just committed to. Considering our history…banging against a dumpster, kissing in the crematory… There really is no telling.

"You and Miss Priss. Dinner at my place." He grins. "To show you what I'm working on and let Prissy play with the pooch."

"Uh," I stammer, fiddling with the hem of my top while trying to think up a way out of the mess I've just landed myself in. Okay, so, I don't actually *want* out. But involving my daughter any further in whatever this is between us has red flags shooting up all over the place.

"*Sure…*"

"I knew it," he laughs. "I don't know where you are, but it sure ain't here with me."

"Oh, I was with you, all right," I mutter, closing the AC vents to keep the heat from blowing on my already flushed cheeks.

"Is that what this is about?" he asks, whipping into a spot in front of Willa's Honky Tonk.

I catch my lower lip between my teeth as I gaze at his profile, the way his jaw ticks and the easy smile that moves across the lower half of his face as he maneuvers his beast of a truck between two others. He always looks like he's having the time of his life when he drives this old thing.

Come to think of it, I can't recall a time he hasn't looked like he was enjoying himself. It's incredibly appealing, his zest for life.

Resisting the urge to fan myself, I shift in my seat and swallow the lump building in the back of my throat.

"You gonna be all weird now cuz I kissed you?" His tongue darts out to wet his lips, and it's all I can do not to jump him. *Get a grip, woman.*

Instead, I toy with the pendant on my necklace, sliding it back and forth along the silver chain. "I'm not trying to be."

"We screwed against a trash bin, for crying out loud." He shoves the gear shift up into park, twisting his entire body to face me. He just threw that out there so casually, without an ounce of mirth. "If we could get past that…" His gray-green eyes meet with mine, and I cease my fidgeting, completely entranced by the seriousness of his ruggedly handsome face. "It was a kiss."

A kiss that, by my estimation, was far more intimate than some drunken fuck.

Then we were strangers looking for nothing more than a good time. But now? Now, I'm actually getting to know the man behind the six-pack abs and chiseled jaw, and finding that I like him—I like him *a lot*, actually. And so does my kid.

Wyatt could be *the one*…or our complete undoing. There's no in between. If I decide to take a chance—to go all in—the result could be the family I've always dreamed of for me and Prissy or complete annihilation of what little faith in love I have left.

"You're right," I say, rather than reveal any of what I'm thinking. "I'm being silly."

He stares at me for a beat before tipping his head, turning for his door, and exiting the cab.

I take a few deep breaths, adjusting the part in my hair in

the visor mirror while waiting for him to come around to let me out. There's a good chance he's ruined me for all other men. I can't imagine any other guy in this day and age will ever live up to the standards he's setting.

Wyatt Landry, unfortunately for the women of today, is a dying breed, and I'm constantly fighting the urge to grab hold of him with both hands and see how far this thing might go.

Maybe it's time I quit fighting?

"How was it?" he asks when my door swings open, holding out a hand for mine. "Scale of one to ten." He waggles his brows suggestively. "Ten being orgasmic."

I scoff, because I'm too flustered to speak.

"Come on…you have to have an answer, being it's all you seem to think about."

I give him my glariest glare as I step down into the gravel lot with his assistance.

He doesn't even flinch. "Maybe you could use a refresher?" he offers, pinning me against the side of his truck with his chest pressed to mine. My heart starts beating double-time.

I lick my lips, practically panting for it and shake my head. "A three."

"Bullshit." The deep timbre of his voice rumbles against my temple, sending my blood rushing.

I can't be sure, but I'm almost positive I feel the tip of his tongue trail along the shell of my ear. My head thumps against the window, and I look up at his scruffy chin. Without thought, my hand follows my line of vision, and I'm running a thumb back and forth in that stubble, imagining the way the coarse hair would feel on other parts of my body…brushing along my hard nipples, scraping the delicate skin between my thighs. "Seven," I amend, still taunting him.

My voice is pure gravel. My limbs, putty.

My breath heady with desire.

He dips his head, and I shut my eyes, every cell of my body springing to life with awareness. His warm, minty breath clouds what remains of my senses. All I want in this moment is to taste him. To feel him. To surrender all my inhibitions.

"Ten," he says, before clasping my face between his massive hands and crashing his mouth to mine.

Without hesitation, my lips part, easily succumbing to his advance. I vaguely hear the moans of desperation sneaking out from the back of my own throat. With my toes curled snugly in my boots and my fingers fisted into the front of his shirt, I'm once again becoming lost in this man. Whether it be the delicate caress of his fingers, the gyration of his hips, or the warm whisper of his breath as his lips trail a path across my neck, his every move feels deliberate. *Practiced.* The man knows his way around a woman. If I had my wits, that would probably bother me, but as it stands, I can't feel anything but appreciation for the skillful way he's molding me to his will.

Calloused hands travel along my sides and over my hips before reaching around to cup my ass. He pulls me flush with his body, nipping at my lips before pulling back just a hair's breadth. "That's a ten," he rasps before inclining my chin with the tip of his nose so I'm staring right at him. "Fight me."

I'm never one to back down from a challenge, but at the moment there is no fight in me—none whatsoever. I nod, gripping the back of his head with both of my hands and attempt to bring his mouth back where I want it—where I desperately *need* it.

What is it about this man that has me willing—hell, practically begging—for him to take me right here, out in the open for anyone to see? The way my hips are grinding into his pelvis like they have a mind of their own—*the mind of a slut*—tells me what I think I already knew… I've not learned a damn thing from our past experience.

"Say it," he commands, through a jumble of nipping lips and gnashing teeth.

"T—ten," I agree, sagging into him as I mewl against his lips.

With that, he breaks away, sporting a satisfied smile as he tucks my hand into his. "That's more like it." He tugs my arm, moving toward the entrance, but I'm still too worked up to move, nearly tripping over my own feet. "Come on, we got some rugs to cut."

"What?" I gawk at him like he's speaking another language while adjusting my clothes.

"Cut a rug?" He does a little shimmy. "You know? Dancing."

"Right." I suck in as much of the cool December air as I can as we cross the parking lot, attempting to regain my wits before entering the bar. "You ever been before?"

He inclines his head, looking up at the flashing neon pink sign. "Here specifically? Or line dancing?"

"Either…both."

"Neither," he admits, gripping the lapels of my jean jacket and pulling me in to plant a kiss on the tip of my nose. "I'm not really one for formal dancing."

"Great," I rasp, reaching around him for the door handle. "This should be a *blast*."

My adrenaline starts pumping when we step inside, greeted by the flashing strobe lights and the familiar tune of "Boot Scootin' Boogie" blaring through the speakers. My hips start swaying along to the sound of boot heels stamping on the wood floor in time with the beat.

Dancing might not be his thing, but I was born for it.

"Keep that up," he teases, pulling me back into his chest with a finger hooked through the beltloop at the small of my back,

"And I'm gonna have to find the owner of this place...see if they have a dumpster out back."

"Don't tempt me," I tease, feeling emboldened by the lively atmosphere, and also still more than a bit worked up.

He nibbles my ear lobe before jutting his chin out straight ahead toward my petite brunette bestie who's standing on a stool, flailing her arms in the air like a maniac to get our attention. "Wonder if she noticed us walk in?" he muses.

Kate and Beau have somehow managed to snag one of the coveted high-tops right off the dance floor. They must've gotten here as soon as the place opened.

They are adorable...all matchy, she in black leggings, a plaid tunic, western boots, and her hair in twin braids draped over each shoulder. Beau's dressed down from his usual lawyer garb, in a black button down tucked into a pair of Wranglers and cowboy boots. His habitually styled hair is wind-tousled, giving him a playful charm. "Damn, Beau," I tease, leaning in for a hug. "You look almost human tonight."

"Could say the same about you," he counters, looking me over from head to toe. "Where's the pencil skirt and red bottom heels?"

"Ahem," Kate hacks, loudly. "We're standing right here, assholes. Stop flirting...damn."

I roll my eyes, making my way around to give her a tight squeeze. "You look very pretty." It's nothing new where she's concerned, but I'm always sure to say it anyway. I'm a good friend like that.

"Thanks," she beams. "So do you."

"Ahem," Wyatt interrupts. "We're standing right here. Damn, Kate, stop flirting with my woman."

My best friend's eyes widen. "Are you two...?"

"No!" I rush out at the same time that he answers in the affirmative.

CHAPTER SIXTEEN

Wyatt

"WE ARE *NOT* DATING," SHE INSISTS, GLOWERING at me.

"We totally are," I argue, getting a kick out of the matching shit-eating grins on our best friends' faces. "I held another man's dick in the palm of my hand to earn the right to say that."

Alcohol sprays out of Kate's mouth. "I'm sorry, you did what?"

Whitney shields her face with both hands.

"You didn't tell her?" I wince, becoming a bit anxious because I think I may have just landed myself in a heap of trouble. "I assumed—"

"And you know what they say about assuming," she snaps back, her hands moving to rest on the curves of her hips.

I look around for a little help, finding none from these two clowns. "No, actually I don't… What *do* they say?"

"Precisely." She winks.

I can only imagine how dumb I must look at the moment, because whatever point she thinks she's just proven has gone way over my head.

"Means you shouldn't assume," Beau says, finally jumping in with the save. Better late than never, I guess.

"Well, one of y'all better start talkin', cuz my imagination's runnin' wild!" Kate holds both palms out, flashing her fingers opened and closed with her curious eyes bouncing between us.

"It wasn't an *actual* dick," Whit shouts just as the music fades out. At least five heads whip in our direction, and I cannot control my hysterical laughter at her expense.

"Oh, for heaven's sake. Mind y'all's own damn business," Kate growls, shooing them with a flick of her wrist. "Buncha freaking busy-bodies." She redirects her attention to Whitney, who by the looks of it would like nothing more than to evaporate into thin air. "Go on…"

"I'm not trying to spread anyone's business," Whitney shoots me a pair of laser eyes that warn I'd better not either.

"Too late." Beau's worse than a woman once his interest is piqued. "Out with it."

"Relax…it was just a dildo." One look at Beau and Kate's wide-eyed, slack-jawed expressions lets me know that I should have just kept my big mouth shut…*again*.

"I wasn't gonna say anything," Whit offers, slinking back around the table to lace her arm through mine. "Didn't feel it was my place…" She pats the top of my hand with hers, as if trying to comfort me. "But I guess the cat's outta the bag. Y'all, Wyatt here is one kinky mofo."

"Is he now?" my nosy cousin-in-law croons, resting her forearms on the table and leaning in close.

"You think you know someone," Beau adds, scrubbing a

hand over his jaw like he's trying to figure me out. "We'll revisit this topic later."

"The fuck we will."

Whitney's back vibrates against my chest while she fights to control her laughter. "Let's not embarrass him, y'all. We came here to have a good time."

"Speaking of a good time"—Kate pushes a glass across the table—"I took the honor of ordering you a Crown and Coke." She dangles her drink in the air. "Heavy on the Crown. You got some catchin' up to do."

"Been here a while?" Whit asks, before bringing the tumbler to her lips.

She sniffs the liquid, pulling a sour face before shrugging and taking an impressive pull from the straw.

Kate doesn't get the chance to answer before the familiar intro to "Cotton Eye Joe" filters through the speakers. A stampede of patrons rush to the floor, arranging themselves in neat rows. I find myself drawn to their energy as I watch them collectively clapping their hands above their heads and howling at the moon like a bunch of fools.

"Let's go." Whitney gives me no chance to decline before taking my hand and dragging me out there with her. The four of us line up in front of our table, on the other side of the guard rail. I appreciate that she's considerate enough to stick to the back of the pack, because without a doubt, I'm about to embarrass us all. Won't be long before she's questioning her own judgment in bringing me here.

"I have no clue what I'm doing," I warn.

"Follow my lead," she says, hooking her thumbs through her belt loops and bouncing in place to the beat. Her smile is radiant and her energy infectious.

Being the nut that I am, I tuck my thumbs in my front

pockets and hula hoop my hips while waiting for the actual dancing to begin. The sound of my girl's laughter spurs me on. I'm so busy acting the ass that I completely miss the start of the dance.

"They show no mercy," Beau laughs, when I'm damn near bowled over by a line of dancers. "Just move. You'll eventually pick up on the steps."

"Front, front," Whit sings, tapping the heel of her boot out in front of her. "Back, back," she says, swinging it back and this time tapping the toe twice. "Cross in front, cross in back." She follows along, slapping her ankles while explaining what she's doing with every step. "This way," she shouts, spinning and criss-crossing this way and that.

Just as soon as I start to get the hang of it, they go switching shit up on me, and we're trading places with the people in front of us.

"You're a damn idiot," Beau shouts when I give up on the steps altogether in favor of a little freestyling.

My date doesn't seem to mind my improvising. It's obvious she's in her element, not missing a beat. I, on the other hand, miss more than I hit, constantly catching myself staring at the woman.

She's beautiful in any light. But the way she looks right now—so playful and carefree? Well, she's positively magnetic.

"You did great!" she huffs, out of breath as we make our way back to the table.

"You're a shit liar," I say. Feeling emboldened by her flirtation this evening, I give her a firm swat to the ass. "But it was fun."

She looks up at me from under her makeup-darkened lashes as she slips out of her jacket, draping it over her chair, leaving her in a pale pink sleeveless top with a deliciously low cut neckline.

My mouth waters as I drink her in. I'm entranced as her ample cleavage rises and falls, glistening with a sheen of sweat beneath the lights—her every labored breath has me catching my own. That flush in her cheeks and the sexy smile she can't seem to wipe from her face have me fighting the urge to take her in my arms…to slide my tongue—

"I need the bathroom," Kate blurts, interrupting the eye-fucking that was likely becoming a bit awkward for our company.

I adjust myself discretely, because hell, now I'm uncomfortable as well.

"You know where it is," Whit says, catching a heated glare from her best friend.

"I'll just go with her," she amends, giving my hand a squeeze before the two of them disappear into the crowd.

"So…"

I raise my brows at my cousin's not-so-subtle intrusion into my business.

"What's the deal with you and Whitney? You seem a bit *cozier* than y'all were the last time we got together. Don't think we didn't see that ass slap." He laughs. "It's no doubt what prompted that little visit to the ladies' room."

I puff up with pride. "I been telling your ass for years—the ladies can't refuse my charm."

He laughs, scrubbing a hand over his chin. "How serious have things gotten?"

"Not serious at all."

He nods, taking a swig from the beer he's been nursing since we arrived. "But you want it to be?"

I gnaw on my lip, a little afraid to speak my desires into existence. "Yeah," I finally confess. "I think I just might."

My admission brings on a brief silence. If Beau's still talking, I'm not paying a lick of attention.

"Be right back," I say, not even sticking around for a response before rushing off to put in a special request with the DJ before the ladies return.

When I return to the table they're still not here, and I start wondering what happens inside women's bathrooms that takes so long.

"Hey!" Whitney's greeting has me nearly falling off my stool.

I take a moment to right myself then sling an arm around her neck. "Hey yourself, beautiful."

She sets a beer on a cocktail napkin in front of me. "Thought you could use a drink."

"Thanks," I say, taking a swig. "But I'm switching to water after this."

Her eyes widen.

"Miss Priss," is my only explanation.

She bursts out laughing. "My kid's such a buzzkill."

"She's wise beyond her years." I tip her chin, staring into her baby blues. "You're doing an excellent job raising her. I'm a better man for knowing her already."

Her throat moves with a hard swallow, and her eyes begin to glaze over. "Dance with me?" she rasps, squeezing my bicep in her tiny hand.

"That's not how this works."

Her head jerks back, brows furrowed.

"A gentleman always asks a lady to dance."

Her face splits into a dimpled smile. "Another one of your Mimi's lessons in chivalry?"

I nod.

"Well, you'd better hurry. They only play a few slow songs before the line dancin' starts up again. Beau and Kate are already out there."

"Patience," I whisper placing a placating finger at her lips. "Our song's next."

"Our song?" she gasps. "Wyatt Landry, what did you do? We don't have a—"

"May I have this dance?" I ask, rising from my seat just as Perfect Stranger's "You Have the Right to Remain Silent" begins filtering through the speakers.

"Thought you'd never ask…"

With her trembling hand in mine, I lead her out to the floor, give her a quick twirl, and pull her body flush with mine. Her arms lace around my neck, her fingers threading into my hair while I splay one across her back, resting the other at her waist.

My heart lurches as I whisper the lyrics into her ear, each one piercing it with truths. "So many times, my eyes have held you. Tonight, please give my arms that chance," I croon.

"Wyatt," she starts.

"Shhh." I push her hair back from her face, brushing my lips over hers. "Just listen."

She rests her head against my chest, her arms tightening around my neck while I sing into her ear about remaining silent and allowing our hearts to do the talking while we dance.

By the end of the song, something's shifted between us. I can't quite put my finger on what exactly, but her gaze suddenly burns hotter and lingers a little longer. Every touch is slightly more intimate and purposeful.

All I know is it feels like I'm finally making my way out of the friend zone, and absolutely nothing could thrill me more.

CHAPTER SEVENTEEN

Whitney

THE FRONT DOOR SWINGS OPEN BEFORE MY FIST HAS even met with the weathered wood to knock, revealing a freshly showered Wyatt. "Y'all made it!"

I greet him with a smile, allowing myself a quick second to catalog his appearance beginning with his still damp hair and piano key smile surrounded by a couple days-old scruff. Today's tee is gray and fitted with a V-neck. He's traded his usual worn denim for black and gray tapered Adidas track pants. His feet are bare, and ridiculously hot. Because of course they are. Why am I even surprised that the least flattering body part in existence is drool worthy on this man? He hit the genetics jackpot for sure. *I mean, is one crooked toe too much to ask for?*

"Barely," Prissy complains, drawing me from my examination. She rolls her eyes at me in dramatic fashion before slipping past Wyatt, right into his house, like she owns the place.

That girl…

"Hey." I shift my weight from foot to foot, trying to determine how embarrassed I should be by his demeanor. Acid rolls in my tummy, serving as a reminder of the potentially poor choices I might've made last night at the bar. I'm not sure whether it's a blessing or a curse that I can't seem to recall a huge portion of the evening before. Definitely blaming the extra Crown Kate put in my first drink. And my second. And *third*. "Sorry about last night," I offer, erring on the side of caution. Judging by the hangover I'm suffering this morning, I'm sure I did something to warrant it. "I don't get out much, and I guess I went a bit overboard on the alcohol."

"Why are you apologizing?" He drops back, ushering me inside. "I had a blast."

As I step around him and take a deep inhale to calm my nerves, I get a whiff of Irish Spring soap and coffee. *Always coffee.* My stomach begins to settle at the comforting aroma.

With a timid smile, I cross my arms over my chest as I take a stroll around his quaint kitchen, absorbing all the details, like the floral wallpaper that's starting to peel at the corners and thick wood trim surrounding the doors and framing the bay window above the sink. "I *think* I did too…"

"You don't remember?"

"Bits and pieces," I admit. Flashes of riding home with my head hanging out the window of his truck fill me with mortification. Momma had to help me scrub the chunks from my hair when I stumbled in last night at a quarter past two. She was still making fun of me when she *literally* had to haul my ass out of bed this morning by my ankles. I fully anticipate her bringing it up for the rest of my life. "I kind of blacked out after the Electric Slide…*until the ride home*, that is."

"Ouch." He winces, covering a smile. "That was pretty brutal."

"Yeah. If I had to forget anything, why couldn't it have been that part?"

"It's fine," he assures me. "Happens to all of us at some point."

"Prissy thinks I was just sick," I mutter, foolishly believing she won't be able to hear me from the living room.

"I ain't stupid," she says, her and the mutt both popping their heads through the doorway. "I know you got drunk."

I stand there, slack-jawed, while she pauses to love on the dog, totally oblivious to her own rudeness. "Anyway, Paw said it was okay because you are a grown-ass woman and you had a designated driver, so I have to let it go."

"Paw's right. And you'd do well to stay out of adult conversation. And mind your mouth, please."

She shrugs. "I heard my name. If you're talkin' 'bout me, that makes it my business."

"Hey Miss Priss," Wyatt interrupts with a perfectly timed distraction. "Rufus has a basket of toys next to the fireplace. I'm sure he'd love for you to take him out back and play fetch."

Thank you, I mouth when my little *demonling* takes his suggestion, hauling off at a sprint. "Still think I'm doing a great job?" I ask, echoing his sentiment from last night.

"I know it." He pours us each a cup of coffee, adding two creams and two sugars to mine, just the way I like it. Wyatt motions for me to follow before setting them both on the table. "You look like you could use this."

After pulling out my chair, he takes the one across from it. "Thanks."

"That kid is confident…loved…free to express herself. Not to mention smart as a whip."

The corners of my lips pull up in a smile. "You forgot willful, sassy…"

His grin vanishes. "Why do you do that?" he asks, running

his pointer finger around the rim of his mug while staring at the black liquid like it holds the answer to his question.

"Why do I do what?"

"Keep trying to scare me off of her."

His words hit like a punch to the gut, leaving me winded. "Do I?"

He nods, lifting his eyes to meet mine. "Constantly."

"I don't know. I guess I'm just waiting for the other shoe to drop." My eyes well with tears. Being called out on my parenting is a soft spot. "It's true what they say, you know? That when you hear something enough you start to believe it…"

"And what is it you're hearing?"

I sigh, fighting the urge to let the blasted tears fall. "I let her get away with too much… That I should be treating her more like a child and less like a friend…" I clear my throat. "She spends too much time around death."

"Who's telling you these things?"

"Her school. Other parents. Sometimes they say they're just concerned, other times they try to play it off as a joke." I shrug, taking a sip from my mug. "I just had her so young, you know? The truth is, I think she's perfect just the way she is, and I could never be with anyone who didn't feel the same. The way you accept her, quirks and all… Well," I sigh. "It just seems too good to be true."

"You're testing me?"

I consider his suggestion for a moment before answering with a nod. "Yeah, I guess I am."

Wyatt flops back in his seat, crossing his arms behind his head. The movement causes his shirt to ride up, revealing a delectable sliver of abs and happy trail. "Well?"

"Well, what?" My face flushes. I can tell by his lopsided smirk that he knows exactly what I've gotten distracted by.

"How am I doing?"

"To be determined."

He chuckles. "Fair enough." After a brief silence, he slaps both hands down on the table and rises to his feet. "You ready?"

"For?"

"To tour your future residence, of course."

I choke on my drink. "Your confidence has gotten out of control."

"Listen, when you know, you know."

I grip the arms of my chair and stare up at him. "And what is it you think you know?"

"We fit." He says it like it's a matter of fact while reaching for my hand.

The sky is blue. The grass is green. Wyatt and Whitney are meant to be.

His declaration has me frozen in place, unsure of how to respond—too smitten to ruin whatever is happening between us with an outright denial, yet still too leery to agree.

"It's okay," he says with a conspiratorial grin. "I'll keep that bit of info classified till you come to the same realization." His head motions to the back yard, where my daughter is squealing with laughter, having the time of her life with Rufus. "This doesn't have to go further than us."

"You're something else," I say, finally placing my hand in his outstretched palm and allowing him to lead me from the room.

"I like you, Whit." He gives my fingers a gentle squeeze. "I'm not going to waste another second pretending otherwise. You have every reason to be cautious." He leans down kissing the top of my head. "I have time. I just want to be sure you know where I stand. No crossed signals. No games."

"This feels really serious all of a sudden," I hedge, stepping down into the massive living area behind him.

"Of course it's serious. I'd never play games with anyone's affections. Least of all a child's."

His transparency is a breath of fresh air. I can't help but to envision us sharing the space, like he suggested, as he begins pointing out the changes he's made thus far—stripping and staining the original wood floors, removing the wallpaper and replacing it with sheetrock, and a few coats of light caramel paint. The fireplace has been completely redone with repurposed brick that gives off just the right vibe, keeping with the age of the house. The mantle is a thick cedar plank, stained to match the beams in the ceiling.

"This is incredible" I say, running a hand over the mantle, pausing at the lone framed photograph in the center. "Is this your family?"

"Yeah," he says, joining me. "Mimi had it framed on the one-year anniversary of the accident and hung it in my bedroom above my dresser. Stayed there til the day I left. I haven't done much decorating in here yet," he offers, running a thumb along my spine. "I'll save that part for you."

I stuff an elbow into his ribs. His responding laugh is hearty and genuine.

"That picture is the only thing I needed to make this place feel like home."

His admission brings a smile to my face. "That's you?" I point to the little boy with a mop of cotton white shoulder-length curls. He's wearing a white and blue striped button down with matching navy bowtie. *Cuteness overload.*

He nods.

"Aww. You were adorable."

"Were?" he mocks, smoothing a hand over his chest, standing tall and proud. "Dare I say, some things never change?"

"You really shouldn't be so modest, Wyatt." I wink. "You

might want to consider therapy. I'd hate for your lack of self-esteem to lead to depression."

"If I were any less depressed, I'd fart glittery rainbows."

"Now that's a visual," I giggle, shaking my head.

He touches a finger to the toddler in his mother's arms once our laughter has fizzled out. "Her name was Annie."

She is an absolute doll, in her pink frilly dress and huge matching bow. Her hair's a golden blonde and her skin porcelain white, but for a rosy hue on her cheeks. I can't quite tell if it's natural or an added affect. Either way, she's so perfect, it's hard to believe she was real.

The professional in me goes right to work painting the scene of the funeral, planning it all out in my head. Her little coffin on display between the two larger ones that would've held his parents. I'm gutted by the visual and trying desperately not to let it show.

"How old was she?"

"In this picture? Eighteen months. It was taken at my grandparents' house the Christmas before we lost them. She'd just turned two a few weeks before the accident."

A huge lump forms in my throat, and the urge to wrap my arms around that four-year-old little boy who lost his entire world in an instant is overwhelmingly strong. "Life can be so cruel."

"That it can, *mon chérie*." My dear.

Wyatt's getting awful comfortable with me as of late. I can't say the term of endearment doesn't set off a flutter in my chest, leaving me feeling both flattered and admittedly a little uneasy. It's been so long since I've truly entertained any man's attention.

"I'm sorry," I whisper, reaching for his hand and lacing my fingers with his. The need to acknowledge his pain is so strong.

He gives me an appreciative nod before turning to face the opposite wall. "Ready to check out our room?"

"Wyatt," I growl.

"Hey," he says, tugging me along, "a guy is nothing without his dreams."

"Show me the damn master."

He guides me to his room where he points out the newly refurbished floors and shiplapped walls. The king-sized bed has a simple wood frame that really fits the feel of the space. The adjoining master bath features a clawfoot tub that appears to be the original, if the green patina on the copper feet is any indication.

"There's no way you fit in that thing." I peer around the cramped room, looking for a standing shower, finding none. The state of disrepair makes it clear he hasn't started renovating in here yet.

"I'm really good at squeezing myself into tight spaces."

I bite my lip and shake my head. "I can't…I don't even know what to say to you."

"Allow me to demonstrate?" He hooks a thumb over his shoulder, pointing it toward the bed looming ten feet behind us.

"My kid is here."

"Oh, yeah…next time, then."

I neither accept nor decline his shameless offer, shaking my head to myself at how forward he's become while inwardly chastising myself for liking it so much.

"This is my next project," he says. "I'm going to extend the room, add in a walk-in shower fit for a king, and an enormous closet for *my queen*."

Once again, I decide it best not to respond, instead moving on to the next room, knowing he'll follow.

"This'll be the nursery, since it's closest to the master."

"Will it?" My mind starts filling the space with furniture—a crib on the far wall, a round braided rug with a little wooden rocking horse in the center. Model planes hanging from the ceiling. Lord, my imagination is running wild today. "So, you're planning on multiple kids?"

"Maybe." His shoulders rise and fall in a shrug. "With the right woman." He restates his position from Thanksgiving dinner while his eyes not so subtly journey over my form.

Heat radiates from my ears and my heart squeezes. I feel myself softening to the idea a little more with each brazen proposition being thrown at me. Before I can do anything foolish, my flight response kicks into overdrive.

"Next!" I say, choosing self-preservation and hightailing it down the hall.

"These two rooms are a little bigger," he says, peering over my shoulder, "and share a Jack and Jill bath." Wyatt crosses the room, opening the door to the bathroom, which contains a tub-shower combo and all of his manly soaps and shampoos. There's even a towel draped over the curtain rod and a little steam still fogging the mirror. *Hah. I knew he wasn't fitting his ass in that tub.* "Prissy can have her choice, or even both, until we have to free up the nursery again."

"Sounds like you plan on keeping your future wife busy."

He waggles his brows. "I promise, I'll leave no room for complaints."

Well, then.

CHAPTER EIGHTEEN

Wyatt

Having Whitney and Prissy here in my space feels right. Two months doesn't seem like a lot of time—certainly not enough to be envisioning forever with a person. Neither does it seem sufficient to be prepared to commit to taking on a six-year-old child. But every move I make, every change, every addition to this old house, is with them in mind—much to my Mimi's displeasure.

My grandmother's worried I'm moving too fast. She says I need to slow down and stop letting my emotions lead. But I know that once she has the chance to meet the new ladies in my life, she'll be just as smitten as I am.

"Shhhh!" I say when Miss Priss comes thundering in with Rufus following closely behind. "She fell asleep." I point to the living room, where Whitney is curled up snoring on the sectional.

"Sorry." She scrunches her shoulders. "Wanna see what I taught Sprinkles?"

I look around to see what the heck she's talking about. *Did she find a new pet in the woods?*

"Just watch," she orders, grabbing a handful of treats from the jar on the counter that was so full it could barely close this morning and is now damn near empty. "Sprinkles, sit!"

My usually obstinate pup obediently plops his ass on the floor, wagging his tail as he stares at her expectantly.

"Good boy," Prissy praises, placing a Milkbone on his tongue and giving him a scrub behind the ears.

"*What* did you just call him?"

"Rufus is a stupid name," she says with a shrug.

I choke on air. "Excuse me?"

"You heard me. What even *is* a Rufus anyway?"

"A name," I answer. "A *manly* name for a *manly* dog."

"He looks like vanilla ice cream with chocolate sprinkles. It had to be changed."

"You can't just change a dog's name. He's eight months old. He likes his name. He knows it."

"Does he?" she asks, arching a brow. Jesus, she looks so much like her mother right now it's almost scary.

"Rufus." I whistle. "Come here boy."

He lets out a whimper, but stays rooted in place, his eyes trained on the girl with the snacks.

"Sprinkles, come." Priss points to the floor.

That traitor rises to all fours, looking more regal than Queen Elizabeth herself as he marches to her side. *Man's best friend, my ass.*

"Good boy," she says, stuffing another treat into his mouth. "Sprinkles, sit."

He sits.

"Shake," she says, holding out her hand for his paw.

"You taught him all of that in less than two hours?"

"Uh-huh. Wasn't hard. I watched some dog training videos."

"Let me guess, YouTube?"

She grins. "Well, it worked."

"I see that."

"So…Sprinkles?" She steeples her hands in front of her face, poking out her lip for added drama.

And that, ladies and gentlemen, is the story of how my beast of a dog became a pansy.

"You're a disgrace," I grumble at the pooch while nodding my head at the little girl. "Guess I can't change what's already done."

She beams, wrapping her arms around my waist. "I've always wanted a dog. Think maybe we can share yours?"

What I think is I'd find a way to give this child the fucking moon if she asked for it. "Don't see why not."

"Thanks, Wyatt. You're the best!"

"I try."

"Hey," she says, disentangling herself. "You don't have a tree."

I can hardly keep up with the kid and the way she jumps from one topic straight into a new one. "A what?" I ask, staring through the still open door. "I have a yard full of them."

"A *Christmas* tree, Wyatt."

"Oh." Well, she's got me there.

"It's in three weeks, you know? Where's Santa gonna leave Sprinkles's presents?" The disapproval in her tone has me ready to right this misstep immediately.

"That's because I was…waiting for you and your momma to help me. It's no fun putting a tree up all alone."

"Really?" she squeals. "Where is it? In the attic?"

"The tree lot."

She frowns.

"Come on," I say, motioning for her to follow. I grab the keys from the hook and my wallet from the counter, slipping it into my back pocket on my way to the living room.

"Hey," I say, squatting beside the woman sawing wood on my couch. I can smell the alcohol still seeping from her pores when I give her shoulder a gentle shake.

"Huh?" She jumps with a start, nearly rolling to the floor. I give her a moment to orient herself while her daughter practically pisses herself laughing.

"Is it okay if I take Priss with me to the store?"

"Uh, yeah…sure," she says, wiping the drool from her chin with the back of a hand. "Want me to come?"

"Nah. We won't be long. Rest up for tonight."

Shopping with a kid is an adventure. An expensive adventure.

Three stores and nearly four hours later, we come trudging back into the house with our arms overflowing with bags and a monstrous tree strapped down in the bed of the truck.

"What's all this?"

"I could ask the same question," I counter when I find Whitney wide awake, whipping up an impressive spread of breakfast for dinner.

She shrugs, "Didn't know what to do with myself when I got up. This was the best I could do for a meal. You didn't have much to work with." Her eyes widen, like she's just come to some major realization. "I hope you weren't planning on us going out to eat." She starts nibbling on her lip, making the vision before me even more tempting.

"This is so much better than anything I had planned," I

assure her, because damn, seeing this woman scrambling eggs and frying up bacon on my stove feels like a little preview of the domesticated life I've been fantasizing about lately.

"Planning on doing some decorating?" she asks, peeking into the bags.

"We're gonna do it!" Prissy says, dropping the lot she's carrying to the floor. "Wyatt was waiting for us to come over to put up his tree."

"Was he now?" she asks, eying me skeptically.

"I was," I readily agree, fighting the urge to kiss that knowing smile off her face. It's getting harder to behave myself when her little girl's around. Now that she's gotten comfortable with me touching her, it's a constant urge.

All in due time.

"Hope you're ready to deck the halls," I say, dropping my load and heading back out to the truck for the rest.

"*The Nightmare Before Christmas?*" Whitney shakes her head as she continues pulling items from bags once we've finished stuffing ourselves into a food coma. "I don't even need to ask whose idea this was."

"It was mine," Prissy beams.

"You don't say?" Whit runs a hand through her daughter's hair before pressing a kiss to her cheek.

"Hey," I interrupt, feeling left out. "I picked the topper."

"Well, let's see it," Whitney urges.

I finish tightening the last screw in the base of the tree's trunk before getting up and dusting the needles and dirt from my pants.

"Here," Prissy says, passing me the white box the clerk carefully packaged it in.

"Where did y'all even find this stuff?" Whit's eyes light up when she sees the ornate black velvet top hat with Jack's face front and center. His bowtie is made of purple, teal, and orange ribbon, and there are glittery swirls around the hat in the same colors. It's bright and festive. *And so Prissy.*

"The girl said she wanted a *Nightmare Before Christmas* tree, so I went online and found a little boutique in the French Quarter that carried it." I shrug. "That's where we found most of this stuff."

"I love these!" Whit's face lights up when she finds the balls, some hand painted with Jack's face and some with Sally's. There are others made of handblown glass in the shape of the characters. "You must've spent a fortune on all this."

"He let me run wild," Prissy says. "We even found a Jack outfit for Sprinkles."

"Sprinkles?" Her brow furrows. "Who's that?"

"Come here, Sprinkles," I call, luring the big lug from his bed. "Whitney, I'd like to introduce you to Sprinkles, the beast formerly known as Rufus."

Her forehead wrinkles. "I am so confused."

"Wyatt let me change his name!"

"Wha—?" She looks from her daughter to me—back and forth a few times. "Prissy, he's just being nice. You can't just change a dog's name."

"That's what I said."

Whit releases a relieved sigh. "Thank you. Finally, someone's speaking some sense."

"And then she proved me wrong." I hold my hands out, palms up in surrender.

"You don't have to give her everything she wants, Wyatt." The concern on her face is adorable.

"Can I show her?" The little girl is bursting at the seams with pride.

When I nod, she runs off to the kitchen, returning with a handful of treats from one of the boxes we just purchased. Then proceeds to demonstrate all the new things she's managed to teach the big galoot.

"Turns out he's not simple-minded after all," I say. "Just needed the right teacher."

"And name," Prissy adds. "Don't forget the name."

"That too."

Whitney shakes her head at the both of us. "I still think it's confusing as hell for the poor animal, but what do I know?"

"Nothin', Momma. You don't even like animals."

"This one's not so bad," she says, seeming surprised by her own admission. "Look at him." She points to the dog, who's just curled up on his bed in front of the fireplace, resting his head on his favorite stuffed bear. "He's even a little cute when he's not jumping and slobbering on people."

Well, I've just mentally checked off another box. Get her on board with the idea of having a horse-sized dog…*check*. Although she might not know that he's not full-grown yet. We'll save that conversation for another day.

CHAPTER NINETEEN

Whitney

With only two weeks remaining until Christmas, the funeral home has been a complete mad house. In the last week alone, we've had two suicides and a group of three high school seniors who smashed into a tree after a night of partying. There were no survivors.

That one shook me to my core. I've still not gotten over it. Daddy fixed them up beautifully, and I spent an entire night in the prep room with those girls, fussing over their makeup as if they were my own.

Sometimes I wonder what it would be like to have a normal profession. To be able to go to work and return home without having the weight of grief resting on my shoulders. As tempting as that idea can be at times, I know I'll never actually leave. Too much of who I am I owe to this place. And, as silly as it may sound, I don't want to entrust the job to anyone else.

"Mornin', gorgeous." The deep baritone greeting is accompanied by a light rap to the door frame.

Drawing in a deep breath, I look up from my planner to find the most welcome sight there is, Wyatt Landry in a toolbelt.

Yum. Yum. Gimme some.

Although nothing's been made official yet, it's safe to say the two of us are an unlabeled item. I believe what we're doing in fancier circles would be referred to as courting. I'm fairly certain my parents have drawn the same conclusion as a result of our frequent lunch dates.

As long as Prissy is none the wiser, I could care less who knows. I'm not quite ready to cross that bridge with her yet.

"Hey, yourself." His unexpected drop-in brings a much-needed smile to my face and a warm fuzzy sensation spreading throughout my body. "Isn't this a pleasant surprise?" I set my pen down, offering him my undivided attention.

"Is it?" He steps inside, shutting the door behind himself. "Come gimme some suga, suga."

"You're so corny." Giggling, I hop up from my chair and round my desk at warp speed. The man makes me feel giddy, like a young girl completely addicted to the rush of endorphins one gets while falling for the boy of her dreams.

And that's exactly what he's turning out to be. Only I'm not a girl, and he's certainly no boy. And the possible repercussions that hang on the outcome of this particular bout of puppy love are enormous.

"Replace that C in corny with an H and you would be correct." He pulls me close, pressing his pelvis into my waist to demonstrate before molding his lips to mine. His kiss is warm and tender and over far sooner than I'd like. The groan that slips out as he pulls away relays as much.

"There are two sobbing women in the lobby." With a frustrated laugh, he presses a final smooch to the tip of my nose. "They're here to make Mr. Boudreaux's arrangements."

"Renovating the chapel, collecting dead bodies, and now acting as my personal secretary…" I run my hands over his shoulders and along his arms while staring into his hungry eyes. "Is there anything you don't do, Mr. Landry?"

"Yes." His answer is immediate and leaves my cheeks burning on account of the ravenous smolder that accompanies it.

"Shameless," I hiss, swatting him on the ass before slinking away and slipping into the chair behind my desk. "You may see them in…and feel free to make arrangements for my lunch break." I touch a finger to my chin, smiling coyly. "Why don't you invite that hot handyman working in the chapel?"

"Now who's shameless?" he teases, twisting the doorknob. "Pick ya up at noon."

"Don't be late!"

As soon as he's gone, I have the urge to call him back—not that I can act on it, seeing how I have less than a minute to switch myself back into work mode.

"Ms. Daigle?"

"In here," I call out to the feminine shadow hovering just outside my door.

A woman who can't be much older than I am peeks her head into my office. She's a little mousy, with layered, shoulder-length hair and the same red-rimmed eyes I encounter on a regular basis. "Come on in," I say, waving her inside. "Please, have a seat."

An older version of her slips in right after.

"Both of you," I add, directing them to the two chairs across from mine.

"I'm Maria," the younger of the two offers, "and this is my mom, Vicky."

The grieving widow lifts one finger in greeting while blowing snot into a hanky.

"It's a pleasure to meet you both," I say, offering them a

box of tissue. "I'm very sorry it had to be under such awful circumstances."

"Thank you," Maria says, cringing when her mother sets her bag down and it *barks*.

"Mom," she grits, nearly expiring from mortification.

"It's fine," I assure her. I rise from my seat, peering over the top of my desk to seem more welcoming. "Who do we have here?" I ask when not one, but two little Yorkshire terriers climb up onto her lap.

"Lucy and Ricky," Mrs. Boudreaux says. "Harold was so fond of his puppies." She pauses to dab at her face. "He took them everywhere."

"That's lovely."

"I couldn't leave them behind."

"Of course not," I say. "They are more than welcome."

That comment earns me my first wobbly smile from the woman.

It's not uncommon for the bereaved to latch onto something that makes them feel closer to a lost loved one. They'll wear their clothes or drive their cars. Serve all of their favorite foods during the reception. We once had a father insist to having his son's dirt bike beside the casket. This is the first time we've had a client bring along a pet, or two rather, to schedule funeral arrangements, but we are in the habit of making whatever allowances possible to make this painful process a little more bearable.

"Well, they are precious," I say, smiling huge while sending up a silent prayer that they don't relieve themselves in my office.

"Yes." She twirls the tail of the smaller one between her fingers. "They are."

"So," I say, determined to move things along as quickly and efficiently as possible, "it is my understanding we're to have a traditional viewing and burial?"

Maria nods while Vicky fawns over her companions, not seeming to be paying one iota of attention.

"Well, then. Why don't we head over to the casket room so you can make a selection? Afterward, we can come back here to go over the financials and finalize plans."

In no time at all, the women settle on a mid-priced pine casket. It's sturdy and masculine and what they both feel he'd choose for himself.

We are back in my office in record time, and I'm counting my blessings that so far, our tiny guests have left no souvenirs.

"I have a request," Vicky says, just as we're beginning to wrap things up.

The command in her tone catches me off guard, but I'm honestly relieved that she's finally coming out of the fog she's been in and partaking in this meeting. "Name it." I give her my most sincere smile. "We will do whatever possible to make it happen."

"Harold—he wanted to be buried with his babies." She runs a hand lovingly over Lucy's head, then adjusts the bows on her ears.

"The dogs," Maria quickly clarifies. "She doesn't mean *actual* babies."

Like that somehow makes this request any more acceptable.

My eyes volley between the two of them and then focus on the little purse puppies cuddled together in Vicky's lap. I can taste the bile rising in the back of my throat—climbing higher and higher with every second that ticks by. I'm not even sure what I'm waiting for…the hook, maybe? There's no way they are serious.

They can't be.

Once the silence becomes unbearably uncomfortable, I have little choice but to accept that this is in fact not a joke and that these women are completely deranged.

I don't care that my father is in the back embalming this man as we speak. If they decide to take their business elsewhere, so be it. Daddy will just have to work it out. I refuse to entertain this for even a moment longer.

"I'm sorry," I say, choking on disgust. "There's no way I can go along with this."

"But you just sai—" Harold's widow starts.

The tips of my ears are as hot as Hades. "I know what I said, but I cannot allow you to murder those poor puppies."

Maria snorts before losing herself to a fit of hysterical laughter. She's folded over, hooting like a complete loon.

I feel like I've just transported to an alternate universe. *What the hell is wrong with these people?* I understand grief—probably better than most. But this…never in my wildest dreams did I imagine such a request.

"I don't see how you could possibly find any of this funny." I'm literally seconds away from calling the authorities on Lucy and Ricky's behalf. Horrified doesn't come close to defining what I feel.

"Not *these* puppies," Maria finally squeaks out. "They're already dead."

"Oh, thank God." My body literally deflates as I collapse into my seat with relief. I reach for a stack of paper from my desk and start fanning myself with it.

"We're not monsters," Vicky snaps, clearly offended. The eyes she has aimed at me reflect the derision I felt just moments ago.

"I'm very sorry, Mrs. Boudreaux. I misunderstood."

The woman sneers before stuffing her pets back into their bag. "I'll be right back."

"Yes, ma'am."

"Don't mind her," Maria tells me, sensing my discomfort. "It was an honest mistake, and quite hilarious. God, I needed that laugh, today of all days. Thank you."

I nod and try to force a smile while still staring after the angry woman. "I feel awful."

"Don't," Maria says. "She's been completely out of sorts."

"That's understandable."

Maria and I make small talk while awaiting her mother's return. I assume she's gone out for a breather or even a cigarette. Maybe to let the puppies have a potty break. I am not at all prepared for what happens when she comes back into the room, though I thought I'd seen just about everything by now.

"This is Wilma and Fred."

I turn toward the door to find Vicky lugging two taxidermied Malteses—one tucked beneath each arm.

"I see," I say, trying like hell to conceal the tremor in my voice.

"We'd like to place them next to the casket at the viewing and then bury them with my husband."

"Well..." I clear my throat. "I certainly have no problem with that."

"Perfect!" The woman sets them on the floor. "We'll just leave them here rather than toting them back and forth."

"Great," I croak. "Anything else?"

"That'll be all," Vicky says, leaving without so much as a farewell.

"Thanks for everything," Maria says, reaching out to shake my hand. "And sorry about all of this." Her eyes dart to the stuffed dogs eyeballing me from a few feet away. "My parents are a bit *eccentric*."

"Yep. Don't even worry about it. Get some rest. You have a long couple of days ahead of you."

"Ready to roll?—Oh, hold up." Wyatt pinches his chin with the thumb and forefinger of one hand while pointing to my new roommates with the other. "Those weren't here this morning."

"No," I agree. "They most certainly were not."

"Something you ordered for Prissy?" he asks, bending down to touch them. He pulls a face. "Why are they so hard?"

"They're not for Prissy."

"Okay…" He picks one up, examining it more closely. "They look so real."

"Mmmhmm," I agree, literally suffocating on the laughter I'm suppressing. "Would you mind turning them to face the wall while you're down there?"

Their lifeless eyes have my skin crawling. I realize that my aversion to them is absurd, considering I spend so much of my time with the deceased. Irrational as it may be, having these poor puppies sharing my space is weirding me out.

I have questions. *So many questions.*

How long have they been dead? Were they displayed on a bookshelf? Collecting dust in an attic? Do they dress them up like baby dolls for the holidays?

Wyatt does as I ask then rises to his feet. "This is some strange décor for someone who doesn't really have a fondness for animals."

"They are *not* décor." I shut my books and grab my purse before walking around to lace my arm through his. I can't get out of here fast enough. "They are Wilma and Fred, and their funeral is tomorrow."

CHAPTER TWENTY

Wyatt

After rolling up to my usual spot in front of the funeral home, I shift the truck into park and let it idle, flipping my visor down to check my hair. I rotate my head this way and that, taking the time to make sure each strand is perfectly placed. There's a slight chance that I may be stalling.

With my hand finally positioned on the door handle, I do a quick count backward from ten, fully intent upon flinging it open, but I chicken out and tug the visor back down, this time under the guise of checking the status of my black bow tie. I give that a little adjustment, as well as the collar to my matching oxford.

It's not even fifty degrees out and I'm wiping sweat off my palms onto my dress pants.

Why am I so nervous?

Just yesterday, I spent well over an hour at the flower shop trying to decide on what color roses to get for her bouquet. Who knew that was such an involved process? *Certainly not me.* My first instinct was black, since it's her current obsession. Pretty obvious, right? Then I read the back of the card, learned they represent death, and couldn't do it. There's no way I was bringing that child death flowers. Prissy's not one for bright and colorful. So, where some shade of pink would be the clear choice for most little girls, they wouldn't work for my date. In the end, I settled on ivory. Hazel, the florist, said they would be the perfect color to show someone you care without romantic intentions.

Have I put too much thought into this? *Absolutely.*

The fact that I'm behaving like a crazy person is not lost on me, but that doesn't prevent the need for a pep talk from yours truly just to work up enough nerve to get out of my vehicle and ring the damn doorbell.

The self-imposed pressure I feel to impress this child is more than any date I've ever been on. I've done all I can think of to make her night magical—to give her a memory she'll look back on fondly for years to come. Every little girl deserves to feel like a princess at least once—even tomboys with morbid curiosities and a fondness for four-letter-words.

I take a deep gulp of the cool December air, brush off the last-minute jitters, then crush my finger to the button and wait.

And wait.

And wait.

"What the hell are you doing, boy?" The door gives way to Hank's puckered face. "Since when do you ring the bell?" He grunts like a boar. "Making me come down all them dang stairs."

"I was trying to make a good impression on the family." I give him a pointed look, to which he rolls his eyes and hangs his head, slowly rotating it side to side. I can't tell whether he's impressed or disgusted with my shenanigans—the niggling worry stirs a little frenzy in my gut.

"Stay right here. I'll go get her." The door slams in my face, then instantly swings back open. "You look real nice, by the way."

Well, that was *unexpected.* "Thanks."

He nods. "Almost forgive ya for stealin' my date."

"You waitin' on an apology to go along with that whine?" I ask when he continues to stand there glowering at me.

Once more the heavy oak door slams leaving me chuckling to myself on the threshold. *Yep, he'll do just fine for a father-in-law.*

When it creaks open again—for what is likely the first time in my life—I find myself completely lost for words.

A sudden knot forms in my throat. I didn't expect to be so affected by the sight of this little girl all dolled up. Nor to feel the sense of pride in the way she's beaming up at me that's swelling my chest to near bursting.

Prissy's long blonde hair has been curled and styled half up with loose bits around her face. True to her word, she let her momma add a touch of pink to her cheeks and gloss on her lips. It's just enough to enhance her natural beauty. She looks polished, but not overdone. Her dress is black—*no surprise there*—fitted at the top with sequins, flaring out at the waist into a poufy tulle skirt that ends mid-calf.

"We match!" she screams, jutting a booted foot out into the space between us. Dimples dent her cheeks when she stares down at the combat boots I acquired for myself just for the occasion.

"Got a leather jacket sitting on the seat of my truck too." I quirk a brow. "If your momma's okay with you wearing yours, of course."

Her wide eager eyes light up. "Can I?"

I've never seen a bigger smile on Whitney's face. "Go get it," she says, while her eyes well with tears.

"How are you even real?" Once the little one has scampered

off, Whitney steps forward, reaching out to cup my cheeks in her hands. "You thought of everything."

Her touch is soft and warm, and sets my heart pumping a little faster. "I tried."

She drags a thumb over my lower lip, giving a gentle tug downward. "She'll be talking about this for weeks."

I grin, fighting the urge to lean down and suck her plump lower lip into my mouth. "I hope longer than that."

She visibly trembles when I brush her hair back from her shoulder, gifting myself with a whiff of her sweet perfume.

"Got it!" Prissy yells.

Whitney drops her hands to her sides, stepping back like she's just been burned.

"Go get yours," Prissy orders, heaving for breath from her mad dash down the stairs. "So Momma can take the picture.

"Wait," I say, crouching to her level while whipping the arm around that's been hidden behind my back for so long now it's gone numb. "Almost forgot. These are for you."

"You got me flowers?"

"I did."

Without warning, she flings her arms around my neck. I swear my heart grows three sizes. "Thank you, Wyatt."

I rub a hand over her back, patting it gently. "You're welcome, squirt."

"I'll go put these in a vase while you get your jacket," Whitney says, taking the bouquet from Prissy and rushing off, I'm assuming to avoid us seeing her become emotional.

If that's what helps her sleep at night, I'll never mention the tears I watched her swat away on her way to the kitchen.

"Well don't you look beautiful, Priscilla," Principal Wyler greets as we walk through the gym doors into a winter wonderland. "Where's Hank tonight?"

"Embalming Joel Dugas," Priss answers with a sly grin.

God, I love the fire in this kid. Her snappy response has me beaming with pride like I had anything at all to do with her badassery.

The middle-aged woman blanches before checking herself and plastering on one of the most unnatural smiles I've ever borne witness to. "Aren't you going to introduce your date?"

"Oh, yeah!" Her little hand tightens around mine. "This is Wyatt. He's my momma's boyfriend, and when they get married, he's gonna be my stepdad."

From her lips to God's ears.

"Oh?" She brings a hand to her chest. "I didn't even know your momma was dating anyone."

"Just friends," I say, in a whisper carefully concealed behind the back of my hand just in case this conversation gets back to Whitney. It's a precarious position to be in, for sure—not wanting to hurt Prissy but terrified of pissing her momma off.

"Of course you are." Mrs. Wyler gives a discrete wink before pointing us in the direction of the photographer. "Enjoy y'all's evening."

My answering smile is forced. I'm not in the practice of putting on airs, but I can't help but think she's one of the ones making Whitney self-conscious about her parenting skills. Apparently I'm now holding grudges on her behalf.

I think that pretty much makes me husband material. I'll have to let her know.

After waiting in line and having our picture taken, we head toward the big round tables set up in the back. At the center of each is wide array of hot chocolate toppings meant to customize the drinks that are delivered to us piping hot as soon as the mom in charge sees me pull out my date's chair.

"You're not adding any of this yummy stuff?" Priss gapes at me while shoving a handful of caramel chips into hers.

"I'm good." I take a sip from the foam cup to prove it.

She shrugs, adds a few blocks of Hershey's chocolate and a handful of marshmallows, then begins mixing the chunky concoction with a peppermint stick

This kid is gonna be *lit* in a few minutes.

"Hey," I say when I notice girls clustering together at the other tables, "don't you wanna go sit with some of your friends?"

She quits her stirring, drops the stick, and stares up at me with the most pitiful of expressions. "They think I'm weird."

The air whooshes from my chest. "All of them?"

She nods, then shrugs it off. "Paw says they're just jealous cuz I'm the smartest. I let him believe that because I think it makes him feel better about things. But I know they just don't like me."

Adrenaline floods my veins. I'm angry enough to break shit—ready to go to war for this kid. "You have no friends?" I ask, trying to keep a steady tone while secretly dying inside.

"Oh, no…I do." Her eyes that were once twinkling with excitement are glistening for an entirely other reason now. "Jacob and Preston are my BFFs, but this is a girl thing, so…"

"So, they couldn't come?"

She nods.

While digesting this new information, I become hyper-aware of what's taking place behind us. The whispers about her "ugly" black dress. Her "boy" boots. The mystery behind her date…me.

One of those awful little girls whisper-yells to her friends,

"She thinks she's so cool because she got someone besides her creepy grandpa to come with her."

I'm already seeing red when the little brat's father laughs at her antics. It takes every ounce of restraint I possess not to punch him square in his jaw. Instead, I turn and level him with a pair of warning eyes when Prissy isn't paying attention. He has enough sense to look ashamed.

"Come on," I say, reaching for her hand when that Whip Nae Nae song comes on and flurry of pink rushes by, headed for the dance floor.

She stares at me like a deer in headlights, unmoving.

"You know the steps; I've seen you do it a million times in the lobby after school."

Prissy brings her thumbnail to her mouth, chewing nervously. "You'll come with me?"

"Well, duh." I make my voice loud enough for the mean dads to hear. "What kind of man sits on his butt and watches his date dance?"

Finally, a grin. Albeit small and wobbly, but right now I'll take it.

"Okay." She sighs deeply before slapping her little hand into mine. "Let's do this."

With the upmost pride, I lead my date to the dance floor, front and center. She glances up at me, gnawing on her lip, while together we wait for the chorus to hit. Then, I put my nightly YouTube dance lessons to the test.

"You know the steps," Prissy squeals in shock, while nae-nae'ing like a fucking boss.

"Learned it just for you."

"Wyatt?" she calls while we're breaking down the Stanky Legg and all the little snooty girls crowd around, cheering us on.

"Yeah?"

"You're a really good fake dad."

I'm so deeply touched by her words that I can't do anything but offer her a smile, fight back tears, and keep on moving.

When I agreed to this date, I went all in, determined to give Prissy a magical night she wouldn't soon forget, never expecting it'd turn out to be one of the most memorable of *my* life.

CHAPTER TWENTY-ONE

Whitney

"Where should I put her?"

This image of Wyatt, with my sleeping child cradled in his arms, will be etched in my mind for as long as there is a heart pushing blood through my veins.

"How was it?" I whisper, trying not to become emotional while signaling for him to follow me up to the apartment.

"Best night of my whole entire life!" the little faker proclaims.

"That so?" I laugh, holding the door open so he can pass through, then trailing them to her room. "In all your six years, huh?"

"Yep!" She yawns, peering at me over his shoulder. "You shoud'a seen Lydia's stupid face when me and him showed out on the dance floor."

I narrow my eyes toward the man in question. "Thought you couldn't dance?"

He simply shrugs.

"Wait for me in the living room?" I ask, once he's deposited her on her bed. "I shouldn't be long."

"You got it." Wyatt bends down to press a kiss to the top of Prissy's head, causing every last cell in my being to swoon. "Had a great time, Priss. We'll have to do it again," he says as he crosses the room.

"Just me and you?"

He pauses in the doorway looking back at me for permission, which I unwaveringly grant, with a bob of my head.

"Just me and you," he echoes back.

My baby is smitten. "Night, Wyatt."

"So, you really had a good time?" I ask once he's left the room.

"Uh-huh."

"And he *danced?*" I remove the pins she's scratching at from her hair.

"Yep! I was so surprised," she says, stepping out of the dress I just unzipped. "Wyatt's got moves, Momma."

"Does he?" I chuckle. "Slip your arms through," I instruct after passing her nightgown over her head.

"It was just like in the movies, with everyone crowded around us." The dreamy look in her eyes resembles the sensation warming my chest, and I think I know just how she feels.

"He's really good to you," I muse, shaking out her dress and draping it over the chair.

"Yeah," she agrees, hopping back into bed. "And he's super nice to you, too," she presses.

"The best."

"And soooo handsome."

My cheeks flush. "He is definitely that as well." I smooth her hair back, tugging the covers up to her neck before leaning down to smother her perfect little face in kisses.

"Momma?" Her voice beckons to me as I reach the door.

"Yeah, baby?"

"You think he likes us?"

"I know he does."

She shifts to her side, propping her head up on her bent elbow. "No, I mean *likes us*, likes us?"

"I'm not sure what you're asking." Although I am. I'm just stalling for a minute—or ten—to come up with an answer.

She sighs. "I mean enough to be your boyfriend."

"Well—I… Prissy, it's just—"

"We're not getting any younger, Momma."

I snort. "We're hardly a pair of old grannies."

"He's a fun dad."

Dear Lord. This is exactly what I was afraid of. "Prissy, he's *not* your dad."

"Well, he didn't get mad when I told everyone he was your boyfriend and was gonna be."

"Priscilla Louise Daigle!" I'm suddenly weak and feeling a bit woozy. "Why on earth would you say that?"

"Because I want him to be."

Tears prick the backs of my eyes as I stand there wordlessly staring into my daughter's pleading face.

"Can you just consider it?"

I'm certainly not about to tell my six-year-old that it's practically all I think about anymore. "Good night, child of mine," I answer in a tone that bodes no argument.

"Night, mother of mine," she grumbles in turn.

After shutting the door, I sag against it, replaying that conversation a dozen times, wondering if the way I handled it was acceptable, worrying I'm ruining my child's life.

"Whit?" Wyatt calls. My heart rate increases with each footstep that draws near. "Hey." The smile he flashed as he rounded the corner falters.

"Hey, you." The mere sight of him has me shaking like a leaf.

"Did you change your mind about that talk? I can head on home if you're tired."

"No." My reply is immediate. "You think maybe I could come with you?"

"Home?" He studies my features, no doubt trying to determine whether or not I'm serious.

I nod, swallowing hard. "To…to talk."

"Yeah," he says while nodding his head. "Mi casa es su casa."

Dare I even hope?

My parents, of course, are more than willing to keep an eye on their beloved granddaughter so I can hang out with Wyatt for a bit. I knew they would be. It wouldn't surprise me to learn that one of them was responsible for planting this little fantasy of the three of us becoming a family in her head to begin with.

Being the upstanding man that he is, Wyatt insists I ride with him, even though he'll have to bring me right back in a couple hours.

The man really is perfection personified. He's charming. Beautiful, both inside and out. Thoughtful. And he makes it no secret that he adores my kid. I could certainly do worse. Come to think of it, I don't think I could possibly do better.

So, what am I waiting for?

"Penis for your thoughts."

"Huh?" I ask with a jump, knocking my head on the window. I must've misheard him.

"Just trying to get your attention."

I shake my head, rubbing out the sting. "Well, that got it, all right."

"We're here." He points through the windshield toward the house ten feet in front of us.

The truck is in park.

The motor's off.

"How long have we been sitting here?"

"Not long, but I'm fucking freezing. Think we could go inside?"

"Of course." I wink. "Was waitin' on you."

"Why are you acting so weird with me tonight?" he asks when we reach the living room and I can't stop pacing. "Sit down." He pats the couch beside him. "Please. You're giving me anxiety."

I nod, perching on the very edge of the cushion. My knees won't stop vibrating while I search for the nerve to say what I came here to say.

"Why does it feel like you're about to break up with me?"

"Jesus," I groan, running a hand through my hair. "Have the whole bunch of you gone mad?"

His eyes widen as he stares after me, awaiting an explanation for my attitude.

"We're not together."

My pulse thrums as the corners of his mouth curve into a smile. "But we should be…and you know it."

Shameless. "Prissy *would* like me to give this a shot."

His jaw ticks. It's the first time I've ever seen him anything that even resembles frustrated with me. "At the moment, I'm a little more interested in what *you* think."

With a contrite bob of my head, I spring back to my feet, crossing the room to stand in front of the fireplace. It's imperative I put a little distance between us in order to get a handle on my thoughts. I can't concentrate through the cloud of longing that takes over whenever he's near. "I think…" I pause, choking back tears. "I think that I—I could be falling in love with you." Worrying my hands, I have to force myself not to divert my gaze to the floor. I said it. *Now, I'm going to own it.*

The man who carries the lead role in my every dream rises

from the couch, sauntering toward me with purpose. "Good. Because I'm already there." He tilts my chin upward. "I've been for quite some time."

"Is it?" My voice warbles and I can hardly breathe as the first of many tears blazes a path down my cheek. "Is it good, I mean? Because I've never been more terrified." My hand flies to my mouth to cover a sob. "Not even at sixteen with a baby growing inside me, knowing her father wanted nothing to do with us."

His thumbs swipe away the emotion pooling beneath my eyes, and he nods—ever so patient, so understanding. "It isn't yourself that you have issues trusting."

His words bounce around in my head, ringing out with glaring truth. "You're right. The thought of letting anyone else into our lives, of exposing Prissy or even myself to that kind of pain…" I shudder at the thought, before hugging my arms to my chest. "I—I'm afraid."

"Jump," he pleads, curling his hands beneath my hair and around my nape. "And I promise to catch you." His knuckles stroke over my jaw, slowly, fueling the fire burning inside me. "Let me love you, Whitney. Without restraint—the way you deserve. The way you *both* deserve."

"Okay." I nod, sniveling. "Okay," I repeat with a little more conviction, because in coming here tonight, I've realized I'm already so far gone for this man that the only alternative is heartache. I tried. Oh God, how I tried, but I've failed *miserably* at locking him out. "Just don't hurt my little girl."

He tugs me closer, until my face is but an inch from his. "You have my word."

"Then you have my heart."

In an instant his lips are on mine, so soft and lush. His tongue is warm and seeking. And his hands—they're everywhere all at once. And yet, it isn't enough.

"Wyatt." There's an undeniable desperation to my voice as he scorches a path along my jaw to the shell of my ear. The heat of his breath has me buckling at the knees, quite literally melting for him.

In one fell swoop, I'm in his arms, with my eyes bolted on his.

"I want you," I cry, my body trembling from the top of my head to the tips of my toes with unrestrained need. "Please." Frantically, I begin fooling with the buttons of his dress shirt, eager to feel his skin on mine. One by one I pop them open and begin to trace his defined abs with my fingertips.

"No need to beg, love." He nips at my lip before pulling back slightly.

My body screams out in protest.

"Bed, or couch?"

"Bed, *definitely*."

He carries me to his room, gently placing me in the center of the mattress, the bulge of his biceps stretching through the fabric of his shirt as he crawls in over me. "You're sure?" he asks, like I'm some delicate flower.

"Now isn't the time for your games," I warn, reaching to unfasten his belt and pop the button on his pants.

He chuckles, the deep warble thick with lust before trailing off as his intense gaze locks with mine. He lowers his body, his chest expanding with strength as he hovers over me, claiming my mouth once again.

My hips arch instinctively toward the ceiling as his roving hands reach around my waist and to my back, sliding underneath my cotton tee shirt. The access allows his skilled fingers ample space to quickly skim the band of my bra before finding the hook, releasing it with a simple flick.

Gritting my teeth, I shudder at the feeling of soft lace

trailing against skin as he lowers my bra and pulls it from under my shirt. Every nerve is heightened. I writhe and squirm, my stomach twisting in knots with the need for his hands to be back on me. When his warm, calloused palm covers my breast, desire pools between my legs. Gently, he tugs at my nipple sending a jolt of pleasure shooting right to my core.

"Jesus," he growls when I begin grinding my hips into the impressive bulge that's been digging into my waist.

His sexy moans spur me on, giving me the courage to sneak a hand between us and cup him through his slacks.

Laughter rumbles from his chest when I gasp at his size, at how thick and solid, and just *large* he is. Dumpster sex didn't give me a chance to take this all in properly.

"Does it meet your approval?" he rasps when I take my time exploring the tool now peeking out of the top of his waistband.

I run my tongue over my lips while staring up at him, his intense emerald eyes burning into mine. "It'll do."

His teeth clamp down on his lower lip and a whisp of hair falls over his forehead. "Oh, it'll more than do," he answers, nudging his knee between the apex of my thighs.

Without breaking from his gaze, I grip his zipper, sliding it down at an agonizing pace. "I want to see you," I say, unsure where this boldness is coming from.

His brow quirks as if to say, *"I'm right here."*

"All of you." Our first encounter didn't allow for any exploring. This time I want to feast my eyes upon every glorious inch of this man. I desire nothing less than the full experience.

"I'll show you mine if you show me yours," he says, reaching to switch on the lamp on his bedside table, ever the tease.

I yank my shirt over my head, flinging it across his room. "Your turn."

His eyes morph into twin pools of liquid lust, never leaving from my chest when he moves to stand at the side of the bed, shrugging the shirt that's barely still draped over his body to the floor and stepping out of his slacks.

"Don't quit now."

He hooks his thumbs into the band of his briefs, skimming them back and forth a few times to fuck with me. "I believe it's your move." The elastic pops as he withdraws his hands, lowering them to his sides.

"So it is." I roll over to all fours, crawling across the bed until I'm close enough to stick out my tongue and taste him. Rising up to my knees, I bring my lips to his pecs and begin peppering gentle kisses over the expanse of smooth tanned skin.

His muscles flex, and I can feel his heart pounding a little faster with every touch. "Whitney," he moans, fisting my hair in his hands. His head falls back as I continue my path lower. *Lower.*

"So strong," I whisper, slipping my fingers into the band of his boxer briefs. "Your body is flawless, Mr. Landry."

"Ahh," he sighs when I stretch the elastic over his ass and pull them down to his knees. That remarkable cock of his springs free from the confines of the fabric, jutting right at me. *Taunting me.*

"I haven't done this in a really long time." My tone is an apology in itself. Truly I should be more nervous, but I'm practically drooling at the thought of taking him into my mouth.

"Please." His moan is a desperate plea.

"No need to beg, love." A smile curls his lips when I throw his words from earlier back at him. "It would be my absolute pleasure."

I run the tip of my tongue the length of his shaft, swirling it over the head before wrapping my lips around his cock.

With a hiss, he kneads his fingers into my scalp, gently urging me forward.

There's an undeniable sense of power that comes with

knowing I'm the one responsible for the sexy little groans and grunts coming from this big, strong man. That, even if only for the moment, he's completely at my mercy.

I curl my fist around the base, stroking to match the stride with which he's driving into my mouth. When I feel his cock tense, I suck harder, hollowing my cheeks and taking him all the way to the back of my throat.

"Oh, God." His dick begins to spasm, and his grip on my hair tightens to the point of pain. All it does is give me the encouragement I need to work harder and faster.

"Stop." He huffs, panting for breath as he withdraws from my mouth with a pop. "Not like this."

My face crumples. "I don't understand… I thought you were enjoying it."

Chest heaving, he bends to grip my chin in one hand. "I enjoyed it immensely," he says, followed by a soft chuckle. "I don't want to wait to be inside you, Whitney."

I pull in my lips and nod, my faltering confidence restored. "Well, all right then… Your move," I whisper, trailing my fingertips over his scruffy jaw.

His answering grin is predatorial and gets my adrenaline pumping. "Lay back."

I do, scooting myself until my head rests on his pillow.

I crane my neck to watch as he crawls in from the foot of the bed, only stopping when his face is hovering above my sex. When he hooks his fingers into the band of my leggings and moves to lower them, my heart becomes a jackhammer in my chest, echoing in my ears, pulsing in my throat, effectively drowning out any and all thought but here and now.

"Don't," I gasp when I realize his intent, suddenly becoming self-conscious. But the whispered plea lacks any conviction, my wanton desires swiftly overtaking any semblance of modesty.

"Just a little taste," he says, spreading my knees apart and dipping his head between my thighs. He runs his tongue over my throbbing pussy, the lace of my panties only adding to the friction. The heat of his breath in my most intimate areas has me damn near convulsing as he blazes a path higher and higher. He presses a slow kiss just below my navel before gripping the elastic in his teeth and dragging the lace the length of my leg, flinging it to the floor.

I nearly jump clean out of my skin at the first swipe of his tongue over my bare flesh. And when he begins flicking it back and forth over my clit, the heavens explode behind my eyes.

"Wyatt, I'm gonna come," I warn, only serving to incite the man.

"Touch yourself," he mumbles with a mouth full of *me*. He stretches one arm toward my chest, covering the hand that rests on my breast with his own. While still lapping at the throbbing bud, he takes my finger with his and begins stroking over my pebbled nipple. "Just like that," he croons when I lose all inhibitions and give in to his demand, tweaking the firm peaks while grinding into his face. Within seconds I come apart on his tongue. Tremor after tremor rocks through my core while he keeps at it, draining every ounce of pleasure from my body.

"That was just a prequel," he says with a wink, reaching for the drawer on his nightstand. I watch with rapt attention as he retrieves a foil packet while still licking my release from his glistening lips. "Do you want to put it on?"

"Umm. I'm not sure I know how." I brace myself on my elbows. "No one's ever offered before."

"It's not hard," he says, and I snort, staring at the massive erection pointing right at me.

He shakes his head. "*That's* definitely hard."

"I'll say."

"You just roll it on." He tosses the little packet at me. "I want you to know you're protected."

Of all the things he might have said in this moment, I don't think anything else could have possibly meant more. This man shows me his heart in a million ways each and every day. "Okay," I say, climbing to my knees. "You ready?"

He grunts. "Don't I look it?"

"Yes," I confirm, my eyes widening as I get a closer look. "*Yes, you do.*" Still nodding, I rip the foil open, careful not to damage the condom. "Here I go."

His dick bobs lightly with the soft rumble emerging from his chest.

"Are you laughing at me?"

"Yes," he deadpans, watching as I hesitate just above the head of his penis. "Here," he says guiding my hand with his own along his shaft. "Rolls on just like *that*." Each word becomes more strained as he hardens further beneath my touch.

"That was easy enough." I grab the wrapper from the bed. "Where should I put this?"

"I don't fucking care." With a throaty growl, he hooks an arm around my back, flopping us both onto the mattress.

"I'll just pick that up when we're through," I say, unsure of where it ended up. "Ohh," I groan when his lips smash against mine.

Someone's in no mood for conversation.

"I can't wait any longer." There's an entirely unnecessary apology in his tone.

"Then don't." I lift my head to nip at his jaw while he seats himself at my entrance. It takes a herculean effort not to elevate my hips and force him inside.

Wyatt props himself on his forearms, stroking my hair while staring directly into my eyes, nudging inside just a fraction of an inch. He stills, his body trembling over me while I relish the feel of his warm skin on my skin—of his heartbeat drumming in time with my own.

"Here's to forever, Whit."

As he pushes forward, my nails score his back, breaking the skin on his shoulder blades. "Wyatt," I whimper at the full feeling of having him sheathed inside me. My pussy begins to pulse around him, and I can scarcely draw breath I'm so caught up in the overwhelming sensation of being so connected to this man.

Then he starts to move—rocking in and out of my body at a deliciously slow pace. It's a gift in the most exquisite form of torture.

"You feel so good," he grunts, his eyes wild with desire. "So right."

I grip two hands full of his hair, lowering his lips to mine. His tongue plunges in and out of my mouth while his hand sneaks between us, gripping my breast.

"So perfect," he rasps.

My head whips side to side when Wyatt moves lower, sucking one pert nipple into his mouth. Then he moves to the other, lavishing it with the same attention.

My mounting climax continues to build, and my body starts to quake. The occasional spasm shocks my core, squeezing his shaft.

"Now," I cry out as my walls clench tightly around his cock. "I'm gonna—oh God!"

His entire body locks up while waves of pleasure ricochet between us.

Forever feels like freefalling straight off a cliff, all the while knowing there'll always be someone at the bottom to break my fall.

That someone is him.

CHAPTER TWENTY-TWO

Wyatt

"Hello future father of mine."

The corners of my mouth give a little tug as I set down my drill and rotate my body toward the chapel entrance, where I see Prissy twirling a blue Tootsie Pop in her mouth.

"What's up, Miss Priss?" At Whitney's request, I don't encourage this father business. I just don't exactly *discourage* it either.

"I'm bored." She plants herself on the top step of the brand-new altar. "How much you got left? Looks like you're almost done in here."

"Just gotta finish installing these windows and do a few touch-ups, then she's good to go." I wipe my hands off on my jeans before taking a swig from my bottle of water.

She pouts. "What are you gonna do when you're done?"

I shrug my shoulders. "Finish fixing my house, most likely. Probably pop in three or four times a day to annoy your momma."

My eyes meet with hers. "See if a certain little heathen needs help with her math homework."

That brings a satisfied smile to her face. It warms me to know she's dreading my not being around as much as I am.

Speaking of... "What's your momma up to? I haven't seen her yet this morning."

"Making arrangements for Jimmy and June's baby girl." She folds her arms over her knees, resting her head on top. "They been in there for *hours*." Her eyes widen to further express the amount of time that's lapsed before she gets real quiet, staring off into space for beat. "Hey, Wyatt?"

"Yeah?"

"Did you know that roughly 350 children under the age of five drown in home swimming pools each year?"

"I didn't." My chest becomes tight as the final memory I have of my own baby sister in that little white casket flashes through my mind. Suddenly I'm filled with alarm, thinking about what happened to Jimmy and June's toddler. "Hey, Priss?"

"Yeah?"

"You ever had swimming lessons?"

She shakes her head. "Where you think I'm gonna drown? The bathtub? We ain't got no pool."

"No, but my property meets up with the bayou, and if I have anything to say about it, you'll be spending a lotta time there. Everyone should know how to swim, anyway." I scratch the back of my head. "I'm gonna mention it to your mom."

"You do that." She jumps up from her perch. "Think I just heard Paw and Mr. Rusty pull up in the van. I'm gonna go see if they need help unloading."

"You do that."

I, myself, plan to stay as far away from that retrieval van as humanly possible.

Rather than jump right back into work, something tells me I should pop in and check in on Whitney. My intuition is spot on. When I reach the lobby, I peek through the front window to see the only unfamiliar vehicle out front pulling away.

"Everything, all right in here?" I tap lightly on the door frame before peering into Whit's office to find her with her head bent over a stack of papers, deep in thought.

"Not really," she answers, lifting her gaze. Her normally vibrant blue eyes are red-rimmed and swimming in tears. The stress of what she's just had to endure is etched in every detail of her face. "That was *brutal*." The hitch in her voice hits me hard right in the pit of my chest. It's so easy to lose sight of the fact that she's not just a funeral director, but an actual person with real feelings and emotions. Whitney's always so strong for those around her, because she has to be. But the pitiful sight before me has me wondering how many times she's wept alone in this office.

"Tell me what I can do to help." I step into the room, shutting the door behind me.

Her one-shouldered shrug is pitiful. "Hold me?" Her jaw trembles as a steady stream of sorrow begins to line her cheeks.

I move my hands in a come-hither motion. She's around her desk, wrapped in my arms, and full-on sobbing into the bend of my neck seemingly before I draw my next breath.

I smooth my hand in circles over her back, pressing kisses to her temple. I have no clue what to say. I don't dare tell her it's okay, because there's not one thing about the death of a two-year-old that could ever be anything other than tragic. "Wanna talk about it?" I ask once she winds down, reaching for the box of Kleenex at the corner of her desk.

She gives her head a slight shake. "Sorry about that," she says, dabbing at her nose. "I can't believe I just broke down all over you."

"Better out than in, right?" I push her hair back off her tear-sticky cheeks so I can see her pretty face.

Her upper lip curls. "Isn't that saying about farts?"

"Meh," I shrug. "I think it's some solid, multidimensional advice…applies to all the bad stuff."

She nods, shaking her head at me. "I don't know what's wrong with me. I held it together just fine until you walked in…" Her lips pucker, before turning to one side.

I'm her safe space.

Hearing her say as much in not so many words just further proves what I've known all along. We belong together. "That's what I'm here for."

She stares up at me and quirks a brow. Whitney doesn't even have to say it for me to know she's thinking about what went down on that rug in front of my fireplace last night. Bad timing or not, I can't help the laugh that erupts from my chest. "I didn't say that was *all* I'm here for."

She pulls back just a little and begins smoothing her hands up and down my arms, obviously deep in thought. I doubt even she realizes what she's doing. I'm more than happy to let her relieve a little stress in the repetitive motion while she ruminates. "June just kept saying over and over that she didn't want her last memory to be of her baby in a box." She frowns. "Can you even imagine?"

I nod, clearing my throat. "It's a vision that never leaves you."

I barely remember what my parents looked like that awful day. I still think of them as healthy and alive, but with Annie…it's the only image I can conjure.

Her nails dig into my bicep. "Oh, Wyatt." She shakes her head. "You are the last person I should be dumping this on."

"I'm not gonna break, love." I smooth her hair back, planting a kiss on her forehead. "Actually, I think I might have an idea."

"I'm listening." Her arms drop, and she perches on the end of her desk granting me with her full attention.

"What if you laid her out in a cradle instead? Made it a little more intimate." When she remains quiet, I start to backtrack. "It was just an ide—"

"No," she exclaims cutting me off. "Wyatt, this is brilliant."

"It is?" *I mean, of course it is.*

She nods, already picking up the phone and dialing someone. "Jimmy!" she greets. "Hey. This is Whitney…Daigle." She rounds the desk, collapsing into her chair. "Yeah. One of our employees just had the idea to—"

I give her a little wave before sneaking out and leaving her to finish her call.

As a general rule, I keep as far away from the viewing areas as possible. With the exception of the time I helped retrieve that damn flying squirrel, I haven't stepped foot in either one. So, when Whitney insists I pay the little girl a visit before the family starts arriving, I'm extremely hesitant.

"I'm good," I insist. "I didn't even know her."

"You should see your work," she says, referring to the cradle I went home and built in my shop yesterday evening.

"I've seen it." I dig my feet into the floor. "I'm the one who built it, remember?"

"Please," she begs, tugging my arm. "It would mean a lot to me."

"Why?"

She blows out a frustrated breath. "Because I think it'll help you."

"I assure you I don't need any help." I turn to head off in the direction of the chapel when her words stop me from taking the first step.

"I haven't been in there yet." She grabs one of my hands in both of hers, fiddling with my fingers. "Not since Momma and Daddy set it all up and laid her out. I could barely make it through the makeup application last night."

"I'm sorry." And I am. I know how hard this little girl's death has hit her. How could it not?

"I have to be in and out of that room all day today, and I'd really like you to be there holding my hand the first time I go in."

I suck my tongue to my teeth, shaking my head down at her. "You fight dirty."

"Isn't this the kind of thing boyfriends do?" She fans her lashes. "I *need* you, Wyatt."

Well, hell.

"Fine," I growl. "But only because I have a really big soft spot for those baby blues of yours."

"I'll take it." She throws her arms around my neck, bringing her lips to my ear. "Don't worry. I won't leave your side."

I narrow my eyes as she takes hold of my hand. "Shouldn't I be saying that to you?"

"Mm-hmm." Her thumb brushes over the inside of my wrist a few times. "We got this…*together.*" Something tells me this is about a whole lot more than her being nervous to be around that body.

The walk down to the viewing area is quiet but for the sound of Whitney's heels clicking and the buzzing of the fans overhead. A feeling of dread falls over me when we reach the massive double doors.

Whit squeezes my fingers, saying nothing as she pulls one open, and we step inside. There's a ton of lead sitting in my chest as we walk hand in hand up to the cradle to pay our respects.

The baby is brunette. I didn't know that until now. I hadn't thought to ask. Her hair is shoulder length and curls at the ends. "She looks asleep," I whisper.

Whitney's head bobs. "Isn't she beautiful?" she asks, leaning forward to adjust the bow on the top of her head.

I nod. Her pink dress is very similar to the one Annie was buried in. This little girl is wrapped in a white crochet blanket, and there's a well-loved gray elephant lovie at her side. To the right of the cradle is a glider rocker upholstered in plush pink fabric.

"Jimmy brought that from her nursery, so June can rock her."

I stare into her sparkling eyes and give her hand a squeeze. "You are great at what you do."

She blushes. "This was all you."

I shake my head. "I may have built the cradle, but the way you care for your clients…the love you put into each and every one of them." I hang my head, searching for the right words. "You have a special soul, Whit. You can't see it, because that same spark resides in the people who raised you. It's just a part of who y'all are. And it's already there in Prissy, even at such a young age."

She clears her throat. "The idea was to get me ready to *not* cry today, *Shakespeare*."

I ignore her feeble attempt at changing the subject. "I know this one's been tough. I just wanted to say—you're good at what you do. Sometimes we all need to hear it." Lord knows her clients aren't in any position to be thinking about how hard the death of their loved ones might be on someone in Whitney's position.

She smiles. "Yeah, well…" Her eyes scour the scene before us. "I think it's safe to say we make a pretty good team."

"I'm glad you think so." I give her arm a little tug toward the doors, more than ready to make my escape.

"Are you?" she asks, following me out.

"I might've signed Prissy up for swimming lessons at Flippers starting after the new year."

"You did?" Her eyes go wide.

I nod. "Signed Lucy up too. I haven't told Kate yet either."

"Don't you think she's a little young?"

I twist my head back toward the room we just left. "Are you seriously asking me that right now?"

"Fair point."

"One more thing," I say, backing her up against the door to her office.

"Yes?"

"Next time you feel like counseling me… I'm much more responsive to play therapy."

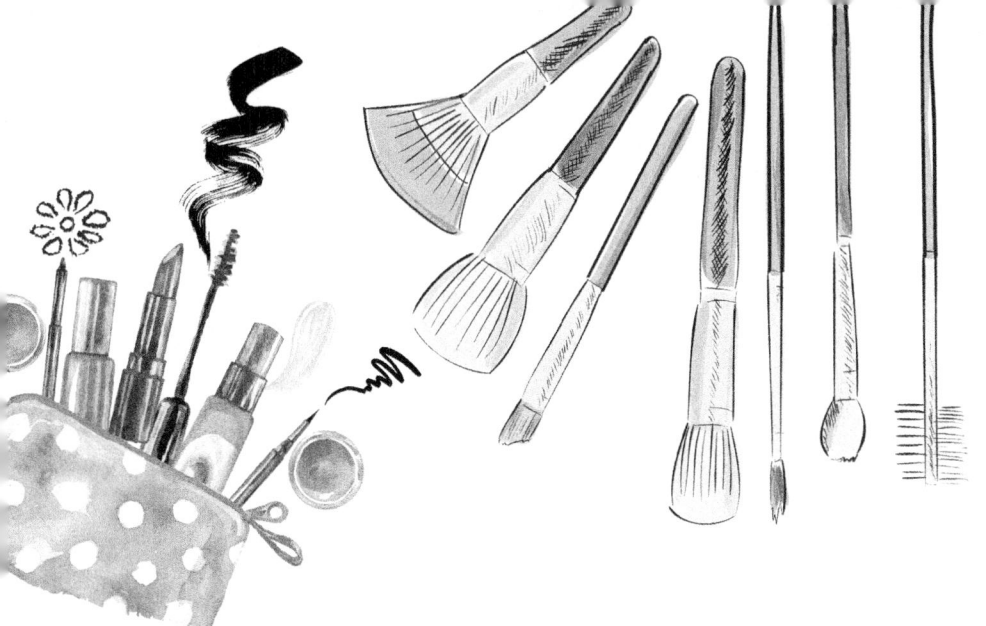

CHAPTER TWENTY-THREE

Whitney

"Wyatt's here." Momma's voice echoes through to the back of the apartment, where I'm still struggling with Prissy over her outfit.

"Coming," I answer, glaring down at my obstinate daughter. "There are two perfectly acceptable choices laid out on that bed. Put one of them on."

"But I wanna wear my hoodie," she whines.

I scowl at the ratty, faded sweater in question balled up in the corner of the room. "Absolutely not. We're meeting Wyatt's grandparents for the first time tonight, and you will not go looking like a homeless person."

With her arms folded over her chest, she props herself against the wall. Her stance says she's not planning on yielding anytime soon. Too bad for her, six years of dealing with that attitude of hers has made me a seasoned pro.

"Very well," I stoop and press a kiss to the top of her head, enjoying a brief whiff of strawberry-scented shampoo. "You can just spend Christmas Eve here with Maw-Maw and Paw-Paw. Don't stay up too late." I flounce my hair, not giving her a backward glance. "I'll bring you back a plate of food."

"Wait!" she hollers when I make to turn down the hall. "I'll wear that one."

I halt, slowly pivoting in her direction to see her pointing at the black leggings and white and black checked tunic.

"What a wonderful choice." I try not to look *too* smug when I rush right back in to help her get changed.

After donning her boots and slinking into her leather jacket, she quickly rips a brush through her tangles and declares herself presentable. "Let's go!"

We find Wyatt waiting in front of the Christmas tree, examining one of Prissy's handmade ornaments from preschool. He's dressed in black dress pants and a burgundy button down, looking like dessert—a real tease seeing as there will be no chance for sampling any of that yumminess tonight. "Well, aren't you looking spiffy?"

"Could say the same for the two of you." His hungry eyes give me a thorough once-over that sends butterflies flooding my tummy.

I run my hands over the front of my black dress, smoothing out any wrinkles, and adjust the gold belt at my waist. "Thank you."

"Can y'all stop flirting so I can go meet my future great-grandparents?"

Dating with a child isn't for the faint of heart.

Wyatt snorts. "You heard the lady." He rests a hand between my shoulder blades guiding me toward the door. "Let's go."

When we arrive at Wyatt's house, there's a little old man sitting on the porch swing just waving away. He's adorable, with a head full of snowy white hair, little round spectacles, and stereotypical plaid flannel and khakis.

"Home sweet home," Wyatt says, killing the engine.

There's a little extra pep in his step as he rounds the truck to let me and Prissy out. The man is simply glowing with pride over finally being able to show off the people who raised him.

I, on the other hand, am seconds away from a nuclear-level meltdown. This fit of nerves is ridiculous. I meet new people every day. That is *literally* my job. But I can't stop thinking about a conversation I had with Kate the other night—the one where she let it slip how uneasy his Mimi was about the rate at which our relationship has progressed. As a fellow mother hen, I'm now petrified to enter that house.

"Whitney, Prissy… I'd like you both to meet my Pop, Charles Hazelwood."

"Pleasure to meet you, sir." I swallow my nerves, steel my spine, and reach for his hand.

"My, she is a pretty one, Wyatt," he announces, clamping his other hand over mine so it's sandwiched between both of his.

"Thank you."

"And who do we have here?" Charles shuffles over to stand in front of my daughter, exerting a heck of a lot of effort to bend his old body to her level. It makes me smile to see where Wyatt gets his finer qualities, always making it a point to be sure that child knows she has his undivided attention.

"I'm Prissy."

He nods, patting her head with a shaky hand. "That's some fine, sturdy footwear you've got there."

Beaming, she twists the toe of one combat-booted foot into the ground. "Thank you." I can't remember the last time I've seen my daughter blush. It's sweet.

"Pretty sure you've just made a friend for life, Pop." Wyatt swipes his knuckles along my spine, eliciting a full body chill. "Y'all wanna get inside, outta this cold?"

"Boy's such a wuss," the old man tuts, easily earning a laugh from my little girl, while trailing his grandson to the door.

"Woah!" Wyatt shouts when Ru—*Sprinkles* nearly knocks us all over trying to get to Prissy. "Down, boy."

"Sprinkles, sit!" Prissy commands, snapping her fingers and holding out a hand for Wyatt to get her a treat. "Good boy," she says kissing all over that slobbery muzzle of his. "That's a good boy."

"You could learn a thing or two from that precious little girl there about controlling that beast."

"You ain't lyin,'" Wyatt says to the elderly woman hobbling out from behind the stove. "Mimi, I'd like you to meet my girls."

Well, if my dang heart doesn't swell to bursting with that proclamation.

"Whitney, this is my Mimi, Melinda. Mimi, Whitney." Sweat beads over my brow while I extend my hand. I wish Kate hadn't said anything, because I'm not usually so awkward.

"Oh, darlin,' I don't do none of that hand shakin' business. If you're gonna make it in this family, you're gonna have to get acquainted with my huggin.'" The short round woman wraps me up tighter than a boa constrictor while Wyatt observes with the hugest smile on his face—completely oblivious to the mounting tension. "Don't you go hurtin' my little boy," she murmurs in my ear, so quietly there's no way possible anyone heard it but me.

I clear the frog from my throat and nod discreetly. *She certainly won't be hopping aboard the Whitney train any time soon.*

"Your turn, little missy," Melinda threatens, aiming her attention at my daughter.

"Hi, Mimi," my darling child greets, throwing her arms around the woman's waist without even being prompted. "I'm so happy to meet you."

She, too, is well-versed in meeting new people.

"Well," the woman says, patting Prissy on the back of the head, her eyes suddenly twinkling. "Aren't you somethin'?"

My baby girl looks up, staring into the old woman's eyes with nothing but sincere admiration. "People tell me that a lot."

Wyatt and I reach for each other at the same time, hooking our fingers together, both fighting back laughter.

"Well, I guess they do," Mimi offers. "I bet you're a handful."

Prissy nods. "Yes, ma'am. My teacher says I'm a real piece'a work."

Leave it to my child to try selling herself with every back-handed compliment she's ever received.

"Well, I'll tell ya one thing—you sure are cute as a button." Her once-hesitant smile now stretches ear to ear. *I think it's safe to say one of us has won her over. Spoiler alert: it wasn't me.*

"I love your pink flowery dress." My kid is lying trough her gosh-darn teeth. But I love her all the more for it.

"I'm so glad to hear it!" the clever old bat announces. "Cuz I got you one just like it for Christmas."

Prissy's forced smile looks positively constipated. "Th—thank you."

"I'm joking," Mimi cackles, pinching her cheek. "Wyatt talks about your naughty little tail all the time. I know you don't like pink."

"Sorry."

"There's nothin' to be sorry about. Don't ever apologize for being just who you are."

Prissy nods. "Yes, ma'am."

"The real question is…do you like cookies?"

My little girl bounces on her toes. "Uh-huh."

"Good," she answers, heading for the oven. "If youd'a said no, that one might'a been a deal breaker."

"Shouldn't she eat dinner first?" Wyatt says when his grandmother hands Prissy a chocolate chip cookie right off the pan.

"Wyatt Jude, I know you ain't tryin' to tell me how to spoil my new grandbaby."

I swat his leg and give him a stern look. The last thing I need is the woman thinking he's questioning her judgment on my behalf.

"Wouldn't dream of it," he responds, appropriately chastened.

Once the awkwardness of introductions has passed, the evening isn't so bad. We have a nice sit-down meal of beef tenderloin, mashed potatoes with gravy, and green beans. Prissy keeps the grandparents entertained asking all sorts of questions about their grandson and what he was like as a child while Wyatt and I engage in an hour-long game of footsie beneath the table. I honestly don't know how I held off on the guy's advances for so long. I've become quite the addict, constantly yearning for even the slightest touch.

After dinner, he assists me in loading the dishwasher while Mimi and Pop set up a fold-out table and chairs in the living room for some top-secret activity they have planned.

"What's up, losers?" The back door flies open, sending in a gush of icy cold air, along with my best friend and her little family. "It's freaking freezing out there."

"Well, hello there, Lulu-magu," I croon, going straight for the baby, who cranes her back, gripping her mother's shirt with tiny fists that are impossible to pry open. Per usual, the child wants nothing to do with me.

"Just take her," Kate orders, shoving the flailing tot into my arms before kissing my cheek. "You know her spoiled butt ain't going willingly. Merry Christmas, Morticia."

"Merry Christmas, Cruella."

She snorts. "Cruella, really? Sure you ain't talkin' bout yourself?"

I shrug. "Was the best I could come up with on the spot." After shushing and coddling Lucy for a few minutes, I give up and set the little tyrant to the floor to do her worst.

"Auntie Kate! Uncle Beau! I didn't know y'all was coming. Did you bring me presents?" I shoot Prissy a Mom Look but she's undeterred.

"Does a bear make poo in the woods?" Beau answers, sounding like a total dweeb.

Kate's got the man so scared to say a bad word in front of that baby she has him saying shit like "make poo."

"I vow to never steal your man card like that, babe." I eye our friends, shaking my head in disgust.

"'Preciate it, love." He slings an arm around my shoulders, pulling me close while Beau gags on air.

"Could you two be more nauseating?"

"Is that a challenge?" Wyatt asks, before slapping his cousin behind the head. "If so, we have some stiff competition with the two of you."

"Y'all gonna just stand around here insulting each other?" Mimi inquires, entering from the living room.

"Mimi!" Kate squeals, skittering across the kitchen in her heeled boots to give the woman a giant hug. "It's so good to see you." The two rock side to side, drawing the greeting out.

Nope. I'm not jealous at all.

After Mimi and Pop have made their rounds hugging and kissing on the new arrivals, they drag us all into the living room for the grand reveal: a gingerbread house building competition.

"We did this every year growing up," Wyatt explains. "Our neighbors would come over and judge afterward." From the look of sheer joy plastered on his face, I can tell there are some very fond memories there.

"Listen up," Pop says, trying to grab everyone's attention. "Y'all got one hour to build your houses. Then Wyatt's arranged for Hank and Marie to come over and do the judgin'."

Wyatt beams down at my stunned face.

"My parents are coming over?"

He nods. "They couldn't make it for dinner and the competition cuz of that body they had to pick up at the retirement home, but they said they'd come by to meet my grandparents and visit for a bit after. Worked out perfectly." He squeezes my hand. "We needed judges…and I've never met anyone more judgy than your father."

Has he met his grandmother?

"This could be the best Christmas ever." I press a chaste kiss to his plump lips while trying not to swoon over the fact that he thought to invite my mom and dad.

Our holidays are usually spent at the funeral home—just me and Prissy and my folks. It's extremely rare that they aren't interrupted with business of some kind. And while it's nice to be out surrounded by loved ones, doing normal festive things, I still feel guilty for leaving them out.

"That's what I'm hoping." He grips my chin, sending a wave of desire rushing through me. "The first of many best Christmases ever."

"You two 'bout done?" Mimi intrudes, smashing her hands to her hips and tapping her right foot against the floor.

My cheeks flame when I notice the rest of the room staring at the two of us. "Yep," I say, backing away from temptation. "All done."

"As I was sayin'," Pop continues. "The winner gets this here trophy." He holds up a little six-inch gold gingerbread man in the

Heisman stance on a stone block. "And bragging rights for a year. Clock starts…now!"

With that we each grab a seat and set to working on constructing our houses.

"At least Rufus is good for something," Kate muses, watching her daughter—who's almost never far enough away she can't make one quick turn and crawl back up in that uterus of hers—climbing all over him.

"Uh, do you mean Sprinkles?" my little sasshole asks while blobbing icing on the corners of her walls.

"My bad," Kate giggles. "Forgot he's a sissy dog now."

Prissy rolls her eyes before promptly getting back to work.

"How'd you get yours to hold together so well?" I ask Wyatt, who's already moved on to lining the edges of his house with gumdrops, while I can't get my damn roof to stop sliding off.

He shrugs. "You gotta get the icing and cookie lined up right. It's all about balance."

Prissy's having about as much luck as I am, so I don't say a word when I see her little genius self chewing up pieces of gum and sneaking them on the inner corners of her house to use as glue when she thinks no one's watching.

"I concede!" I announce, ready to throw the damn thing into the trash. "I don't have the patience for this."

"You can reconstruct an entire face, but can't get a few pieces of cookie to hold together?" Kate taunts.

Braggy little bitch.

I toss a peppermint stick in her direction, nailing her right between the tits.

Pop bows out right about the same time I do. His little pile of rubble is nearly as pitiful as mine.

Wyatt and Mimi have the most traditional looking houses, by far, but it's totally not fair because they've done this before.

Beau's roof is lopsided, and it looks like Lucy decorated the damn thing; but I truly have no room to talk. Mine appears to have been hit with a wrecking ball. Kate's house isn't too bad…I guess.

Okay, fine. It's adorable as fuck.

If there was an originality award, it'd definitely go to my daughter. She's iced the entire thing in black and added nothing but white gumdrops and candy pearls, and a few randomly placed stalks of black licorice. She's nothing if not consistent.

When my parents arrive, I let them in to wait in the kitchen, since they aren't allowed to see who's building which house.

"Time!" I hear Mr. Charles shout.

In the next second they're all packed into the kitchen, wishing my parents a Merry Christmas. Momma and Daddy seem to hit it off really well with Charles and Melinda. This thrills me to no end. They don't get the chance to socialize much, so I'm feeling extra emotional and taking care to commit every moment of this special night to memory.

"All right," Daddy's deep voice booms through the tiny kitchen. "Let's have a look at these houses."

Like a herd of cattle, the crowd moves to the living room.

"I'm gonna murder that stupid mutt," Kate shouts, pacing along the table edge, taking in the wreckage. She's usually gaga for that puppy, so her outrage is extra hilarious.

"See," I gloat. "Cruella."

"He *ate* my masterpiece!"

Sprinkles cowers, tucking tail and slinking away to hide behind the couch.

"Maybe it was Lucifer," Prissy argues. "You ever think of that?"

"Oh, yeah. The *baby* climbed up on the table and gobbled up every house but yours."

Prissy shrugs. "I'm just sayin', if you didn't see it happen, you can't go accusin.'"

"Well," Daddy announces, through a roar of laughter, "guess my girl Prissy wins by default."

"Only because her house is so creepy, not even the dog would touch it."

Oh, what would we do without our Kate?

CHAPTER TWENTY-FOUR

Wyatt

"Go on and get yourself ready for the day," Mimi orders. There's no question where I get my habit of early rising from. The two of us are already working on our second cups of coffee before the sun's come up.

"For what?" I glance down at the candy cane striped pajamas she gifted me last night, smoothing a hand over my chest. "It's Christmas. We never wear real clothes on Christmas."

"Occasionally you gotta adapt with the times, son." Pop comes strolling out of the guest room, looking sharp as a tack with his hair gelled to one side and a fresh thermal. The smell of Old Spice is so thick I can practically see it floating around him like a cloud.

My eyes volley between my two parental figures. I feel the divot forming between my brows. They've always been sticklers for routine and heavy on tradition. "What're you guys up to?"

"You belong with your girls, Wyatt." My grandmother

reaches across the table to pat the top of my hand. "You're not being apart from 'em, today of all days. Certainly not on our account."

"It's a nice gesture." I give her fingers a little squeeze to show I appreciate it. "But I'm not leaving you two alone on Christmas."

Her head jolts back, appalled by the suggestion. "Well, of course you're not. I didn't say we were just gonna hand you over like we're some pair of worn-out shoes you've gone and tossed in the trash ."

Damn, but my grandmother can be some kinda drama queen when she wants to be.

"Marie typed me a note on my phone this mornin' to see if we wanted to swing by. Said that girlfriend of yours was moping around the house like someone gone and died while waiting for Prissy to wake up."

"*You* learned how to text?"

She huffs. "Well, *no*. I had to call her so we could talk. You know my eyes ain't as good as they used to be. Anyway, she's invited the three of us over for breakfast and to watch that sweet child open her gifts."

"I'll be ready in ten." I hop up out of my seat and head for the sink to rinse the rest of my coffee down the drain. After putting my mug into the dishwasher, I return to the table and plant a kiss on my Mimi's round cheek. "Told you you'd love 'em," I say before starting in the direction of my room.

"Jury's still out on the older one," she hollers back at me.

"Hey, Mimi?" I return to the kitchen and peer my head inside. "You do realize they're a packaged deal?"

"Yeah, yeah," she answers with a backhanded wave.

"Wyatt?" Whitney's sleepy eyes expand as her lips curl into the sweetest of smiles. "What're you…?"

"Surprise!" Marie peeks her head over her daughter's shoulder. "I was gonna stick this big bow on top his head and give him to ya for Christmas, but you got to the door before me."

Sure, enough the woman's standing there with about a foot-wide red velvet bow clutched to her chest.

"Merry Christmas, beautiful," I say drinking her in from head to foot. The woman is a vision, even with ratty hair and not an ounce of makeup—especially for those reasons. Just the sight of her gets my heart beating faster and makes my throat thicken. It has me dreaming of a day in the future when we make this thing between us official and I'm able to wake up next to this *hot mess* every morning.

"Well, it's definitely merry now!" She tightens the sash on her robe when she sees my grandparents standing behind me then throws herself into my arms. "I'm so happy you're here."

I bury my face in her hair, breathing in her sweet scent. I'd give just about anything to be alone with her right now. It'd be too simple to pull that belt open and slip my hands inside.

"You two lovebirds wanna clear the entryway?" Mimi huffs.

I cough, clearing the lust that's quickly filling my head. If I'm not careful, my heated thoughts will be on display for all to see. With Whitney still dangling from my neck, I shift to the side so my grandparents can sneak by. She giggles when I conceal my face in her neck and bite down gently in the slope of her collar bone.

"Stop it." She squirms. "You're gonna get me all red and flustered."

"What's all this racket?" The guest of honor finally comes trudging down the hall, still wiping sleep from her eyes. "Y'all are loud enough to wake the dead!"

"Now why would you go and say a thing like that knowing you probably got two or three corpses chilling in the freezer downstairs?" I ask, setting her momma to her feet.

"Wyatt?" The little grump tears across the living room like a bat fresh outta hell to get to me. "What're you doing here?" she asks, throwing her arms around my waist. "It's still dark out."

"We came to watch you open presents."

She scours the room until she finds the *we*—my grandparents—chatting with Hank and Marie at the table, donuts in hand. "Mimi and Pop! You're here too?"

"Of course, we are, child," Mimi answers, as if they've always been a part of her life and it's the silliest of notions that she'd be any place else.

My sister and I were their only grandchildren, and I've been grown for quite a while. They'll benefit from this relationship as much, if not more, than Prissy.

"Do I have to eat before openin' presents?" The now very much awake, wide-eyed child asks her momma.

"It's Christmas," Whitney answers, staring at the girl like she's grown two heads. "There are no rules on Christmas."

"I love you, Momma." Prissy curls up into her mother's lap, wrapping one arm around her back and the other over her shoulder.

"Love you too, baby," Whitney responds, gently rocking her with her lips pressed to her forehead. "Merry Christmas."

It feels as if we're all intruding on their tender moment. Even my ruthless old grandmother's dabbing at the corners of her eyes.

Whitney may have had her young, but their bond is one of the strongest I've seen. The love these girls share is palpable. It's simply impossible to be around them and not feel it. Or, as my grandmother is quickly learning, not to want to be even the smallest part of it.

Once she's all snuggled out, Prissy grabs her momma's hand and drags her off the sofa to the tree.

"This one's from me," Whit says, handing her a beautifully wrapped box. The paper is shiny, with candy cane stripes in red, white, and green. It's topped off with a fancy ribbon. One of the ones with a million loops that I'd never be able to pull off.

Prissy has all that hard work she put into the packaging shredded in seconds. "Just what I wanted!" She lifts the yellow box with the phrase "Good Guys" imprinted on the side into the air above her head and starts jumping up and down.

The freckle-faced, orange-haired doll glares at me through the plastic window. "You can't be serious." My eyes land on Whitney, sitting cross-legged on the floor, surrounded by a mountain of gifts.

She *would* come running straight at me with the damn thing. "Will you open this for me?"

Whitney shrugs, stifling a giggle. "It's what she asked for."

"A Chucky doll?" Now I'm shaking my head at that future daughter of mine. "What is wrong with you? This little monster gave me nightmares well into my teens."

She sneers. "It's just a baby doll."

I whip out my phone, doing a quick internet search for "baby doll." "This is a baby doll," I argue, holding it out for her to see.

Her response is one hell of an unimpressed eyeroll.

"Think you could build him a bed?" Priss asks, batting her lashes, with one hand layered over the other on my right knee.

I snort, ripping the box open for her and fighting with all the little twisty bread tie thingies. "Tell ya what...I'll build him a jail cell, how 'bout that?"

"You're so drama," she says, snatching her new friend out of my hand as soon as it's freed from the packaging.

"Open mine next," Hank insists, digging around under the tree, then tossing a box to his granddaughter.

Her face lights up when she opens it to find a brand-new black hoodie that reads, "I put the fun in funeral." Immediately she slips it over her head. "Thanks Paw! I love it."

My grandmother gives me wide-eyed look. If *"Are you fucking kidding me,"* had a face, hers would be it.

I shrug. I wasn't kidding when I told the woman Prissy was a different brand of princess. Maybe she thought I was exaggerating. She'll soon learn those odd quirks are what make her so damn precious.

Just like I did—hell, I don't even think I liked kids all that much before this one. Not that I'd had much experience, but I definitely never wanted to be around them all the time. Well, most of the time—certain activities call for a little privacy.

"Can I go next?" I ask, anxious to see her reaction to the gift I spent the past month agonizing over.

"You got me a present too?" Prissy skips back to the far side of the room where I'm still seated on the stool I drug in from the kitchen.

"Duh," I answer, using one of her most favorite words. "Merry Christmas, Miss Priss." I hand her a giftbag, since my wrapping skills are lackluster at best.

"Don't you know unwrapping the gift is the best part?" Mimi chastises while Prissy flings wadded-up tissue filler to the floor.

"I do now."

When she pulls the worn leather case from the bag, my pulse races and my palms begin to sweat.

"You got me eyeballs!" she screams, rushing to show her Paw-Paw the collection of five porcelain prosthetic eyes.

"Not just any eyes," I say, warming inside over her excitement. "They all date back to the early twentieth century.

There's a sticker with a code on the bottom of each. If you go back to the seller's website, you can read the story of the original owners."

"Well, I don't even know if I wanna give her my gift now." My poor grandmother is looking a rather unhealthy shade of green.

"I'm sure she'll love it," Whitney assures her.

"Thank you, Wyatt! This is the coolest thing I ever got!"

"You're welcome, sweet girl."

By the time she finishes opening her Santa gifts, the entire floor is covered in trash and that little girl has more creepy shit to occupy her time than you could even imagine. It's like Hot Topic threw up all over their living room.

"All right, ma'am," Marie says, retrieving a huge black yard bag from the utility closet and shaking it open. "Time to get all this garbage up before you run off to play with your new stuff."

"Wait," Whit says, "she didn't open the one from Mimi and Pop yet."

"It's just a little something," the old woman mutters, clearly setting herself up for a disappointed reaction.

Prissy couldn't be more gracious when she climbs up in between my grandparents to unwrap her final gift.

"Yes!" she shouts, leaning over to kiss Mimi's cheek, then moving to Pop to do the same. "I got my very own makeup, Momma!"

She is selling this hard. Bless her soul. I learned at Thanksgiving just how much she doesn't like wearing the stuff. Thankfully, my grandparents are none the wiser.

"That's awesome, Priss." Whitney mouths her thanks from across the room.

"Momma doesn't let me play with hers. Now I can practice for when I'm a mortician!"

Hmm. Maybe she's not faking after all.

"Maw-Maw...Mimi...think I could practice on y'all after breakfast?"

And. I. Am. Dead. She actually just asked the two oldest women in the room if she could use them as guinea pigs to hone her mortuary makeup skills.

This kid is fucking brilliant.

"Sure," Mimi says, still glowing over how well her gift was received and not connecting the dots on why the gift is exciting.

"Now you listen here, Priscilla Louise, you think cuz we're old and wrinkly you can just use us for your own entertainment?" Marie, knowing exactly why Prissy chose the two of them, is rightly offended.

The little girl nods. Her confusion over her grandmother's reaction is a reminder of her innocence. It's easy to forget how young she is. "Well, most of the bodies we work on *are* old and wrinkly, Maw-Maw."

"Kid has a point," Hank says between wheezing guffaws. The old man is about to keel over he's laughing so hard.

"Mimi wants to go first," I offer, on my grandmother's behalf.

"Why I gotta go first?" she complains, having just been schooled on the reason her darling new granddaughter wants to play makeup with her.

"It was your gift." I shrug. "Plus, you have the most wrinkles."

"Keep that shit up boy," she warns, pointing a crooked finger at me. "Don't think I won't take off my shoe and bust your tail in front all these people."

The woman talks big, but while she's hootin' and hollerin', she's sinking down into the couch, making herself comfortable for her mortuary makeover.

"Almost forgot," I say, reaching into my coat pocket. "I have a little something for you too."

When I hand Whitney the little blue box, I'm pretty damn sure every adult in the room stops breathing.

"What's this?" Whitney's fingers tremble over the ribbon.

"Not that! Breathe," I say. "Just open it."

She takes a long drawn-out breath before lifting the lid and removing the white gold charm bracelet. "I can't decide if I should kiss you or punch you," she says after examining each trinket: a hammer to represent yours truly, a makeup brush for her, a little combat boot for Prissy, and my personal favorite and the one that has her so conflicted…

"Why'd you give that girl a bracelet with a dumpster on it?" Pop asks, fixing his glasses on his nose to examine it further.

"You son of a bitch," Hank howls, slapping his knee.

CHAPTER TWENTY-FIVE

Whitney

"Dayum, Whit." The fire in Wyatt's gaze as he looks me over in my shimmery silver mini dress and matching stilettos has my blood running hot and warmth pooling between my legs. Or maybe that wetness stems from how delicious he looks in his three-piece suit. *Hubba hubba.* "We could skip the party and stick to the original plan…head back to my place?" His teeth scrape over his lower lip ever so slowly while he backs me up against the door, his fingers slipping just inside the low V that ends at the small of my back. "Make our own fireworks…"

"As tempting as that is," I croon, flattening my palms over his pecs and leaning in close to run the tip of my nose over the bend of his neck, hovering in place when I reach his ear. "My very resourceful boyfriend managed to snag a room and tickets to the most coveted party in the city."

"Is that so? He sounds like a pretty cool guy."

"The coolest. How *did* you manage that so last minute, by the way?"

He splays his fingers over my bare back, nipping at my jaw. "That new job I just landed?" His lips skate along mine, sending sparks of desire firing off every nerve ending in my body. "Building the pool house?"

"Yeah," I rasp, already lust drunk.

"It's for the owner's son."

"*Nice.*" I slip a hand between us, palming the steel rod digging into my hip. "You are so fucking hot; I can't stand it," I growl giving his cock a firm squeeze while pressing my thighs tightly together.

His answering laugh oozes sexual frustration. "And yet…you still want to go to this party?"

"Foreplay," I whisper, grazing my tongue over the shell of his ear. "We're always so rushed. For the first time ever, we have all night." I slip my hands inside his jacket and around to his back, grabbing two fists full of his firm ass. "I'm going to enjoy every second of torturing you, because I know what awaits at the night's end will be well worth it." Clenching my fingers, I glide my tongue along the seam of his lips. "I can't wait to watch you lose control."

I feel his dick twitch against my abdomen before he scrubs a hand over his face with a groan. "Let's go and get this over with." His voice is uncharacteristically gritty, as if his vocal cords have been brushed with sandpaper. Wyatt laces his fingers between mine and brings my hand to his mouth for a kiss. "Before I settle for a quick fuck in the prep room."

I pinch my puckered lips, twisting them to one side. "Now, I might be convinced to be a little late in that case."

The Winchester Regency is the place to be. Anyone who knows anything about New Year's Eve in New Orleans knows this, while few actually get the chance to experience it. The place is known to book up a year or more in advance. So, I must admit, I feel like hot shit checking into a balcony suite on tonight of all nights.

"Wanna give the bed a test run?" Wyatt asks when we pop into our room to rid ourselves of our bags. His brows do a sexy little bounce as he fists his hands out in front of him and begins thrusting his hips.

The man is relentless. And goofy. And so damn gorgeous it drives me to distraction.

"And ruin my makeup and hair?" I scoff. "Not a chance!"

With a grunt, he hangs his head, his handsome face shrouded in a look of defeat. "I don't like this game."

"I promise you'll *love* the way it ends."

"Well, that's a foregone conclusion." He walks up behind me where I'm touching up my makeup, pressing his chest to my back and resting his chin on my shoulder. His warm exhale into my neck has my limbs shaking and my pulse quickening. "I love every second I'm lucky enough to spend in your company."

The lipstick tube fumbles to the counter with a clang. I'm not quite sure whether the action is voluntary or a result of my weak-kneed response to this man. Reaching back, I twist my hand to scruff his hair and rest my lips on his forehead, letting them linger for a beat. "Me too."

His hand skates up my torso, over my breasts, and along my neck until his palm is stroking my jaw and his fingers are buried in my nape. He gives a gentle tug, rotating my face until his lips reach mine. "You can fix it again before we go downstairs to eat," he rasps before covering my mouth with his.

After one hell of a hot and heavy makeout session, we arrive at our reservation only a few minutes late. *I'm calling it a win.* I've never felt as fancy or grown as I do right now. To be sitting here, dressed to the nines in the VIP section of such a swanky place, is surreal. But then again, my entire life has felt like a dream since the moment Wyatt Landry made his reappearance in it.

The tables are covered in white cloths with lit candles and red roses at the center. There are more utensils laid out than I know what to do with. The fact that my date doesn't seem to have a clue what they're for, either, eases the fit of nerves they bring on.

Dinner is a delectable feast of beef with au jus, truffle whipped potatoes, and the most delicious buttery steamed asparagus I've ever had the pleasure of eating. For dessert we share a bananas foster cheesecake and bread pudding—each sampling the other's, because is there any other way to do it when you're young and in love?

Once we've filled our bellies, we take off on a stroll around the grounds to see what kind of trouble we can get into.

For our first adventure of the night, we pop into one of the ballrooms to see a burlesque show. Neither of us has ever been to one before, and it's supposed to be one of the highlights of the venue.

We grab drinks from one of many mobile bartenders posted up around the hotel on the way to our seats. All the while, I do some heavy people watching. The guests are such a diverse bunch, dressed in everything from black tie to feathers and boas.

And can I just say... *So. Many. Titties.*

In the crowd. On the stage. Tits every which way you turn.

My jaw hangs, and the nails of my once-lax hand press into my date's knee when one of the performers lights her freaking tatas on fire! *Okay,* so if you want to get technical, it's actually the tassels that are ablaze. But they're attached to her nipples, so that's practically the same thing.

"Look at her go!" Wyatt's eyes about pop out of his head when she starts helicoptering those flaming gazoongas. Round and round and round they go.

The crowd is going nuts. My heart leaps into my throat. She's one ill-timed flop away from catching that poufy platinum blonde bouffant of hers on fire.

"Can yours do that?" he asks, trailing a finger over my cleavage.

"Seriously? I barely have a C cup. Those are like *very* stretched out Gs."

He snorts, choking on his beer. "*I can do that...*"

I give him a flirty little side eye before fluffing his ego like any good girlfriend would. I do take my new role seriously, after all. "If you were to try that you'd have knocked out everyone sitting in the front row."

"That right there," he says, shaking a finger at me before squishing my cheeks together and kissing my subsequent fish lips, "is why I'm gonna marry your ass someday."

His suggestion has my smile brimming from ear to ear. His near-constant hints at forever no longer send me itching to flee. In fact, I'm beginning to feel downright hopeful. The emotion is so foreign to me. I'm teetering on the edge of fear and forever, praying the latter wins out in the end.

After the show, we decide to skip the casino entirely and find ourselves a spot to dance the night away. There are multiple stages and entertainers to choose from, and people literally everywhere we turn. Wyatt and I end up squeezing our way through until we're right in front of the stage of some really badass 80s cover band. The performers are dressed in vibrant spandex unitards with huge perms and crazy costume makeup.

"These guys are really good," Wyatt says, double-fisting Crown and Cokes while I slake my thirst on cosmos. The first few tasted like pure rubbing alcohol, but I'm halfway through my third and either they've eased up on the liquor or I'm well on my way to shitfaced.

"*You're really good.*" I give him a filthy eye-fucking, holding my drink out to the side while resting my free hand on his shoulder and shaking my ass. My ogle's so lewd I wouldn't be surprised if a cop showed up and cuffed me on a count of indecent exposure.

After a few drinks, he too has loosened up quite a bit. And those moves of his—the ones Prissy bragged so staunchly about—begin to make their appearance.

"You're not a bad dancer," I offer, while he grinds his erection into my ass to the beat of "Pour Some Sugar On Me." A wave of heat starts at my cheeks, trailing down my body. My skin tingles with his every touch. I'm hot to the point of feeling feverish, but it's a welcome burn—the kind that warms you from the inside out. Like being curled up in front of a fire with a steaming cup of hot chocolate, a cozy blanket, and fuzzy socks. Throw in some pussy pulses, and that's me…in a nutshell.

Every now and then I'm jolted from our little bubble of love and slapped with a reminder of just how jam-packed this dancefloor is, like when some overzealous patron nearly knocked me on my ass or when another got a little handsy and Wyatt had to set his ass straight. But for the most part, my vision is singularly focused on one man. When his hands are on my body, the rest of the world fades away. There's only him and me and the endorphins flooding through my veins. This constant build of sexual tension has me feeling a bit like a tea kettle ready to blow.

"Five minutes til midnight," the lead singer shouts into his mic before the band jumps right into a funky rendition of Prince's "1999"—such a classic New Year's jam.

The hair at the nape of my neck soaks with sweat while Wyatt and I join in with the rest of the crowd in some variation of a mosh pit—a little less violent, a whole lot messier. We are literally being showered with every type of alcoholic beverage you could dream of.

My heart pulses harder and faster with the mounting excitement over my first ever New Year's Eve midnight kiss. And thrums even more so if I allow my thoughts to drift to what's to come when we return to that room upstairs.

"Almost time," Wyatt croons, spinning me out and then reeling me back into his arms. My chest slams into his. He holds me close. "I'm going to fuck you so hard."

"Well," I say, buzzing with desire. The bulge protruding into my pelvis assures me the man means what he says. "That was unexpectedly hot…look at you acting all alpha." I waggle my brows. "I should pump you with alcohol more often."

"I'm gonna pump you with something, all right." He bites his lip and winks. It's adorably uncoordinated.

Before I can formulate a witty response, the music stops and the countdown to the new year begins.

"Ten, nine, eight, seven…" The flutters in my tummy ramp up to an all-time high as Wyatt pulls me closer, chanting with the crowd. "Three, two, one! Happy New Year!" The sky explodes and confetti sprays into the air.

Just as the beginning notes to "Auld Lang Syne" fire up, Wyatt crushes his lips to mine. Gripping the sides of my face, he caresses my jaw with the pads of his thumbs while easing his tongue inside. With deliberate slowness he proceeds to make love to my mouth. Fireworks screech overhead and my erratic heart threatens to burst from my chest while he guides me, angling my face with a tenderness that has my toes curling.

"Happy New Year, love." His adept fingers ghost along the

sensitive skin at the back of my arms, tracing lazy circles lower and lower. Then he reaches around to cup my backside, while thrusting his tongue and his hips in a synchronized rhythm.

"Wyatt," I moan, breathless and dizzy with want.

"Mmm?"

"Take me to bed…"

CHAPTER TWENTY-SIX

Wyatt

WHITNEY'S HAND IS IN MY PANTS, RUBBING MY painfully hard cock while I fight to get the damn keycard from out of my wallet. *Why must they make the freaking slots so small?*

With everyone else distracted by the ongoing festivities, we managed to land an empty elevator. Due to that stroke of luck, we've made it to the room with our clothes barely still hanging from our bodies, out of breath and on the brink of combustion.

I won't allow myself to think too long about what a field day the security team must have had if they were watching that blasted camera. I stand by the belief that elevators, like bathrooms, should be allowed privacy.

"Finally!" Whit withdraws her hand when I shove the door open, stumbling over the threshold while kicking off her heels. "Meet me in the shower," she slurs with a sorry excuse for a wink while reaching around like a damn contortionist and lowering the zipper on the back of her dress. It flutters to the floor in a puddle at her feet, leaving her completely bare from the waist up.

Fuck, but she's beautiful. I ache to run my tongue over every creamy inch of skin she's got so boldly on display.

Like a siren, she shimmies along to the music in her head slinking around the corner and out of sight. Her little black thong comes flying out of the bathroom, nailing me in the chest just before the sound of rushing water filters into the room.

Once I manage to pick my jaw up from the floor, I make haste stripping out of my shirt. On my way into the bathroom, I trip trying to pull the narrow hem of my fitted slacks over my heel. Fucking booze has my balance off.

"Everything okay?"

"Just peachy." I'm hella relieved she's not around to see me on my back, rolling about like a turtle flipped on its shell, while still fighting to free myself from these fucking pants.

Once I've managed to disrobe, I bound to my feet, happening a glance at the floor-length mirror as I finish the short trek to the bathroom.

My erection's looking a tad deflated following that scuffle, so I give him a few good pumps, making him just a bit more presentable. Can't be waltzing in there all willy-nilly, failing to put our best dick forward, now can we?

"Well, hello there," I croon, slipping into the steaming shower behind the sudsy vixen, who appears to have gotten the party started without me.

"Oh," she says, jumping at my appearance. "Fancy meeting you here."

"Please"—I wave a finger—"carry on," I say, referring to the sultry little dance I seem to have interrupted with my arrival. "I was enjoying that very much."

"I can tell." Twin fiery blue flames home in on my very enthusiastic cock.

Inwardly I'm patting myself on the back over that last-minute decision to beef him up a bit.

"Can I?" she asks, soaping a clean rag and gesturing toward my rock-hard dick.

"By all means," I say, lifting my arms and bracing them on opposite walls of the shower.

With a satisfied smirk, she drops to her knees, letting the bar of soap drop to the floor while gently scrubbing my cock. If it didn't feel so fucking incredible, I'd be in hysterics over the way she's giggling while completing her task.

"The royal penis is clean, your highness," she snickers, letting the towel drop with a *splat*.

"*Coming To America*," I snort. "Nice."

"You have no idea how long I've wanted to reenact that scene," she says, squinting with rapt fascination as she runs her hand over my hardon, watching the suds rinse away. "I'm really enjoying this relationship thing."

"Yeah?" I ask, reaching down and stroking a finger over her cheek. "I'm enjoying you too."

"Like wow!" She sinks down, now sitting on her heels. "I have a *whole man* to myself." She shakes her head as if she can't believe it. "It's incredible."

The innocence of this woman drives me absolutely wild—makes me want to satisfy her in ways she'd never dare to imagine. "Anything else you'd like to try?"

"Can I be on top?" she garbles, wrapping her lips around the tip of my cock and sucking me into the warmth of her mouth.

My hips jerk from the unexpected treat. "You've never—?" I rasp, panting as my heart takes off at a frenzied pace.

She gives her head a shake, nearly choking on the effort. Her cheeks cave in and her head bobs as she puts her all into working me with her mouth.

I weave a hand into her hair, steadying myself with the other against the slippery tile. With gentle persuasion, I guide her, syncing our movements. "The night is yours," I say, grunting when she moans and her lips vibrate like a cock ring around me. "Ahh," I yank her hair, popping her off my dick. "Fuck, baby. Your mouth."

She beams up at me, licking my precum off her lips. "It's my night, remember?"

I nod.

"I want to finish."

Who am I to argue with that logic?

She curls the fingers of one hand around my shaft, giving a few good strokes before adding her mouth back into the mix. She takes her time, winding her tongue in circles over the engorged tip before taking me all the way to the back of her throat.

"Whitney," I moan. "Like that, love. Just." I grind my molars as a rush of heat fills my shaft. "Like. That."

With a whimper, she picks up speed, pumping the base with her fist. The pressure in my cock builds to impossible heights when she hollows her cheeks, sucking me harder and faster.

"Tell me if it's too much," I say as I begin plunging in and out, fucking her mouth.

Whitney is a *goddess*, meeting me thrust for thrust, never once faltering.

I try to pull out when I feel my impending release, but she grips my ass, telling me without words she wants it.

"Ohhh," I groan as thick hot come juts out in spurts, shooting right to the back of her throat. She continues sucking, not letting up until she's swallowed every drop. Only then does she relax and allow my cock to slip from her mouth.

"That was—" I'm truly at a loss for words, sagging against the shower wall.

She smiles, smacking her lips. "Salty?"

I snort. "Get up here."

With my help she rises to her feet, and I pull her close, kissing her passionately beneath the spray. "It was incredible," I say, nipping at her lips. "*You* are incredible."

She reaches around me to twist the knob on the faucet, shutting off the water. "I'm ready to ride," she announces, making a giddy-up motion and twirling an invisible lasso.

I sigh, hating that I have to disappoint her. "I'm gonna need at least thirty minutes to round up your ride, cowgirl."

She deflates with a pout. "Okay…well, wanna watch some TV?"

I shake my head, reaching for the big towels and wrapping one around her before tying the other around my waist. "No, Whitney, I don't want to watch fucking TV."

"Then what do you wanna do?" she asks, nibbling her lower lip.

"I have a better idea."

Her eyes widen as she takes my outstretched hand, following me into the room. "I'm listening."

"I want to taste you," I say, tipping her chin and placing a kiss on her lips. "I want to bring you to the brink over and over and over again until you're screaming so loud every person on this floor knows who's making you come. I want you desperate and writhing, begging for my cock because you know it's the only thing that will satisfy the ache."

She clears her throat, muttering unintelligible sounds.

"Is that a yes?"

"Y—yes," she mutters, staring up at me with hooded eyes.

"Get in the bed." I rip her towel off on my way to open the

sliding glass doors leading out to the balcony, dropping my own before climbing in to join her. "A little ambiance," I say as the sky lights up with flashes of gold.

Gripping her thighs in both hands, I pull her toward me. "Relax your legs, love." I lift her right knee to my lips, peppering soft kisses along her inner thigh until I reach her center.

Her hips jerk toward my face when I trail my nose along her slit. "You smell delicious."

She cries out my name when I flick my tongue over her swollen bud. Once…twice… "Oh, God," she cries as she starts to lose control, rolling her hips to the rhythm of my ministrations.

I pull back, not ready for her to find her release just yet.

"Wyatt," she whines, her hips grinding against me, her tone one of utter frustration.

I grin up at her from between her spread legs. "Foreplay," I whisper, throwing her earlier justification back at her.

Her lips part, no doubt to offer some witty reply, but I silence her, slipping two fingers inside of her, curling them as I bring my lips to hers. "It's going to be so fucking good, Whit."

I feast on her for what feels like days, but is more likely only minutes, working her to the brink over and over without letting her climax.

Until, finally, neither of us can wait another second.

"Wyatt," she moans, sounding desperate and greedy. "Wyatt, fuck me, please."

I slide my fingers from her heat and roll to my back, grinning at her all the while. "Mount up, love." I nod my head toward my dick, which is once again proudly standing at attention.

Whit grabs the foil packet from the top of the nightstand and tears into the wrapper, wasting not a single second before rolling the condom down over my cock, straddling my hips, and impaling herself on my erection.

"Wow," she muses, a seductive lilt to her voice as she rocks her hips slightly, testing the new position. "This is…*different*."

"Good different?" I ask, thrusting my hips upward, encouraging her to move.

"God, yes." She plants her hands on my chest. "What do I do?"

"Whatever feels good."

She starts off tentatively swirling her hips, before dropping her weight onto my chest to support herself as she bobs up and down. "It's so deep," she moans, still searching for a tempo that works for her.

I reach out, brushing my thumbs over her nipples. Her body reacts on instinct, her head falling back, her pussy tightening.

"Yes," she moans, arching her back and digging her nails into my thighs.

I lower one hand, applying pressure to her clit, and a switch flips—she's bucking against me, crying out every time our hips meet.

She's a mad woman, chasing her release with a violent fervor. I can tell she's close when her walls squeeze my dick nearly to the point of pain.

I reach for her face, pulling her down to my own so I can taste her sweet lips as she cries out my name.

As if it was planned, the sky explodes, bursting with color at the exact moment she comes. "Oh, God!" Her cries of pleasure turn to garbled murmurs as she collapses against my chest.

"So beautiful," I whisper, grinding into her from below. Her pussy flutters around me as she rides out the aftershocks of her orgasm, milking me for all I'm worth until I fill the condom with my release.

"That was beautiful," she whispers, staring out at the night sky.

"It was," I agree, but I'm not referring to the light show.

For long minutes we lay there, content to remain just as we are.

"Are you snoring?" she screeches, jarring me awake.

"No way." I blink a few times, clearing the fog from my eyes.

She giggles, running a finger along my chest while staring up at me. "You fell asleep with your *thing* buried in my hoohah."

I shake my head, gently rolling her off of me. "That was so far from sexy—*oh, shit*."

"What?" she asks, alarmed by my tone. "What's wrong?"

"Did we forget the condom?"

Her eyes widen with alarm before she shakes her head. "No…I put it on myself."

"It's gone."

She's breathing heavy, on the verge of hyperventilating. "What the hell do you mean it's gone?"

Frantically we both rip the covers and sheets from the bed, shaking them out.

"Where's the condom, Wyatt?" Her voice is strangled.

A sick feeling washes over me. "I think maybe it stayed… inside."

"Huh?"

"Of you," I add for clarification.

Her eyes widen. "That can happen?"

I shrug my shoulders, pacing the room. "I don't know, but where the hell else could it be?"

"Oh God," she cries. "I'm going to be sick."

Think quick, Wyatt… "Should we go to the hospital?"

Her jaw drops. "And tell them I think I might have a come-filled condom stuck inside my vagina?"

I cringe. "I could maybe…fish it out?"

"I like that idea much better," she says, flopping back on the bed and opening her legs like I've seen on shows when women are preparing to give birth. "Use the flashlight on your cell phone."

"Right." I fumble around on the end table until I find it and switch on the light.

Her hand grips me around the wrist firmly. She cranes her neck, lifting her head to meet my gaze. "Don't you dare snap any pictures while you're down there."

After a quick look-see, I toss the phone to the side, deciding it's more helpful to have the use of both hands than a spotlight. "Relax," I say again, attempting to insert two fingers into her pussy to no avail. She's got that thing locked up tighter than Fort Knox. "Baby, you have to ease up, or we'll have no choice but to make a trip to the emergency room."

"I'm trying," she cries, and I hear a sniffle.

The sight of her tears fucking guts me. "There!" I say, as I slide the slippery rubber out. "And still completely intact." I hold it out for her examination.

Whitney pinches the bottom where my release is still puddled inside before drying her eyes on the sheet and collapsing with relief.

"Add condom fisher-outer to your list of jobs."

CHAPTER TWENTY-SEVEN

Wyatt

Waking up to Whitney draped across my chest is my new favorite thing in life. The warmth of her bare breasts. Her hair tickling my nose with every intake of breath. The steady cadence of her heartbeat thrumming against my ribs…

My own version of heaven.

It's a little after six in the morning, but the room is already bathed in sunlight thanks to neither of us thinking to shut the balcony before passing out last night. No matter. I'd be awake either way. At least the orangey glow allows me to enjoy the view while I trail my fingertips along her spine and watch her squirm.

"Good morning," she rasps, stretching her legs out with a yawn. Her sex-tousled hair falls around her face in a veritable rat's nest. "*Someone's* happy to see me." She trails a hand over my morning wood, causing me to leap up and haul it to the bathroom in a hurry.

"*Someone's* gotta pee," I chant on my way, laughing at her loud, exaggerated groan.

"I was about to take advantage of that," she grumps.

"No worries." I return with a lingering semi dangling between my legs while drying my freshly washed hands on a towel. "You're only a few pumps away from paradise."

Her answering laugher fills my soul, as I leap into the bed beside her and proceed to demonstrate just how quickly our little dilemma can be remedied.

"These things are sinfully delicious," she garbles around a mouth full of food while we look for a decent spot on the New Year's Day parade route. It isn't for a few hours yet, but pretty soon there won't be a square foot of sidewalk to stand on. We post up next to each other on the curb in a nice shaded spot to wait it out.

"You have a little something right there." I start to dust the falling powdered sugar from her breasts, but she swats my hand away.

"I was saving that for later."

"For me? Or yourself?"

She waggles her brows. "Here," she says grabbing a beignet from her little white pastry bag. "Eat one so I don't feel like such a pig."

Between bites we talk about everything and anything from the antics she and Kate got into as little girls to my stint in rehab when Mimi found pot in my room.

"She sent you to rehab for a little pot?"

I widen my eyes and gawk at her. "You met the woman! Mimi don't play. And for what it's worth, it worked. I never touched the stuff again."

She giggles. "I was raising a baby while my friends were going through that phase." Her smile wobbles. "I used to think I missed out on so much, but now I really believe Prissy saved me from a world of heartache and bad decisions."

"It's true," I agree fervently. "You're so much more mature than other girls I've dated that were your age."

"And inexperienced," she adds, her cheeks turning rosy.

"*That's* a positive."

"Is it?" *Fuck, she's adorable.*

"Hell yeah!" I tip her chin up and meet her gaze. "Now I get to show you the ropes."

She shakes her head to herself. "I've had plenty of sex, Wyatt."

No need to brag, Whit.

"You don't have to be a virgin to be innocent, love."

She folds her arms over her knees, resting her head on top and angling it my way. "Explain."

"Well, your lack of interest in relationships has kept your heart pure." I brush a lock of hair behind her ear to better see her features. "I don't take the honor of being your first love, lightly."

"How do you know I didn't love Prissy's dad?" she counters.

I wave that pesky thought away. "Impossible. You're way too smart to fall for someone like that."

"Yeah, he was…" She cringes. "A good time, but a really bad choice."

"Hey, that really bad choice left you with a priceless gift."

She nods. "I occasionally wonder if he ever thinks about her, or if he just went off to college without ever looking back." She brings her thumbnail to her mouth and nibbles on the end.

"His loss is my gain." I don't think she could possibly know how sincerely I mean that.

She smiles, reaching for my hand. "You really love her."

"I do." My answer comes with zero hesitation. "And I love you."

She nods, giving my fingers a squeeze while she clears the emotion from her throat. "I love you too, Wyatt."

I bend to press a kiss to the top of her head, then stroke my hand over her back.

"Can you believe this all started with a dumpster fuck?" She spits a laugh. "God, when I walked out to meet our new construction guy, and saw *you* standing there…" She shakes her head.

"I wasn't even sure I was gonna take the job until I realized it was you, all high and mighty in your pencil skirt and lace blouse." I chuckle. "Such a stark contrast from the party girl I hooked up with in that alley. I almost didn't believe it."

"Then I opened my mouth."

"And I knew."

"Knew what exactly?" Her sly grin stretches ear to ear while she looks at me expectantly.

"That I was gonna have to fuck the hoity-toity outta your uptight ass."

She chokes. "You took the job because you wanted to have sex with me?"

"I took the job because I saw a damsel in distress." I give her a little jab with my elbow. "You needed saving, and I was just the man for the job. Don't be twistin' my words."

"And your plan was to save me with your *penis*."

I nod. "That sounds about right."

Her look is one of stunned disbelief. "You're a real prince, Wyatt Landry."

"You're welcome." I give her the best bow I can manage from my seated position.

"So, why'd you stay?" She hedges. "*After.*"

"Because," I drawl. "You flipped the script and made me fall in love with you first."

"I love that."

"You know, they say you find love in the least likely of places."

She grunts. "We just happened to find it behind a dumpster."

"Nah. That was unfettered lust. Love came later. We found *that* in a funeral home."

"We're just a real fucking fairy tale."

I don't know if my uncontrollable laughter is from what she said or how she said it. "Can't wait to tell our fuckin' grandkids," I finally say, when I can catch my breath.

"Excuse me." A very irate woman walks up, tapping me on the shoulder. "There are children present."

"I'm so sorry." I glance around at the crowd that's collected while we've been sitting here lost in our own little world.

After that we stick to safer topics. Sports. The weather.

Until the telltale sirens announce the start of the parade.

As the first float nears, Whitney turns to the woman we upset earlier and her children behind us, offering them our spot. I'm assuming it's to make amends for our potty mouths. But it could also be that she's just that freaking sweet. Whatever the reason, it makes me proud to be with such a thoughtful woman. Especially when I see the kids raking in beads and candy galore.

"Thanks," says their mother, whose face now has a megawatt smile in the place of her early grimace.

"It's no problem," Whitney assures her.

"Mount up, cowgirl," I tease crouching so she can climb up onto my shoulders.

"What am I going to even do with you?" she asks, blushing

while she moves to make her ascent. "I can't do it." She circles around me, sizing me up. "I'm gonna hurt you…or break my neck."

"Sure, ya can. Put your hands on my head and then just froggy hop up."

"Riiiiiight."

It takes a few tries, and our uncontrollable laughter after every miss certainly doesn't help matters. But before the next float arrives, her thighs are wrapped around my neck, her hands fisted in my hair.

And me? Well, I'm considering looking for the nearest dumpster, of course.

CHAPTER TWENTY-EIGHT

Whitney

"Hey there, handsome." I pound a fist on the open door of the old barn turned shop in order to be heard over the buzzing of his power tools.

At the sound of my voice, Wyatt kills the saw, lifting his dust covered goggles to rest on top of his head, and whirls around.

It's a rather warm day for January, even in Louisiana, with it being in the mid-seventies. I'm extra thankful for that fact when I catch sight of him shirtless and dripping in sweat. I'm literally salivating. He's in a pair of work jeans. They're worn and sitting low on his hips. And his abs. *Dear Lord Almighty.*

The man makes filthy look like a *snack*.

"To what do I owe this surprise?" With wide eyes, he looks to me and Prissy, back and forth a few times, his smile growing with every twist of his head.

"We wanted to come see what you're doing over here," Prissy

announces, charging into his waiting arms. "We missed you, Wyatt."

It's been two whole days since we saw him last, and my little girl and I have been going out of our minds with Wyatt withdrawals. *It's a thing, okay?*

The funeral home and, well, life in general are—in the words of my child—*boring* without him. I must say, I concur.

"I hope this is okay…" I twist the toe of my Converse into the ground, breaking up dirt.

"You kidding?" He crosses the shop to kiss my cheek, leaving me longing for so much more. He's really good about toning things down for my daughter, maybe even better than I am. Despite it being a very chaste peck, she's still ooooh-ing and giggling up a storm. "I can't even think of a better surprise than my favorite girls showing up unannounced."

"Well, I know you're busy with building these cabinets." I swipe some sawdust off his brow and take a glance around the cluttered space. He's got cabinets in every stage of development from raw wood stacked in one corner to frames awaiting doors, some put together just needing to be finished, and even some completed pieces drying in the sun after being stained. "I promise we won't be in the way." I tilt my head and bat my lashes. "I even brought the stuff to whip up spaghetti. I mean, you've still gotta eat, right?"

"I know what this is really about," Wyatt taunts, bringing his lips close to my ear. "You're in mourning."

I narrow my eyes. "For whom?"

"Not who…what."

"Okay," I amend, "for what?"

"My wood," he rasps before flicking his tongue discreetly over my lobe.

I snort, slapping him on the chest. "No! That's definitely not what this is about."

"So, you're not?" He pushes his lip out into the most pitiful of pouts.

"Well, I mean…" I feel the flush taking over my cheeks. "I could definitely go for some of that too…but that's not why *we're* here."

He nods, backing away as he clears his throat. "Dinner sounds amazing, and Priss?"

"Yeah, Wyatt?"

"Sprinkles could use a training session. He's been awful obstinate lately."

"On it," she chirps, sprinting across the yard for the back door of his little house that's looking a lot less like a fixer-upper with each passing day.

"Get over here, woman." His ravenous gaze has me burning up with need.

"She could come back at any—"

"I just want a kiss," he says, sauntering back toward me. My head rests against the cypress wall of his shop when he tips my chin up with a finger and his hungry lips descend on mine. He kisses me deeply, thoroughly, and with so much passion, I have horny tears building in my eyes when he finally forces himself to break away. "I've missed you, Whit. Don't ever doubt that. If I didn't have to have these damn things finished by tomorrow, there's no way I'd have stayed away."

"I know." I cup his cheek in my hand. "You get back to it. I'm going to go get dinner started."

"Careful…" He swats me on the ass with a flick of his T-shirt on my way out the door. When I turn back to see what he's babbling about, he grins and says, "A man could get used to this."

I leave him with a flirty wink and proceed to the house, floating on a cloud.

Upon entering, I'm greeted with the sound of Prissy and Sprinkles horseplaying in the living room. She truly *loves* that dog. It's good to see her smiling and engaging with someone other than her grandparents and myself, even if her new friend is a miniature pony.

Wyatt's house smells like him. Like leather and sunshine, sawdust and man. I can't even look toward his bedroom without aching for his touch. *I miss him.* To the point it's kinda scary. Two days isn't long. Yet somehow it feels like a lifetime.

I busy myself with washing up the few dishes Wyatt left soaking in the sink. Then, I get right to work, browning and draining the meat and boiling noodles. After adding a couple of cans of Ragu—hey, I never said I was some master chef—I lower the heat and cover the pot.

With nothing left to do but make sure the house doesn't catch fire, I plop down into a chair at the table and, for just a few minutes, allow myself to imagine what life here, in this house with Wyatt and Prissy, might be like.

"So, there's something I wanted to talk to the two of you about," Wyatt says, taking his seat beside me at the table after pulling out both mine and my little girl's chairs. The scent of Irish Spring engulfs me. The ends of his hair are still dripping, and his fresh shirt is damp. Did no one ever teach this man how to dry himself?

I would be all too happy to volunteer for the job.

"What is it?" Prissy asks while I give his thigh a little squeeze under the table.

"It's been recently brought to my attention that *someone* has a birthday coming up."

"It's me!" Prissy answers, bouncing in her chair. "I'm gonna be seven." She Cabbage-Patches her arms in circles over her plate.

"I know." He grins, clearly amused by her enthusiasm. "How would you feel about us taking a little trip?"

"Like a vacation?" she squeals, before turning to me with reluctance. Her face droops. "We don't take vacations…"

I feel sick. The last thing I want is to have to be the one to disappoint them both. "Wyatt…I can't just leave."

"But what if you could?" he asks, not losing a bit of steam. He's got a confident air that tells me he's convinced this is already a done deal.

"You've seen what goes on at the funeral home on a day-to-day basis. It's too unpredictable." I swallow a lump. "People rely on us—on *me*."

"Your parents are already onboard," he announces before I can get too upset. "They think the two of you getting out of that depressing place for a few days is worth Marie coming out of retirement for just as many."

"Really?" While she still helps out here and there, Momma was more than ready to retire when I took over. The stress of the job was beginning to take a real toll on her.

Wyatt leaves me to stir in my thoughts, while getting up from the table to retrieve a few brochures from the junk drawer in the kitchen. "Check it out," he says handing one to each of us. "Great Bear Lodge. It's an indoor waterpark where our little mermaid here can put her recent swimming lessons to good use."

"Look at this big water slide, Momma!" Prissy is out of her mind with excitement.

"What about school?" I'm really not trying to be Debbie Downer—just thinking of anything that might prevent this trip from happening before allowing myself to get too excited.

"School." Wyatt scoffs and rolls his eyes. "No one should have to go to class on their birthday." He turns to my little girl, who gives her head an enthusiastic nod of agreement. "It's a four-day weekend. She'd only have to miss two days. It's not far—just outside of Dallas. We'll travel at night…"

"Wow," I sigh. "You've really thought this through."

He reaches across the table for Prissy's hand and to my lap for mine, giving them both a squeeze. "Well, what'd'ya say, Momma? Can we?" he asks, bringing his fingers together at a point beneath his chin. "Huh? Huh? Can we?"

"Can we?" Prissy joins in. "Huh? Huh?"

"Fine!" I shout, with a laugh. "When do you propose we take this trip?"

"Second weekend of February. Friday to Monday."

I nod. "How much is it? When do we book?"

"Already taken care of," he says, booping me on the nose. "Now let's eat. I'm starving."

CHAPTER TWENTY-NINE

Wyatt

WE DECIDE TO MAKE THE TRIP TO GREAT BEAR Lodge in Whitney's Camry, since it's newer and more dependable than my old rust bucket. After dropping Sprinkles off to stay with Beau and Kate, we line up in carpool to scoop Prissy up from school and head out. With an eight-hour drive ahead of us, we aren't wanting to waste any time waiting around for her bus.

"Free at last," the little heathen chants when she throws her backpack on the seat and clambers in after it. This girl always looks like she got into a scuffle with a cat *and lost* by the time the school day ends. She has more hair out of her ponytail than in it.

"How was your day?" Whitney turns completely around in her seat to make sure Priss is buckled in properly. The restraint it takes not to reach out and slap that fine ass of hers... It's practically begging for it, all firm and round in those tight-fitting jeans.

"It was good, but Mrs. Wyler said she's gonna have a talk with you about responsible parenting when we get back."

"Damn it, Prissy! You weren't supposed to tell anyone about our trip." With a loud harumph, the angry blonde flops back into her seat, effectively stealing my view while she refastens her belt. "What happened to pretending to have the flu?"

"I'm sorry, Momma. I'm just not a good liar like you."

I actually feel Whitney's gaze burning a hole in the side of my face when I spit out a laugh. "What?" I ask recoiling toward my window. "Oh, come on, you have to admit, that was funny."

"It's not funny! That woman hates me."

"Hey," I say, reaching across the car to tickle the back of her neck. That sour face of hers just isn't sitting well with me. This is supposed to be a happy trip. "You let me handle Mrs. Wyler, okay?"

"I wish I could...*my* kid, remember?" She shoves my hand away, trying not to laugh. "Keep 'em on the wheel, sir."

All jokes aside, I can't wait for the day we can formally remedy this little situation. For the day I can officially call that kid my own. It's not something I've brought up with Whitney yet, only because I'm still not so patiently waiting for enough time to lapse that she might not turn me down when I work up the nerve to ask her to be my wife. "Right," I say, chewing on the inside of my cheek. "Well, I'll accompany you to said meeting, and we can handle that witch together. How's that?"

"Deal."

After about a half-hour of idle chit-chat, the car falls silent. Whitney's busy reading some romance book on her Kindle, and Prissy's occupied playing games on her momma's phone.

I switch the radio on to some good old-fashioned rock and roll and proceed to cruise, watching the mile markers tick on by.

"Pull over," Whitney groans, folded at the waist with a hand clamped over her mouth.

I take the next exit, pulling onto the shoulder of a wooded area, where she promptly flings the door open and proceeds to empty the contents of her stomach.

"Are you okay?" I wish I could do more to look after her, but as it stands I'm presently hanging my head out the window, fighting the urge to lose my own lunch. The smell alone is enough to curdle my gut.

"Yeah," she says, wiping her face with a Wet One she retrieved from the glove compartment. "Food must've stayed on my stomach."

This is only the first of many pit stops. There are a few for Prissy to pee, but most are on account of Whitney's newfound penchant for car sickness.

"I'm so sorry. I would've taken some motion sickness medicine, but I've never been on a long enough trip to know I needed it."

"No worries, love. I just feel bad for you. You look awful."

Her eyes widen. "Uhh…thanks?"

"You know what I mean."

Our last stop is a gas station connected to a Wendy's, where we feed Prissy dinner and get Whitney some sleeping medicine to hopefully knock her out for the remainder of the drive.

"Honeys, we're here!" I chant to the two beauties sawing wood like they're competing for a gold medal in some Olympic event for snorers. How anything so beautiful can produce such vile sounds is beyond me.

"Wow," Priss says, opening her eyes and squeezing herself between the front seats to have a better look at the massive grizzly bear statues as tall as the roof. She perches herself on the center console to peer through the windshield. "Get up, Momma," she says, shaking Whitney by the shoulders. "Look!"

Whit chokes on a snore before wiping her mouth with the back of a hand. "We're here?" *Poor thing's still half asleep.*

"We are. Let's get inside so we can get some rest." With our many stops, the eight-hour trip quickly grew to over ten, and I'm freaking exhausted.

After a late check-in, we head up to our room. I swear Prissy's mouth hangs open the entire way as she drinks in every detail of her playground for the next few days. The décor is off the chain, the outdoors theme woven into every facet of the place.

But her reaction when she sees our room is the one I don't think I'll soon forget.

I might have splurged on one of the more expensive rooms, with a queen-sized bed and a set of bunks enclosed in this neat little manmade stone alcove.

"Are you kidding me?" The kid seems to have caught a second wind, zipping around the room and checking out every last detail.

I'm so focused on Prissy's reactions that I fail to notice how pale Whitney has become.

"All right, Priss. Your momma's not feeling well, and it's late. I know you're excited, but it's time for bed, okay?"

"Fine," she sulks, trudging to the bathroom with her bag.

"Are you okay?" I plop down beside her on the couch, resting a hand on her knee.

"Yeah," Whitney says, yawning. "Just still really tired from that sleeping pill."

"Go on to bed," I tell her. "I'll take the couch."

"Y'all can stop doing that," Prissy barks, ambling out of the bathroom in her mummy Halloween pajamas, her face screwed up in annoyance. "You can sleep in the same bed. I know y'all do when I'm not there."

Whitney snorts, grabbing her daughter by the arm and hauling her into her lap for a cuddle. "I love you, brat." She nuzzles her face into Prissy's neck.

"I love you too…but you still don't have to treat me like a baby."

"You're right, we do sleep in the same bed when you aren't there," her mother confirms, shocking me speechless. "I just didn't want to make you uncomfortable."

Quiet as a mouse, I sit here, a silent spectator, wondering how this'll play out. I fully expected Whitney to deny, deny, deny. But I really shouldn't be all that surprised by the honesty in her response. She has a respect for her daughter that I've come to admire. Whitney and her parents don't talk down to her or treat her like any less of a person just because she's little. It's made Prissy a confident and very intelligent child, albeit sometimes a little too big for her britches.

Prissy gives an exaggerated shrug. "Why would *I* be uncomfortable? Y'all the ones with each other's feet in your back. I have two whole beds to myself."

"I apologize for treating you like a baby, Miss Priss." Whit peppers her cheeks with kisses. "Can you ever forgive me?"

"Just don't let it happen again." Prissy squirms in her mother's lap, trying to fight her off.

"Yes, ma'am." With a giggle, she sends her off to bed with a playful swat to the behind.

"So…?" I look to Whitney, widening my eyes in question, not wanting to assume anything.

"We can share the bed."

Yes!

By the time we've gotten ourselves ready and climbed in between the sheets, Prissy is already snoring the roof in.

"This is weird," I say, lying flat on my back, staring up at the ceiling with Whitney beside me, but…not. At least a foot separates us. It's more torturous than having her across the room. At this distance I can smell her perfume and feel the heat her body's giving off. The urge to wrap myself around her is so damn strong, but our little cockblock is right on the other side of the wall in her bunkhouse.

I walk my fingers across the mattress until I find Whitney's hand and give it a squeeze, then lift it to my mouth and pepper kisses along her knuckles. "I love you, Whit."

She rolls onto her side to face me. I can just barely make out the whites of her eyes as she props her head in her hand. "I love you too," she whispers, combing her fingers through my hair before stuffing a pillow between us. "Just in case we forget she's here during the night." Her giggle is one laden with frustration. But hey, delayed gratification is just one of those things you get used to with a kid around. Keeps the fire burning hot, desire constantly simmering beneath the surface, and the climax—fucking explosive. Every. Single. Time.

"Good thinking." I'm still not quite sure that'll be enough to keep me from pawing her in my sleep, but I'm willing to give it an honest try.

After leaning over the barrier for a chaste goodnight kiss, she flops onto her pillow. With her fingers intwined in mine, I stroke the underside of her wrist until we drift off to sleep.

CHAPTER THIRTY

Whitney

Never in my life have I been more thankful that my child loves her some sleep than I am right now, as I find myself waking up to Wyatt's face buried in my nape and his morning wood pressing into my ass like a light saber ready to do battle. Desire floods my veins, and the rhythm of my heartbeat borders on erratic.

Powerless to resist, I trail a hand between us, palming the steel rod and caressing him in long languid strokes until he awakens fully.

"Shhh," I whisper at the sound of his moan. "We're not alone."

The reminder pours over him like an icy bucket of cold water, signaling his retreat. My disappointment at the loss of his prodding erection is entirely irrational. To touch him at all was flirting with fire, but the man has a way of making me want to dive headfirst into the flames and savor the burn.

When he disappears into the bathroom to deal with his *situation*, I slip from the bed, creeping into Prissy's nook to sit on the edge of the mattress. I take a quiet moment to reflect as I watch her sleep. It's incomprehensible to me that my baby is already seven years old. It seems like only yesterday I was faced with that positive pregnancy test, while practically still a kid myself. At the time that little plus sign felt like the end of the world. Now I know it was merely the beginning. Despite being young, I can honestly say that not once have I regretted my choice to keep her. When I look back on the years of joy this little girl has brought to my life, I know without question that Prissy's existence was no mistake. She's my greatest accomplishment. My pride and joy. My *legacy*.

"Happy Birthday, Priss." I stroke her wild hair back with my fingers and she stirs. *Grunts.* But makes no attempt to open her eyes.

"Prissy," I say, a little louder. "Rise and shine, birthday girl!" When she still doesn't budge, I go for the heavy artillery and dig my pointers into her sides, tickling her until she's writhing around swatting and kicking in hopes to make me stop.

"Fine!" she laughs. "I'm up! I'm up!"

"*That's* more like it." I bend to retrieve the notebook from the floor beside me. "Because it's time for your interview."

The birthday journal is something I read about online during my pregnancy and started when she turned one. For the first two years, I answered on her behalf, but since the age of three the words have come straight from the horse's mouth. It's a lot of fun to look back at her answers throughout the years, something I know we'll both cherish more and more as she gets older.

"You brought it?" With a wide smile, she scoots herself up to sitting, roughly pushing her tangles away from her face.

"Of course I did."

"Okay," she says, folding her hands and placing them in her lap, all proper-like. "I'm ready."

"Question number one," I say, tapping my pen on the pad. "What was your favorite book this year?"

"That's easy," she says. "The Fudge books by Judy Blume."

Of course, I think, jotting it down. She's only had me read the entire series three times. The girl is obsessed with Fudge and his antics. He probably reminds her of her naughty little self.

"Perfect," I say, moving on to the next. "What was your favorite movie?"

"Chucky!"

"Which one?"

"Umm," she places a finger on her chin, tapping it lightly. "All of them."

Again…no surprise. With a shake of my head, I scrawl her answer on the page. "Who is your best friend?"

She chews her lip and begins to rock back and forth. "Don't get mad, okay?"

"Why would I get mad?"

Her shoulders tense as she brings them to her ears before dropping them back down with a huff. "*Okay…*" She covers her face with her hands, so she won't have to witness my reaction. I half expect her to tell me she befriended a murderer by how crazy she's acting. "It's Wyatt." Her answer escapes as a high-pitched squeak.

Is that all? "Wyatt's a great choice." I'm touched that she was afraid to hurt my feelings in choosing someone other than me. In all honesty, I'm relieved. It warms my heart to know that she's forged such a solid bond with someone other than myself or her Paw. The fact that I, too, have a very deep connection with her new bestie also, serves to soften the blow. The more she loves him, the freer I feel to allow myself to do the same.

I blow out a deep breath when I come to the next one, because unlike with most children, the answer never changes. Asking is simply a formality. "What do you want to be when you grow up?"

She squints her little eyes at me. "A mortician, duh!"

Duh, indeed. My little girl has never dreamed of being anything else. Not a princess or a teacher. She's never wanted to be a cashier or flip burgers at McDonald's. Nope. Unlike myself, who wanted to get as far away as possible from the place until life gave me a reason to stay, she's embraced her birthright from the womb.

After a few more questions, we come to my personal favorite. "Okay," I say, rubbing my palms together to play up the suspense. "Think really hard before answering."

"Okay..."

"What was your *favorite* memory from being six?"

"Oh, I know," she says with a dreamy look in her eyes. "The father-daughter dance with Wyatt, cuz it was like, the best day of my whole life."

Is someone chopping onions in here?

"What looks good?" Wyatt asks Prissy when we enter the cutest little bakery, Bear Paw Sweets & Eats. Evidently, his Mimi gave him treats for breakfast on his birthdays, and we're continuing the practice. The fact that he's passing traditions from his childhood on to my little girl has me floating on air.

"Oh, Mylanta." Prissy's eyes pop as she spins in a circle, taking in the wall-to-wall yumminess that surrounds us. "The ice cream looks really good." She licks her lips staring into the glass case at the mouthwatering display of cupcakes. "But so do those."

"Get whatever you want, kiddo," Wyatt encourages. "It's your day."

Shamelessly my mind jumps straight to the gutter, recollecting New Year's Eve, when he proclaimed it my night. He sure does love to pamper his girls, catering to each of our very different appetites, of course.

"Okay…I want chocolate ice cream with whipped cream and chocolate sauce and sprinkles."

"On it." On my way to the counter to place her order, I notice the indecision on her face. Poor baby looks utterly overwhelmed. "Pick out a few other things. Whatever you don't eat now, we can always drop off in the room for later," I say with a wink.

By the time her enormous sundae is prepared, Wyatt and Prissy are unloading arms full of cupcakes, brownies, and an M&M cookie as big as my head next to the register.

"What are you gonna have?" Prissy asks, apparently not willing to share her haul with her mother.

I shrug. "I'm still feeling a little queasy from the ride."

"You have to eat."

Knowing Wyatt won't accept no for an answer, I grab a Rice Krispy treat to appease him and toss it up there with the rest of it. "There."

When we sit to eat, Wyatt rattles his hands on the table, making a full-blown spectacle before whipping a number seven candle out of the pocket of his shorts. He takes the rainbow cupcake out of her hand just before she opens her mouth to bite it, and stuffs the candle into the center. "Happy birthday to you…" he starts after lighting the wick and setting it down in front of her. Every person in the establishment and even some passersby pop in to sing to my little girl, who looks like she might just explode with glee.

"Make a wish," I say.

She looks at Wyatt and then to me, shamelessly waggling her little brows before blowing her candle out.

Wyatt rubs the toe of his shoe over my ankle beneath the table, making me aware that Prissy's all too obvious hint didn't go unnoticed by him either.

After we've eaten, we start packing up the rest of Prissy's snacks, preparing to bring them to our room, when the lovely woman behind the counter pops by with an offer to hold them in the back, allowing us to go straight to the waterpark. We graciously take her up on that suggestion, eager to get this day started.

The place is *huge*, and the scent of chlorine is so strong my eyes and nose are burning before we've set foot in the water. We stroll right past the little kid area, because my child is seven going on seventeen and cannot be bothered to play with children her own age.

"Let's go on that!" Excitedly she points to a huge yellow and red monstrosity. My stomach revolts at the thought.

"Why don't we start out in the wave pool and work our way up?" I suggest, eying the safe haven across the room.

"'Fraid of heights?" Wyatt jeers, nudging me with an elbow.

"Duh!" Prissy offers before I can respond. "At the fairs, Paw has to go on all the scary stuff with me."

"I'm not scared," I lie. "I'm merely suggesting we allow a little time for our food to digest before riding something with *tornado* in its name…"

"Fine," she concedes, taking off at a sprint, her stringy blonde hair bouncing behind her.

"Thank you for this," I say to Wyatt as he links his fingers with mine. "It means more to her—to us—than you could ever know."

"Of course." He smiles down at me, setting off a swarm of fireflies in my tummy. "I love being with you guys."

"Me too," I say, because I'm an idiot. "With you, I mean. We love being with you."

The soft rumble of laughter that follows heats my blood. "I know what you meant."

The mood changes to something a little more PG when we meet up with my daughter at the set of lounge chairs she's claimed. The girl has already removed her coverup and packed it away and has a pair of lopsided goggles affixed to her face.

I set my bag on the chair beside hers and slink out of my dress, nice and slow to give my man a little tease, knowing there's not a damn thing he can do to act on it for a few days yet. His heated gaze as he ogles my red, ruffle-trimmed bikini tells me my efforts don't go unnoticed.

"You are so wrong for that," he rasps into my ear before reaching over his shoulder and gripping the back of his T-shirt with one hand. He has it over his head in one swift motion.

Saliva pools in my mouth. I don't think I'll ever get my fill of looking at him. His broad chest and tanned skin. The light ripple of definition dusted in a blonde happy trail that disappears beneath turquoise boardshorts.

"Are we gonna go in or are you two just gonna check out each other's bathing suits all day?"

"Yeah," I say, forcing my gaze away with a laugh. "Let's go."

The wave pool isn't all that packed, probably because it's still very early in the day. Not that I'm complaining. Prissy is having a blast swimming laps between wave sessions, and I'm not having any difficulty keeping her in my sight.

"She's a fish," I observe, still amazed by how fast she picked up on the skill.

Wyatt smiles tenderly, watching her with so much pride it

momentarily steals my breath. He's so easily slipping into a parental role with her—one I'm shocked that I'm not more reluctant to share. Their bond is effortless. I have to believe that if things ended up not working out between us, he'd remain a part of her life. I can't allow my mind to think otherwise.

"Now we won't have to worry about her drowning in the bayou."

Comments like this one are why I'll keep my fears and insecurities at bay and ride this train as far as it takes us. What man dates a woman for a few months and spends his time fretting over the safety of his home for her child? *A damn good one.*

"Y'all," Prissy comes up, sputtering, swiping water from her face. "Look at that lady's boobies."

Wyatt's eyes widen. Clearly, he hasn't been privy to my child's recent fixation with getting her boobs.

"What about 'em?" I ask, shoving her hand down. "You know better than to point at people."

"I never saw some like that before." With her palms rounded in front of her chest, she sways side to side as if she's imagining them on her little body. "They're really high. Almost in her chin!"

"Because they're fake," I whisper, this time shoving both of her hands down. "Stop doing that."

But her mind only heard one portion of that conversation. "I know what I want for my birthday now."

Wyatt's choking on a laugh before she gets the words out. He knows as well as I do what ridiculousness is coming.

"Fake boobies." She pokes out her chest doing a little shimmy.

I *can't* with this child. "You can't get fake ones til you're grown. It's a surgical implant...like a pacemaker," I add when her brow crinkles. She loves to accompany my father to the crematory and watch him remove them before cremation. We have to, or they'll explode.

"Fine," she deflates. "My eighteenth birthday then."

"We'll see."

"Ugh," she growls. "That means no."

I wink.

"What's with the boob obsession?" Wyatt mutters close to my ear when the waves begin to roll in and my child's focus shifts. "Just when I think she and I couldn't have more in common," he muses.

"I dunno," I laugh. "She skipped the whole 'all I want for Christmas is my two front teeth' phase and went straight into wanting her very own set of boobies."

"Speaking of," he growls, fixing his hungry eyes on my tits. "Is that some kinda magic bikini top you got on there? The girls are lookin' nice."

"Definitely not," I say, catching him off guard when I shove him under the water.

After a few minutes of riding the surf, my stomach begins to make some waves of its own. I leave Prissy with Wyatt, citing a need to use the restroom, barely making it inside before expelling every bit of my breakfast and then some into the trash can.

After rinsing my mouth a few times, I decide I won't even mention my little bout of nausea to the other two. No sense in messing up their vacation as well.

Sweat beads my brow when I return to the pool, and they're not where I left them. I take slow, practiced breaths as I scour the area while going to my bag to check my phone, expelling a huge sigh of relief when I see that there's a message waiting. "Took her to ride the Howlin' Tornado. You can repay me in sexual favors at a later date.'" A second message follows with a series of three emojis: a winky face, a tongue, and an eggplant.

I get to the attraction just in time to see the two of them come flying down, with identical looks of elation plastered on their faces.

My heart threatens to burst from my chest, but instead it's a cackle that erupts when Wyatt hits the water at just the right angle to have him cupping his junk beneath the water while an attendant fetches his shorts, which are riding the waves without their owner.

I am cursing myself for not bringing my phone along, leaving me no way to record this historic moment that will no doubt be a highlight of this trip…if not our entire lives.

CHAPTER THIRTY-ONE

Whitney

"Well, hello, Morticia!"

My lips twist into a smile at the sound of my best friend's voice. I've only been back at work a few hours, but the intrusion is a welcome distraction from the stack of papers I've been mulling through since ambling in at six this morning. My mother, bless her heart, is not the most organized of people. There isn't enough coffee in the world to deal with this level of chaos before breakfast, but I'm not one to leave shit lingering. I *will* be caught up by day's end. I lift my gaze to find the stunning brunette lurking in the doorway with Lucy on her hip.

"Good morning," I singsong, scrambling from around my desk to steal my godchild and give my best friend a kiss. "To what do I owe the pleasure of your company?" Surprisingly, the baby leaps into my arms *willingly*. And while she only gives me about thirty seconds before wrestling to be set free, I'm claiming this small victory.

"Knew you loved me, turd nugget," I tease, setting her to her feet to do her worst on my office.

"What's not to love?" Kate says, shutting the door so her toddler can't escape before plopping herself in one of the chairs. It's not even ten in the morning and the poor girl looks busted. With her boundless energy, Lucy could exhaust a squirrel.

"Not that I'm not ecstatic to see you both, but what are you doing here?"

She narrows her eyes. "You just took a vacation with your new beau…I want details, missy!"

I roll my eyes as I snatch the Sharpie her daughter just pilfered from the top drawer of my desk. "Prissy was with us. Believe my very despondent vag when I say there wasn't any of *that* going on."

Before I've found a high enough place to stash the potential disastrous marker, she's gotten ahold of a container of paperclips. Evidently, Kate believes herself to be on vacation because she doesn't even move to correct the situation. "No, Lulu. You can't have that either."

"Well, I know that." My friend crosses her legs, making it clear she's here for the long haul.

Lucy's loud wail drowns out whatever drivel comes out of her mouth next.

"Here," I say, shoving the sample dragonfly cremation orb into the raging tot's hand. "Play with that."

"Did you just give my child a dead person to play with?"

"I did." My brow juts for the ceiling, daring her to question my godmothering skills.

She raises her hands in a defensive motion. "Just checking."

"The trip was fine," I say, finally collapsing back into my chair. "The park was really nice. Prissy had the time of her life. And Wyatt…" I feel the dreamy look that overtakes my face. "Well, he was amazing."

"Of course, he was." She perks up, sitting higher in her chair. "Things are getting pretty serious with you two…" she says.

"Yeah…I guess." I grab a pen and begin tapping it on the table. The subject has me all sorts of flustered. "You don't think it's too fast though?"

"What I think," she says, leaning forward to rest her elbows on my desk, "is that it only matters what you and Wyatt and your little girl think."

I feel bile rising in my throat and try swallowing it down. "It's just…*people talk*."

"Bitch," she squeaks, slapping a hand over her mouth when she remembers her kid is in the room. "Sorry, Lulu." She shakes her head at herself. "*Bitch*," she mouths, "this town has been talking about you since you turned up pregnant damn near eight years ago. Face it…they ain't gonna stop till you're dead. And maybe not even then."

"Oh, God," I say, reaching for the trash can at the end of my desk, mostly dry heaving.

"Eww, dat natty," Lucy says, stepping back.

"Sorry," I say knotting the bag and getting up to set it outside of my office door until I can take it out. "I've been car sick."

Kate narrows her eyes. "You got home yesterday."

I shrug. "I've been sick since we left Thursday afternoon."

"Have you now?"

"Why do you look so smug?" I swish my mouth with the little bottle of Listerine that now lives in my purse before spitting it into a disposable cup.

"No reason." She sucks her tongue to her teeth nodding to herself. "When was your last period?" She picks at her nails, calm as can be, like she's just asked about the weather.

I feel an icy chill. "A woman can be sick without it automatically meaning she's pregnant."

"Mm-hmm." She nods. "When was it?"

"I don't know." I grab my calendar out of my top drawer to check—*that can't be…*

"Well?" she asks, getting up to look over my shoulder.

"December." I'm trembling so hard I can't keep the little planner in my hands. "Kate," I hiss, my eyes welling with tears. "We were careful. Every time. It can be stress, right?" I nod, trying to calm myself. "It has to be stress."

Kate's eyes widen like saucers. "Holy fuck!" she says, not even caring that her child is now toddling around repeating the word. "Remember when your pussy gobbled up that condom?"

I stretch my collar, suddenly finding it hard to breath. "His come was still in it. I checked."

"I think she may have swallowed a little."

"No." She's wrong.

"I'm gonna be an Auntie again."

I take a deep breath. Followed by another, trying desperately not to pass out while my friend cheers at my demise. This can't be happening. Not again.

"Are you okay?" she asks, finally noticing I'm damn near catatonic. She waves a hand in front of my face. "Seriously, Whit? What the hell? It's a baby…not a cancer diagnosis."

"I can't," I say, shaking my head.

"You love him."

I nod.

"He is crazy in love with you."

Again, I bob my head. "Seems to be."

"I don't see the problem." She lifts her child into her lap for effect. "A baby is a blessing. Wyatt's not like Jeremy. He'd never leave you high and dry. That man's going to be an amazing father, *if* you're pregnant." She shrugs her shoulders unconvincingly. "I mean, it might still be stress, right?"

"He's going to think I tried to trap him!" My heart is pounding, my fist itching to do the same when Kate bursts into hysterical laughter. Sometimes I really want to punch her.

"I'm sorry." She beats a hand on her chest, dramatically trying to wind down. "But did you just insinuate that man's gonna think you have some condom-snatching talent of some sort?" She snorts, pointing a bossy finger at me. "That pun was totally intended, by the way. I want full credit in all future retellings."

"I'm the one who put it on," I hiss at her.

She shrugs. "And his dumb ass is the one who fell asleep and forgot to remove the damn thing before going soft."

"It wasn't his fault."

"It was no one's fault, Whit. That's my point. It was an accident. Those do happen."

"What am I going to do?"

Kate picks up my phone from the charging dock and holds it out to me across the desk. "You are going to call him, right now while you have me here for moral support, and you're going to tell him."

Moral support, my ass. She just wants to witness the train wreck.

I shake my head while accepting the device. "Maybe you could just go get a test from the drug store? Then we would know for sure… No need to worry him unnecessarily."

"Call him," she urges. "He would want to be the one there with you when you find out. Don't take that from him. And don't push him away when you need him most."

I hate it when she's right. "Okay," I sigh, touching my finger to his contact before I can chicken out. "Here goes…"

She gives me a thumbs up when he answers after the first ring.

"What's up, beautiful? Miss me already?"

"Always," I say with a lump forming in my throat. "Wyatt, I have to tell you something."

"Sounds serious." The fear in his tone cuts right to my heart. "Are we okay? Did I do something wrong?"

"Nothing like that," I insist cutting him off. "Wyatt…I think—"

Kate urges me on with the roll of a hand.

"I'm late," I blurt.

"For what?" *Poor clueless Wyatt.*

"M—my period is late. I've been sick, and you know my boobs are a little swollen and tender, and I don't know why I didn't think to check before, but Kate—she's here, and she brought up the possibility, and I checked, and I missed my period in January."

"Breathe." His one-word response has me full-on sobbing with relief.

"You're not mad?"

"Mad? Why on earth would I be mad? Whitney, I love you."

Kate reaches to my desk, grabbing a tissue to dab at her eyes.

"I love you too." I sag into my seat. "I was so scared."

"Don't be. God, Whit, I don't ever want to hear those words pertaining to me ever again. The last thing I want is for you to ever fear me."

I nod as if he can see. "I'm sorry."

"Can you meet me at my house in…two hours?"

"Sure… Yeah, I'll be there."

"Told you," Kate says, smirking, when I end the call. "That man is your happily ever after, best friend. And I'd just like to point out, you have *me* to thank for that."

When I pull up to his house, Wyatt is waiting on the front porch, pacing back and forth, looking nervous as heck. Maybe now that he's had time to think about it, he's had a change of heart.

Oh, my God. What will I do if I lose him? This can't be it. This can't be how we end.

Paralyzed with fear, I exit the car and make my way to the house with lead in my shoes and a boulder sitting in my chest.

The moment I step onto the deck, Wyatt erases a load of my worries when he takes hold of my face and proceeds to kiss me senseless.

"We're still okay?" I ask when I'm free to speak.

"Told ya we were when we talked earlier." His smile is a soothing balm. "Nothing's changed."

"Okay…you just worried me with the pacing."

"That's got nothing to do with the maybe pregnancy." He waves off my concern. "And everything to do with this." He removes a small box from his coat pocket and offers it to me in a shaky hand.

"What is it?"

He shrugs his shoulders, blowing warm air into his fists to ward off a chill. "Open it and find out."

I pull the ribbon and open the box, identical to the one he gave me at Christmas. "It's a key." I lift the little charm, holding it out between us.

"It is."

"For my bracelet?"

He nods, taking it from my hand and lifting my sleeve to hook it on himself. "To mark what I really hope will be another milestone in our relationship."

"What milestone might that be?"

"Move in with me." He takes hold of both of my hands, rubbing his thumbs nervously over my knuckles.

My eyes widen. "Wyatt, you don't have to do this."

"I want to. I've had that charm since Christmas. It was part of your gift, but then I worried it was too soon and didn't want to spook you."

My mind is reeling. "What about Prissy?"

"What about her?" He jerks back, seeming offended by the question. "She loves me…maybe even more than you do."

"I mean what if you hurt her, Wyatt?"

"Then I'll apologize, beg her forgiveness, and buy her a glass eyeball to add to her collection."

This man. I huff a laugh. "I don't know…"

"Not good enough," he says suddenly very serious. "I want this settled before we go in there. Before we know for sure." His eyes drop to my tummy. "I want there to be no question in that mind of yours that I want you and Prissy, whether there's a baby in the equation or not." His face crumples with raw vulnerability. "And I need to know, Whit. I need to know that you want me too. Either way."

Well, damn. There's something in seeing this big strong man on the verge of tears that hits me with a jolt of clarity.

"Yes," I say, throwing my arms around his neck and letting my emotion run free. "Of course I want you, Wyatt. *We* want you."

After a long, passion-filled kiss, he sets me to my feet.

"Then, it's settled?" he asks, reaching into his pocket.

I nod unable to wipe the smile from my face. "We're officially shacking up."

He places the object he retrieved from his coat into the palm of my hand: a gold key dangling from a keychain that says "Home is where the heart is."

CHAPTER THIRTY-TWO

Wyatt

"Panties for your thoughts?" I'm sitting at the foot of the bed about ready to go crazy with anticipation when she comes out of the bathroom to find her black lace thong dangling from my finger, just like it was the day I taunted her with them in her office.

It seems like a lifetime ago when in reality it hasn't been but four months.

"You're ridiculous," she says, a grin fracturing her severe tone as she walks toward me.

"But you're smiling…" I pat the mattress beside me, urging her to sit. "So, it had the desired effect."

As soon as Whitney stretches to grab them from my hand, I move them out of reach. "Ah-ah," I chide. "Thoughts first."

"Can I just tell you why they were in my pocket?" She plops on the bed beside me.

I tap a finger to her pout. "No can do. That ship has sailed, love. I've upped the ante." Plus, after seeing how easily her pussy weeps for me, I've pretty much sorted that one out on my own.

"Fine." Bringing one knee onto the bed, she rotates her body toward me. With a deep inhale, she pulls her hair to one side, nervously fingering the edges. "You want to know what I'm thinking?"

I nod.

"I'll tell you…I'm thinking this has all moved so fast and a baby is the last thing either of us wanted right now." Her throat bobs with a hard swallow as she moves to fiddle with a frayed string on the comforter. "I'm thinking," she says, her voice breaking, "I've spent years trying to fix my tarnished reputation in this stupid little town, and this is not going to do me any favors."

"Whitney—" I start, and she cuts me off.

"You asked—let me finish." She rests a gentle hand on my thigh, offering me a little reassurance. "But I'm also thinking I've been a fool for caring more about what others might say about the choices I make for my life than myself and the people I love. *And, I. Love. You.*" With tear-filled eyes she cups my cheek, stroking gently. "While our relationship has been brief by most people's standards, you've come to mean more to me than I ever dared to dream possible. And I *know* that no matter what happens when we check that test in another minute, I'm the luckiest woman in the world to have been chosen by you. To be *loved* by you."

The heaviness that began forming in the pit of my chest with the start of her monologue begins to lighten, and my heart flutters in my throat. "Fine," I grumble, biting back emotion. "Take the damn panties." I hook them around one finger and pull back, slingshotting them at her chest.

With a snort she seizes them before punching me in the shoulder. "That's it?"

"Not even close." My God, I have so much to say, but I can't focus, so instead I grab her face, pull her toward me, and smash my lips to hers. Kissing her is my immediate answer to everything.

She stares at me expectantly, wiping the back of a hand over her swollen lips. "*Now* would be the perfect time for some grand declaration about how awesome I am." She folds her hands in her lap, all demure, while nudging me with her shoulder and fanning her lashes.

"I know," I say as the timer on her phone starts to buzz, "but can we check that first? I don't care how politically incorrect it is…I'm really fucking excited."

She takes a deep inhale before blowing it out slowly and accepting my outstretched hand. "I'm shaking," she whispers.

I bring her fingers to my lips and kiss each one in turn. "Breathe," I repeat my earlier sentiment. "One moment—one breath—at a time, we've got this."

Her grip tightens and she nods. "Ready?" Whitney asks, clutching the upside-down stick in between her thumb and forefinger.

"Plus or minus, right?" My pulse surges and my palms begin to sweat. I'm not even certain why I want this so badly. But if my body's reactions mean anything, I do.

"Yep."

"Okay…" I cross my fingers behind my back, sending up positive vibes and nod, giving her the go ahead.

With her lids pulled tight, she flips it over. "Well?"

I blink a few times to be sure my eyes aren't playing tricks on me before shouting my excitement through the roof. "Fuck, yeah!" I grab Whitney at the back of her thighs and lift, wrapping her legs around my waist. Sprinkles is going crazy beating on the door, trying to get in on the action.

She giggles through a torrent of tears while I bounce up and down, spinning in place.

"You're really happy?" She grips my hair on either side, turning my face so she can stare into my eyes.

"Am I not being clear enough?" I ask, carrying her to the bed and dropping her in the center. "Tell me those are happy tears," I beg, laying on my side to face her. I brush a thumb over her cheeks, wiping the wetness away.

"They are…*confused* tears." She dips her head in a sort of apology while fingering the buttons on my shirt. "I'm not sad," she assures me. "Overwhelmed, maybe?"

I nod, the gravity of what this means setting in. "That's fair." I can appreciate what she's going through, but at the same time, I can't stop smiling. "Feel my heart," I say shifting her hand to my chest. "That's for you, for us, for Prissy, and *our baby*." I clear my throat. "You want a grand declaration, this is it, love. It doesn't get more genuine."

She pulls in her lips and nods while emotion drips down her cheeks. "We're going to be okay?" Her voice is so unsteady. That she's unsure guts me. I wish she could share in my excitement, to know without doubt that things will be different this go-round. I'm positive that'll come with time. So I'll be patient, reassuring her every step of the way until she truly believes it.

"We're going to be more than okay," I say, tipping her chin to kiss her tear-soaked lips. "We're going to be a family."

"That's all I've ever wanted," she says, sniffling. "For Prissy… for myself."

"I know." Tenderly, I stroke my knuckles along her arm. "We want the same things, Whit. And I feel like I've finally found a family, in you and in Prissy, and hell, even your kooky parents. And now…this." I shake my head in disbelief. "No, it wasn't planned…but neither was showing up on your doorstep a few months ago." I shrug, and she smiles. "So, yeah," I say, beaming. "I'm happy. How could I not be? When I'm staring at everything I've ever wanted—when it's finally right here, within my grasp." I grip the back of her head, pulling her close to kiss her again, because I can't get enough of those salty lips.

Out of nowhere she chokes on a laugh, catching me completely off guard as she pulls back.

"What's funny?"

She coughs, clearing her throat. "I was just thinking… I mean, this is so…*us*."

"What is?" Fuck, she's beautiful with her blonde hair cascading around her face like a curtain, her dimpled smile on full display, and those expressive blue eyes shining bright with so much emotion. She steals my breath, every time.

"To wind up pregnant *this way*." She can't stop giggling. I'm not complaining; it's a welcome sight over her tears.

"What way might that be?" I taunt, leaning in to nibble on her neck.

"You know what way." She squirms, moaning under my ministrations.

I chuckle. "I just wanna hear you say it."

"So bad," she mutters, nipping at my jaw, playfully. "My *pussy* swallowed that condom like a fucking Venus flytrap."

I roll to my back, hand on my chest, laughing until tears stream down my cheeks. Blushing, she climbs on top of me. "Know what I just realized?" She circles her ass over my cock.

"What?" I grip her at the waist, lifting my hips to offer a little encouragement as desire takes root in my groin, spreading heat throughout my entire body.

Leaning forward, she brings her lips to my ear. "No more condoms."

With an arm hooked around her waist, I flip her around so that I'm hovering over her. "*That* is really good news."

"Is it?" she asks, reaching up hastily, unfastening the buttons before pushing my shirt over my shoulders and down my arms.

With a nod, I stare into her bottomless blue eyes, losing myself in their depth as I shrug the rest of the way out of my flannel. "Our little hobby was about to get expensive."

She quirks her brow, not catching my meaning.

"You live here now, remember?" I nudge her with my erection. "Two or three a day at seven days a week…" I touch each of my fingers to my thumb mocking calculations.

She grins up at me. "Right," she rasps, her eyes clouded with longing as I grope her breast through the fabric of her blouse.

One by one she releases each of the little pearl buttons while I trail a hand the length of her inner thigh, beneath her skirt, and along the scrap of lace covering her heat.

"Yes," she hisses, her head falling back, slowly rotating side to side with every light touch.

I reach around to her back, unfastening the clasp to her bra before shoving it out of my way and bringing my mouth to feast on her breasts.

She's hypersensitive, nearly coming clean off the bed with every brush of my tongue over her pebbled nipples.

"Wyatt…" My name is a desperate plea falling from angel's lips.

She writhes beneath me as I move lower, spreading kisses over every exposed inch of her skin, devoting extra time and attention when I reach her flat stomach.

Settling, she combs her hands into my hair, no longer tugging, but caressing, lavishing me with love and affection while I worship the body that's nourishing our miracle.

With every measured press of my lips, my emotions climb.

"Hey there little one," I say, as tears prick the backs of my eyes. I smooth both hands over her stomach, overcome with the depth of my feelings for a child I've not yet met. "It's me…Daddy."

Whitney chokes on an emotion filled sob, drawing my attention. She shakes her head, motioning for me to continue. "I'm o—okay."

"You're not yet," I say, crawling over her to stare into her eyes, "but you will be."

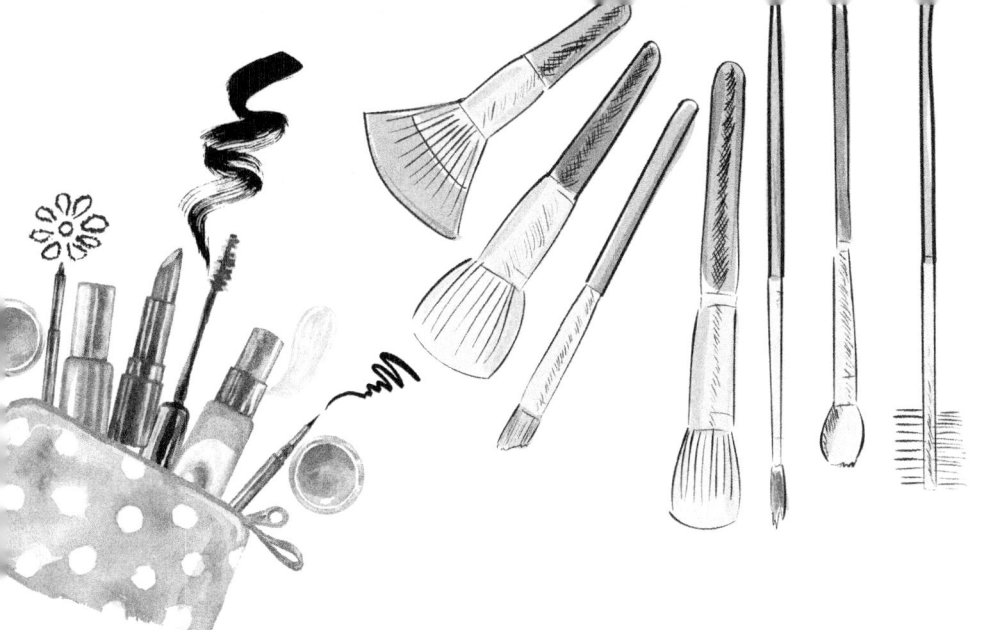

CHAPTER THIRTY-THREE

Whitney

"I GOT ONE!" PRISSY SCREAMS, LEANING BACK WITH dramatic flair as she reels in her pole. She's too stinking cute with her little camouflage ball cap, cut-off shorts, and rubber boots. Her acclimation to country life's been a breeze.

"Be careful," Wyatt urges, setting his own down on the brand-new dock he finished for us last week, coming over to investigate. "Pretty sure you got caught on another log."

"No way," my child argues. "It's so strong. I bet it's an alligator."

"Don't yank like it that, you're gonna snap the line." He stands behind her, gripping her pole and controlling her reel with his big hand covering hers.

"I know what I'm doing, *Dad*."

Yep. Dad. Be still my heart.

It's been four months since we moved in. Prissy started with the dad bit about a month ago. The first time she did it, poor

Wyatt looked like a deer caught in headlights, unsure of how to respond. A simple nod from me was all it took to have him melting on the spot and accepting his new title with gusto.

Who am I to begrudge her—either of them—that relationship? The bond is already there. It's merely a title, and one that man has more than earned—one he wears like a badge of honor.

"You two wanna stop arguing? You're killin' my vibe." I rest my paperback face down on my basketball-sized belly, squinting through the setting sun to glare at the two of them.

"Hear that?" he growls. "You're pissin' the prego off."

Prissy snickers, crawling out from under Wyatt's arm, leaving him to deal with her mess while she runs over to join me at my lounger, her rubber boots clomping on the wood with every step. "How's my sister?" she asks, resting a hand over my navel.

"Could be a brother," Wyatt hollers, cursing up a storm at the massive driftwood he just reeled in.

"Whoops," Prissy giggles, covering her mouth. "Think he's really mad?"

"No way," I say, reaching around to the back of her head to tighten her ponytail. "Put your hand here." I slide her lower and to the right where the baby is practicing its kickboxing technique.

"Does it hurt?" she asks, her eyes widening.

"Not at all."

She cringes. "I'm not gonna have a baby," she announces, moving to show her jealous dog some attention when he dips his head under her arm, nudging her hand. "Cuz, I don't want nothin' coming outta my vagina."

I choke on my tea, sitting up so I don't die. "It's not that bad."

"Imma just take your word for it."

"You'll change your mind one day," I assure her.

"Nuh-uhn."

"Why don't you come in and watch?" If any kid can handle

witnessing a birth, it's this one. With everything she sees and has seen at the funeral home, I'm not worried one bit.

"Watch the baby come out?"

I laugh at her excitement. "Sure," I say, looking to Wyatt for his approval.

"Don't see why not," he shrugs. "She can take over when I pass out." He winks at his daughter. "Two birthing coaches are better than one. Let's tag-team this shit!" He holds out his hand for a very enthusiastic high-five from Priss.

"Great. Now that that's settled," I say, reaching for Wyatt's hand to help me up from the chair. "Let's get some dinner. This baby's starving."

Once we've finished eating, we go through our nightly routine of loading the dishwasher and cleaning the kitchen as a family, then settle around the coffee table for a board game. After spending half an hour trying to decide, Prissy settles on *The Game of Life*. It's one of her favorites, only tonight she adds an unexpected twist when she lands on the "Get Married" space.

After adding her little blue man to her car, she sets her piece down and leaps to her feet. "Speaking of getting married..." She focuses her beady blue eyes on Wyatt. "When are you gonna marry my momma?" Her hands move to rest on her hips. "It's time to shit or get off the pot, dude."

Choking—I am literally choking on my own saliva.

Wyatt's lips curve into an amused smile. "Funny you should mention that, Prissy."

I shoot my precious daughter a look. "I don't think it's very funny at all." *Pretty sure I just died, actually.*

When he disappears from the room, I grab my daughter by

the arm and pull her next to me. "What the heck do you think you're—"

"It's okay," Wyatt says, waltzing back in with something hidden behind his back. "I've been waiting for the right moment…"

He pushes the table over to kneel in front of me and everything goes blurry. Everything but him. On one knee. Looking up at me with a little velvet box in his left hand. The finger of his right preparing to flip the top open. "Whitney," he says, clearing his throat. "You've given me a family. A daughter," he turns, smiling at our little girl, who I might still want to throttle right now. "A baby." His eyes glisten. "A partner in everything but name."

The tears brimming in my eyes spill over, scorching a warm path down my cheeks. "Marry me," he says flipping the box open to reveal a beautiful princess cut engagement ring. "Whitney Daigle," he says, his eyes locked with mine. "Will you do me the honor of becoming my wife? To give you my name would make me the happiest man on earth."

"Yes," I say, blinded by tears as he slides the ring onto my finger. My heart is literally jumping up and down. "Yes," I say again, wrapping my arms around his neck. "I'll marry you. Of course, I'll marry you."

"Oh, my God, y'all are so gross," Prissy groans when he pulls me in to seal our engagement with a kiss. But that little shit grin of hers says she couldn't possibly be happier, and I might even see a tear or two forming in those baby blues of hers.

"We'll pick this up a little later," Wyatt whispers into my ear before dropping back to his knee, this time in front of my daughter.

"Priscilla Louise Daigle," he says, retrieving another velvet box from his pocket. "I already consider myself to be your daddy in every way that counts, but it would mean the world to me if you'd agree to make it official." He opens the box, removing a gold cuff bracelet with "Landry" scrolled in cursive writing in the center, and a sob bursts from my chest.

"Prissy, will you take my name?"

She nods and, completely out of character, starts sobbing when he places the dainty piece of jewelry on her wrist. "Yes," she cries, falling into his outstretched arms. Her little body is vibrating with so much emotion.

"I love you, Daddy."

"I love you, daughter." With her head cradled against his shoulder, he looks up at me, and we share the most intimate moment I've ever experienced, one of love and longing and utter relief. We did it. We let our guards down and, in doing so, found everything our hearts desired—in each other.

My life has been filled with unforeseen twists and turns. But if I've learned anything in navigating the ups and downs, it's that sometimes those unexpected curveballs turn out to be exactly what you never knew was missing.

Not every Prince Charming rides in on a white horse. If that's what you're waiting for, you're likely to miss him altogether. Maybe he's sitting next to you in church, or bagging your groceries at the Piggly Wiggly. And maybe you just might find him during a drunken hookup on Bourbon Street.

All I know for certain is that life didn't sit around waiting for me to figure my shit out. It happened, despite my best efforts at times to thwart it. I wasn't truly living, but merely existing, until I learned to recognize each unexpected blessing and seize them with arms wide open.

EPILOGUE

Wyatt

Delivery Day

"Nine centimeters," our labor and delivery nurse, Gretta, announces, lifting her head from beneath the sheet covering Whitney's business. And I say business in the very literal sense. So many people have done been under that damn cover, you'd swear Whit was running 7-11 out of her vagina.

"What's that mean?" Priss asks, sipping a Coke and munching on gummy bears in the blue plastic recliner that's supposed to double as my bed for the night.

"That means it's show time," she offers, popping her gloves off and tossing them into the trash. "We're about to break down the bed and set up," she adds, addressing Whitney. "Y'all got someone to watch the little one out in the waiting room? It's probably time for her to head out."

"She'll be staying," my *wife* says.

Yep, my wife. It's crazy how much things have changed for me in the last year. I've gone from a bachelor in every sense to a married man with a child…soon to be two.

And let me tell you, people talk about being strapped down like it's a bad thing, but I'll take these shackles any day. Life is so much more meaningful when you have people to share it with. It's all the little things. Take a fart, for instance… Pre-Prissy, it was merely a sound—a smell released into the void. Now? There are squeals and giggles and a feeling of accomplishment.

Gretta's face scrunches with uncertainty. "Are you sure? No offense," she says, glancing toward me, "but most grown men can't even handle it without getting weak."

I choke on a laugh. My grandmother gave us the same speech in the car this morning during the drive to the hospital—cited all the reasons her favorite granddaughter ought to hang out with her and Marie in the waiting room. It's actually quite funny, the way she insists on treating her like a delicate flower, knowing damn well that kid is tough as nails. Mimi can't get enough of that little girl, Whitney either. The woman calls her more than me now. I'm sure that will only increase with the birth of the new baby.

"Listen, I drain and embalm bodies for a living," Prissy sasses, whipping her head so her ponytail swishes side to side. "I think I can handle watching a baby come outta a vagina." She tugs the lapels of her leather jacket, sucking her tongue to her teeth like a total badass.

Whitney shakes her head, grinding her molars, while I have to turn away to keep from laughing. I find myself doing that a lot. "We own a funeral home," she explains, pinching the bridge of her nose. "She doesn't actually embalm the bodies, but she's assisted countless times and will be just fine." She dips her head back toward me. "He's the one you should be concerned about."

I nod, not even pretending otherwise. "It's true."

With a laugh, the middle-aged woman makes for the door. "Sounds like y'all have this all figured out. Be back in a jiff," she says before rushing down the hall.

"This is it," I say, beginning to pack up Prissy's snacks. "Time to meet my son!"

"Daughter," Prissy challenges.

"What're you doing?" my wife asks, eying me curiously. "You aren't going anywhere."

"Putting her food in the bags so it doesn't get splashed on."

"What the hell do you think's about to happen in here?" she guffaws. "If blood splatters into that back corner, we're in big trouble."

"Just seemed like the right thing to do."

"The right thing to do would be to get your sexy hiney over here and give me a kiss."

"Ugh," our child groans. *"Not again…"*

I've barely slipped my tongue between her parted lips when a team of medical people storm into the room.

"Gonna need you to back away for a minute, sir."

I move to stand by Prissy, watching with rapt fascination as huge spotlights descend from the ceiling and her bed is broken into pieces. Whitney's legs are placed into stirrups and a tray with all sorts of tools is wheeled in. There are people in scrubs fluttering around the room, setting up the baby warmer and some tarp contraption under Whit's bottom.

"Ooooh!" Prissy squeals, squeezing my biceps as the room begins to look a little more like the stuff she watches on ER. "This is gonna be so frickin' cool!"

"Just what I was thinking." *Not at all what I was thinking.*

"Dad?" a nurse I haven't met yet calls, waving me over. "You can come stand on this side. You're gonna help hold her leg back like this," she says, bringing Whitney's knee to her chest. "She's numb from the epidural, so she won't be able to do it on her own."

I nod, feeling self-important. "I think I can manage that."

"Perfect." She smiles at me while walking around to the other side of the bed. "I'll just be over here."

"Cool deal." *I've so got this. Best delivery coach ever, comin' atcha!*

"Oh, and see that mirror?" she points between Whitney's legs. "That's so you can watch what's happening without actually being down there. "If you start to feel sick, just don't look."

"Got it." My skin starts to tingle. It feels like little pin pricks all over my body, and my breathing becomes shallow as I rub my wife's arm, trying to comfort her wondering who the hell's gonna comfort me. Now that we're so close I feel like I'm starting to hyperventilate.

"Where do I go?" Prissy asks, pacing like a lost puppy.

"You can stand by your dad," Gretta offers, forcing a smile. She's obviously still not too keen on the idea of her remaining in the room. "If it's too much, just go sit back in your chair, okay, honey?"

"Hear that, Dad?" Prissy taunts. "If it gets too much, just go sit in that chair."

Whitney snorts. "Behave, Priscilla Louise."

"Yes ma'am." She glues herself to my side, curiously taking in everything going on around us.

"On the next contraction, we're going to start pushing," Gretta announces, rolling herself on the little stool to between Whit's legs. "Once we get the baby to crown, Doc'll come in to deliver."

"Okay," my girl says, squeezing my hand with nervous excitement, while the nurses' heads all whip in the direction of the machine that measures the contractions. "You ready?" Whitney's eyes meet with mine. She's glowing with excitement.

I nod. "This is it," I say, with a knot lodged right in the center of my throat. "We're really about to have a baby." I take a deep breath and twist my head side to side, cracking my neck, giving her hand a reassuring squeeze before I too focus on the monitor—my heartrate climbing with the mounting contractions. I swear it's like the thing is directly connected to my pulse.

"Did y'all know..." *Oh, shit.* My stomach drops. "Approximately seven hundred women die every year in the US alone from pregnancy and delivery complications?"

Gretta and the leg-holding nurse both gape at our child in stunned disbelief.

"You've really gotta stay off the damn YouTube," Whitney says, laughing nervously. She reaches to scruff Prissy's head. "It's gonna be okay, baby."

"Just don't be a statistic, Momma." The worry in her little voice is gut-wrenching. And that's what her ill-timed comment comes down to—*She's scared.* It's what all her morbid death knowledge stems from.

"No plans to, baby." My girls share a tearful embrace before the chaos begins.

"Here it comes," Gretta announces, as everyone scurries into position. "Let's see if we can get this baby to come down."

On her command, Whitney bears down, apparently that means to curl into a sit up and clench every muscle in her body, including the ones in her fingers that are damn near cutting off my circulation. It's okay, though. I'll deal. Losing a few digits is a small price to pay to ease her discomfort.

"You're doing so good, love," I croon. She's been pushing for a solid forty minutes and is running out of steam.

"I can't do this," my beautiful wife cries, falling back onto the pillow.

"You're doing so well," the leg nurse, whom I've just learned is named Harloe, encourages. "Won't be long now." She places an oxygen mask over her face. "Just breathe."

"Baby's right there," Gretta announces, sliding over for Dr. Andrews to take her place.

"You're doing great, Whitney," the doctor praises. "We're going to push real hard through the next few contractions. No breaks. Push to ten. One big breath, and immediately go into the next one."

"I can't," she wails. She's dripping in sweat and the whites of her eyes are red from straining so hard.

"Can't is just a state of mind, Momma," Prissy argues. "Now, you just bear down and push my sister out!"

That little pep talk seems to light a fire in her ass. "Okay," Whit sighs, drying her eyes and sucking air from the mask.

The next few pushes are so intense I'm tempted to borrow the oxygen for myself. This is some hard work, and I'm not even doing anything.

"Look at her hair!" Prissy screams. "My sister has hair."

"Brother," I grunt, while petting my wife's damp hair off her face.

"The head is out," Dr. Andrews exclaims. When I glance up to the mirror all I see is her shoving a snot bulb down the baby's throat, suctioning fluid out. "Give me one more push. On three…"

Before she's gotten to two, the baby slithers out right into the doctor's waiting arms, and Prissy folds over, gagging.

"Really, Priss?" Whitney collapses into the bed, heaving for breath, while craning her neck to try to see the baby. "It's just blood."

"Nuh-uhn," my daughter grumbles, still retching. "You—"

I clamp a hand over her mouth, giving her a very severe look that thankfully Whitney doesn't notice, as she's become too focused with what's going on at the foot of the bed.

"Congratulations, you have a beautiful baby boy!"

"A boy." I press a kiss to my wife's forehead. "Whit, we have a son." Tears fall unchecked between us while I kiss her cheeks, her forehead, her lips. "You were amazing," I say, meaning it with every beat of my heart.

When we break apart, Prissy is just standing there, arms crossed, glaring at me. *Lord, that girl hates to be wrong.*

The very petty side of me wants to stick out my tongue and gloat. Of course, I don't. I want her to love him, not see him as a bet she lost. "Look at him, Priss." I wrap my arm around her shoulders, leading her to where the doctor is waiting for me to cut the cord. "You wanna do it?" I ask in a split-second decision, hoping it'll help her bond to her new brother.

"Really?"

I nod. "Go for it...I'll get the next one."

I feel my wife's glare before her words meet my ears. "Over my dead body."

Curious about the fateful night on Bourbon Street that started it all? Click here to download a special bonus scene, THE DUMPSTER[https://dl.bookfunnel.com/yi9g2vic1k].

Preview of *Take Two*

CHAPTER One

Nya

Déjà vu

A BEAM OF LIGHT STREAMS IN THROUGH THE WINDOW, stabbing me right in my barely opened eye. Jackhammers pound inside my head as I squint, peering around the room to take in my surroundings: a king-sized bed with plush white linens, gaudy chandelier, a wall of windows with thick, gold damask drapes pulled back on each end.

What the hell am I doing at a hotel?

A loud snore sounds, nearly scaring me right out of my tingling skin. To my left is a hard body, enveloped in billion-thread-count sheets, facing away from the offending window. That back—those sinewy shoulders and sculpted muscles—I'd recognize anywhere.

"Liam?" I whisper, forcing myself not to run a hand through his tapered hair, to touch my finger to the little mole right at the edge of his hairline. It was once my favorite spot to kiss.

What. The. Fuck? This can't be happening. *Not again.*

Groggy and disoriented, I attempt to roll off the bed to relieve my screaming bladder and rid myself of the dragon breath that only comes after a night of hard partying. One I can't seem to remember. But I can't move. Reaching beneath the comforter to investigate what's weighing me down, I come up with my hands filled with layer upon layer of satin and tulle. *What the hell?*

"A wedding dress?" I screech, panic welling in my throat as my heart damn near leaps from my chest. No way.

Suddenly the mound of man muscle shifts my direction. With a dreamy smile, his large hand creeps across the bed, reaching for mine. The smell of last night's cologne wafts into the air, threatening to weaken my resolve. Holding my breath, refusing to be distracted, I scoot to the edge of the bed. Has he lost his damn mind? Has this idiot forgotten that we've been over since our now-preteen daughter was barely walking?

Well, mostly over. *There was that one time...*but that was a mistake we swore to never speak of again. At any rate, we've proven that me, alcohol, and my ex-husband are not a good mix. The situation is one I try to avoid at all costs.

"'Morning, wife!" Liam stretches his arms above his head, winking a sleepy blue eye my way. His caramel-colored hair is sticking up in all directions, only serving to make the insufferable man more irresistible. He looks...well...*well fucked.*

Wife. That curse has me scrambling to my feet, lugging fifty pounds of dress to the full-length mirror that's attached to the closet door. Adding to my horror, it's a dress that only my very extra—and now former—best friend would pick out.

How could she do this to me?

"Where is she?" I growl, turning to the side and running my hands along the fitted silhouette. Jesus, I'm thirty-three, not twenty. I look like I'm going to the damn prom.

"Who?" Liam glances around the room, seemingly confused by my reaction. Most likely by why I'm not already threatening to castrate him.

"Hannah! Who else? Are there pictures? I swear to God, if there are pictures of me in this thing, I'll kill you both, and no one will ever find your bodies."

My ex-husband snorts. "You wouldn't do that to Ellie."

Our daughter. Ugh. I want to slap that smug look off his too-handsome face.

"How did this happen?" Please, for the love of God, he'd better tell me we went to a freaking costume party or something, but the sense of déjà vu is just too strong. This room all too familiar. The bustling city, haunting me through floor to ceiling windows, bringing back memories of the biggest mistake of my life. My college boyfriend. An impulse trip to Vegas. A little white chapel. No. No. "No." I shake my head, moving to the window to stare down at Sin City.

"Give me six months," the asshole rasps, sneaking up behind me wearing nothing but a thin pair of cotton boxer shorts. He glides his warm hands around my waist, pulling me flush with his chest. As if he has any right. I gulp hard, swallowing down a lump of regret, because something tells me I gave him that right last night. Liam's eyes connect with mine in the glass, and I'm finding it hard to breathe. "We owe it to our little girl."

Jesus, now he's using our kid as a weapon. I should move out of his embrace, but I've always been putty in his arms. "Does she... does she know?"

He spins me around to face him, my resolve weakening with every moment spent wrapped in his embrace. "You don't remember anything, do you?" Liam brushes away the strands of hair blocking his line of sight and studies my eyes.

Heat blooms in my chest. The smell of alcohol on his breath

is oddly arousing. It's not even fair that he's been blessed with sexy morning breath, of all things. He's not at all deserving of such sex appeal. "Please tell me this is a nightmare." My voice cracks as the enormity of this situation creeps in. "And that I'm going to wake up to Ellie begging for me to make her scrambled eggs or to take her to the skating rink with her friends. Liam, tell me this isn't happening."

"Poker?" he asks, swiping a tear from beneath my right eye with the pad of his thumb. "Shots, shots, shots, shots, shots," he sings in his best Lil Jon impression. A hopeful smirk curls his lip as he does a little shimmy to the beat. I try like hell not to let him see me ogling his erect penis flopping side to side with his movement.

Damn him and that appendage, which reduces me to nothing but a puddle of hormones.

"Oh, dear God, did we?" Nausea pools in my stomach as the face of my boyfriend, Ryder, flashes in my mind.

"Not yet." His chiseled brows bounce.

"This isn't funny, Liam!" I shove at his chest weakly. "I have a boyfriend."

The exasperating man barks out a laugh. "Fraid to tell ya... but husband trumps boyfriend."

How can he be so blasé about this? "There's no way."

"No way, what?" he asks, lifting my hand to rest on his chest. The glint of a familiar diamond shimmers in the light of the morning sun. I'm momentarily distracted by the realization that he kept my ring all these years. My heart wants to soften to him, but the anger at this impossible situation swiftly overpowers the foolish organ.

"There's no way I married the same mistake...*twice!*" I shout, breaking away from him to pace the enormous room.

"Six months, darlin'," he repeats, casually dropping the

endearment he hasn't used with me in years, his blue eyes ablaze with hope. "You promised me six months."

"For what?" I ask, panting. "To prove what *idiotas* we are?"

A dimple pops out on his left cheek, and I brace myself for his retort. "Nya—" *Fuck the way his saying my name makes my vagina twitch and my chest ache!* "Babe, I only need about ten minutes to prove what idiots we were…you never did last long."

He ducks, just as I send the Bible from the side table flying in his direction. "Fuck you."

"That's what I'm hoping for."

Great. I cross my arms on my chest. "You married me for sex?"

"Now, we both know I didn't have to marry you for that."

CHAPTER Two

Liam

"Honey, I'm home."

"That's the last of it, man." My roommate Chance claps me on the back with a shake of his head as I roll down the trailer door. "You sure about this?"

The adrenaline vibrating through my veins is all the answer I need. "Yep."

"Okay, well... good luck." He eyes me with a shit grin. "Pretty sure you're gonna need lots of it. I'd come to help unload, but—"

"Nope. I'm good," I interrupt, hopping into the driver's seat, slamming the heavy door behind me. "I got this." I hang a fist out the window, giving him the old thumbs up, willing myself to feel the confidence I'm trying to display. "Thanks for everything, man."

Chance is not only one of my best buds, but also a very sore subject when it comes to Nya. It could have a little something to do with my investing the inheritance I received from my grandfather to go in with him to open a club on the Vegas strip.

Don't look at me like that. It seemed like a great idea at the time, to a fresh out of college finance major with tens of thousands of dollars suddenly burning a hole in his bank account. But apparently, those are not the types of decisions a man makes without consulting his new wife. Believe me, I see the error of my ways, hindsight being twenty-twenty and all, but I still lost my girls. I've been paying for that stupidity for nearly ten years.

I finally have the opportunity to right all the wrongs. I won't screw this up. I can't. I've got to move fast, *quite literally.*

When I turn into the subdivision, I jab my first two fingers on the buttons, lowering the glass on the driver and passenger-side windows. Then I twist the knob, cranking the sound up as loud as it will go just as I round the last curve leading to the cottage-style house Nya and I picked out together not long after discovering she was pregnant. The little house is situated on half an acre in a quiet town just south of Vegas, called Clairmont. "Mama, I'm Coming Home" by Ozzy Osbourne blasts through the speakers as I pull up to the curb, shifting the U-Haul into park. Nothin' like a little mood music to set the tone.

Here goes... I pull in a deep breath before resting an elbow on the horn, smiling to myself as I anxiously await the epic tantrum I know is coming. Three, two—

"Daddy!" Ellie shouts, running through the front door in a pair of pink footy pajamas, her raven hair a tangled mess. She looks so small and not at all like the preteen drama queen she's quickly becoming. "What are you doing here?"

Before I can answer, my heart's in my throat at the sound of her mother's voice approaching behind her.

"Yeah, Liam. What are you doing here?" the love of my

life grits through clenched teeth. Unlike our daughter, her long dark hair is sleek and shiny. Her copper toned skin is free of any makeup save for a light shimmer accentuating her pouty lips. I lick my own instinctively as I take in the skin-tight jeans that cling to her perfectly round ass like a glove.

With a shrug, I climb down, pretending not to notice the fire blazing in her eyes as I approach her and our daughter. "Listen." I cup a hand over my right ear, belting out the chorus. I won't even lie—I'm thoroughly enjoying the horrified look on her face.

"Oh, no. No, Liam. This is not happening." She plants a hand on her cocked hip, eyes narrowed my direction. Lord, I love getting her all riled up like this. The flush in her cheeks and the frustrated breath she blows up toward her hair only spur me on.

"What's not happening?" Ellie asks, confusion marring her pretty face. *So, Nya hasn't even told her yet. This is turning out to be even more fun than I thought.*

"Oh, it's happening," I assure Nya, my eyes briefly connecting with hers before turning to face our little girl. "Remember your wish?"

"Uhh..." she stammers, chewing her lower lip as she waffles between her mother and me. "Yeah?"

I think back to two nights ago. Her eleventh birthday. The day our daughter unknowingly delivered the second chance I've been searching for.

"Make a wish, Ellie," Nya urges. My chest tightens when she latches onto my arm as she gazes adoringly at our little girl pursing her lips to blow out eleven pink, sparkly candles.

Don't get me wrong, we have a great relationship as far as divorced couples go, but she's not usually so touchy-feely with me. Especially not since Ryder came into the picture. So I can't help but allow myself to revel in the moment.

"I know what I'm gonna wish for," Ellie says, looking fondly at her mother and me.

Guilt swirls in my chest, because I already know her wish won't come true. I fucked up any chance of that years ago.

"Don't say it," Hannah, Nya's best friend, orders, worry creasing her brow. "Or it won't come true." Good old Hannah. Always trying to put out fires before they start.

"It won't anyway," Ellie pouts, looking just like the toddler I like to pretend she still is, before she catches a wave of prepubescence and gives her Auntie an eye roll to rival that pale chick from The Exorcist.

"What?" Nya's face jerks back in surprise. "How do you know that?" She runs a hand through our daughter's long dark hair, the same shade as hers, and leans over her shoulder, planting a kiss on her cheek.

"Cuz. I wish for the same thing every single year, and it never happens."

"Oh." My clueless ex-wife's face falls. "Well, maybe just this one time, you can tell us, and we can help to make it come true?" Her big doe eyes find mine, brimming with concern for her little princess. She nods to me for approval, which I swiftly provide. Far be it from me to be the one to stop this train wreck.

"Don't make promis—" Hannah starts to warn her best friend off before my eyes catch hers and I shake my head. She clears her throat, holding her hands up in resignation. "Go 'head, El."

"Okay…" Ellie starts, nibbling her thumb nail nervously as she fixes her stare on the tile floor. "I wished for you and Daddy to get married and for us to be a real family… like we were when I was a baby."

Nya's legs buckle, so I hold her a little tighter. For stability, of course. "Th—that's your w—wish?"

"It's stupid," Ellie mutters, crossing her arms protectively over her heart. "That's why I didn't wanna say it."

"It's not stupid," I assure her, my stomach twisting up into a huge knot. I don't miss the pained look on Nya's speechless face as I release my hold on her and our daughter lunges herself into my arms, sniffling into the crook of my neck.

"N-not all families look the same, Ellie," my ex explains while rubbing circles on her back. "We're still a family even if we don't all live in the same house."

My daughter stiffens at her words, schooling her features. "I know, Mom, but it's not the same."

Nya has worked really hard to make sure Ellie has been raised with two parents. Her guilt over being the one to initiate our divorce has always eaten at her. As hard as it is to be around Nya. To want her and never be able to act on it. To sit at the same fucking table with her and now her new boyfriend, Ryder. I'm here every holiday. Every birthday. Hell, every Sunday for family dinner. It's as close to a two-parent home as we could give her without actually being together, but Ellie's right, it's not the same thing. Nowhere near it.

"Sometimes relationships don't work out, baby. Some people just aren't meant to be—" at that I tune her out, because I will never believe Nya and I aren't meant to be together. I wouldn't still want her so badly after all these years if that were the case.

"She's gonna be okay, right?" Nya asks as she slinks back into the room after tucking Ellie into bed, looking positively defeated. She swiftly takes the procured glass of wine from Hannah before plopping into the chair across from mine for what has become a routine Sunday night card game.

"Sure." I nod before taking a pull from my beer. It's hard to keep the mood light, but the last thing this woman needs is me acting like a petulant child. She's well aware of how much I still want to be with her. From the day we split, I've made that no secret.

"I mean," she adds, fanning her cards in front of her face and arranging them in her hand. "We're doing the right thing…right?"

"Oh, yeah," Hannah agrees, while I practically bite my tongue off.

"You're great parents. Don't ever doubt that. Tons of kids grow up in broken homes these days and most of them turn out just fine."

Ouch. Probably not the best way to support her endorsement. Internally I cringe as Nya balks at her words.

Drinks are flowing more heavily tonight than usual as we play a few rounds of poker. I'm thankful for the empty chair that Ryder's occupied the past couple of months when Nya makes me an offer I'd be a fool to refuse.

"What if we gave it another shot?" she asks, almost inaudibly. Her tan cheeks are flushed crimson. "That'd be stupid, right?" She glances from Hannah to me, worrying her lower lip between her teeth.

"Why not?" I interrupt when she starts backpedaling.

"You could always try it out for say…a year." Hannah pushes her unruly cropped blonde curls behind her ears, and her emerald eyes glow with excitement. She's always been a fan of Nya and me. "And if you don't want to be married when the time's up, you call it quits."

Nya slinks out of her chair, pacing the kitchen. The room falls silent as we all await the verdict. "Six months," she counters, looking to me for approval. Insufferable woman always has to have everything on her terms, but she's finally handing me some terms I can work with.

"What?" Hannah shrieks. "Are you serious?" Bounding out of her chair, she rushes to wrap her arms around her best friend's neck. "This is the best crazy idea you've ever had."

"Right now," I suggest, pushing back from the table, before she has the time to change her mind. I look over to Hannah, who's practically bursting with excitement. "Call the sitter?"

She nods and immediately begins scrolling through her iPhone.

"Vegas?" Nya proposes with something suspiciously close to a twinkle in her eye.

"Vegas!"

Keep Reading! Take Two is available now!

Preview of *Pour Judgment*

PROLOGUE

Rhett

"Oh, Rhett, yesss..."

I squeeze harder, lapping her nipple into a firm bud through her thin top. My cock stiffens as she grinds her hips to the tempo of the music, giving me a sexy as fuck lap dance. Suddenly I have this inexplicable urge to look up, letting Monica's tit slip from my mouth. I feel smothered—like all the air has suddenly been pulled from the room.

Who is that?

"It's fine, Nick—" She digs her heels into the floor. "No, I don't want to meet—"

"Rhett." My drummer, Nick, approaches, dragging the very reluctant blonde behind him by the arm. "I'd like to introduce you to my cousin, Korie Potter. Korie, this is Rhett." He gives her a little shove, landing her on her feet, right in front of my bent knees.

My eyes peruse her sweet little body. Her long blonde hair is pulled back in a low ponytail. There's not an ounce of makeup on her face. Her eyes are a vibrant shade of emerald, and she has the most delectable little freckles dotting her cheekbones. She's wearing a black Rolling Stones tee—slightly fitted, the collar ripped so it droops a little, exposing one shoulder. One creamy, slender, tantalizing shoulder. I clear my throat, reaching around the raven-haired beauty presently situated in my lap for Korie's hand.

"I'm good," she says, not reaching back, her face scrunched like she's just gotten a whiff of something foul. "Just carry on with whatev—umm *whoever* you're doing." She whirls back on her cousin, eyes flaming. "I'm gonna go get some air."

In her haste to get away, she trips over my foot and is sent hurtling face first to the floor. Like in the movies, the music stops and every pair of eyes in the room are on her.

"Oh, shit." I slide Monica to the side. "Scuse me," I rush out, blundering to my feet, the alcohol throwing off my balance as I hop around, trying to right my pants zipper before reaching her. "My fault," I say, shoving the little douche aside who's trying to help her up. "I've got it."

He throws his hands in the air, backing away.

"Are you all right?" My fingers curl around her upper arm, and inexplicably my pulse begins to race.

Then, she turns toward me, and our eyes truly connect for the first time. Fireworks burst in my chest, and I can't seem to locate my voice. The attraction is instantaneous.

Well, it is for me at least.

She visibly stiffens. "Get your hands off of me. I'm fine."

"Just wanted to make sure you were oka—"

She shrugs out of my hold, popping to her feet and righting her clothes. "I said, I'm fine." She glances around at the slew of eyes fixed on her, sneering at all the snooty females whispering, pointing their manicured nails, and giggling in their Louboutin shoes and designer cocktail dresses. What I found hot not even five minutes ago suddenly seems pretentious and well, *boring*. "You're just making it worse," she grits.

"Right." Nodding, I withdraw my hand and bring it to my chest. "You all act like you've never seen a person trip before," I say, addressing the crowd. "Get back to it." I clap my hands loudly toward the DJ, "Music!"

With an annoyed huff, she rolls her eyes and storms off in her black Converse.

Sneakers at a Hollywood party...*Who is this girl?*

"Don't take it personally," Nick says, coming up behind me and clapping me on the shoulder. "She's Jax's daughter."

Jax Potter...Nicholas's washed-up rock star uncle, who hooked us up with our agent and helped get The Rhett Taylor Band off the ground. So, that explains why her name sounded familiar. But still doesn't account for her odd reaction toward me.

"Did I umm...Have we met before?" I stare after her until she disappears through the balcony door. "Did I offend her in some way?" I'm beginning to wonder if we've maybe hooked up and that's the reason, I feel this strange connection. But I'm positive I've never felt like this before, and she certainly doesn't seem like someone I'd easily forget.

"Nah, man. This just isn't her scene. You know Jax...wasn't easy being the one at home with her mom while he uh...did his thing." He shrugs. "I'm honestly surprised to see her here at all."

"Right," I agree as Monica's hands slink around my waist from behind. She's shimmying to the beat of the sultry music, her breasts pressed to my back, but I'm just not in it any longer. "I'll find you later," I lie, kissing the tips of her fingers and sending her off to her friends.

She pouts like a child, running a hand over my chest. "Don't forget me."

Nick laughs after she walks off. "That's probably what uh... what did it. She thinks we're all like her pops." He gives his shoulders another shrug. "Thanks for the party, man. You're the best. I'm gonna go check on Korie."

* * *

"Ahh, there you are," I say, finding Korie perched on a wicker couch with a drink in hand. It's a dark, clear night. She's staring out at the stars, all alone on the balcony off Nick's room. "So, I think maybe we got off on the wrong foot." I take a pull from my beer then clear my throat. "I wanted to find you and reintroduce myself—start over again, you know, in less...*awkward circumstances.*"

Her head slowly rolls in my direction. The look in her eyes tells me she's over this conversation before it even begins. "No need. Everyone with the internet knows who you are. You're Rhett Taylor—bad boy of country music. Playboy. Womanizer."

"Ouch." I suck in a breath, bringing a hand to my chest. "Yeah...well, you see what the media wants people to see."

She rises to her feet, closing the distance between us in a few strides. The wind blows through her hair, and I get a whiff of her floral shampoo. My dick twitches. She's so close—inches away. I have to stop myself from giving in to the urge to reach out and touch her again. "What I saw when I walked in was nothing less than I expected." She plants a hand on her hip. "That wasn't the media. That was a rock star in his natural habitat." She taps a hand lightly on the front of my shirt. "I know it's probably real hard to believe, but I'm not here to go gaga and fall all over you." She smiles a lazy smile. "As disappointing as that may be for your huge...*ego.*"

Did I just imagine her eyes dropping to my crotch?

"I came to see my cousin, who I haven't seen in years. The rest of this"—her hand circles the air—"is just unfortunate."

She stalks back into the house, leaving me to scrape my jaw up from the floor. Something about that sassy mouth of hers only makes me want her more.

I spend the rest of the evening lurking in the shadows of my own home, stalking a girl who wants nothing to do with me. It doesn't take her long to befriend all of the girls who were making fun of her earlier tonight, including Monica. It would seem we're all under her spell. But for some reason she's decided to give them another chance. Me? Well, I think she'd written me off before walking through the door.

I'm green with envy. I don't know what it is about this particular girl that has me feeling things I haven't felt in years… but it makes me realize just how numb I've allowed myself to become.

For the first time since I can't remember when, I'm *feeling*, and even jealousy feels a hell of a lot better than indifference.

CHAPTER 1

Rhett

"You're serious right now?" Anika, my manager, paces the studio in four-inch stilettos while gnawing on the back of a pen. "You want to cancel studio time to go to...to *camp?*"

She's kinda cute when she's all riled up like this, her pale cheeks flaming red and daggers shooting from her amber eyes. I sink down further into the plush couch, crossing my arms on my chest. "It'll be fun. I'm in need of some fun. You said so yourself. A few days on the coast with other single, college-aged adults. Real people, Anika. A break from Hollywood."

"I said *after* we finish the album. Not right in the middle of recording it." Her heels clack on the wood floors as she moves to crouch before me, resting her manicured nails on the arms of my chair. Her frustration is evident in the heaviness of her breaths. She shakes her head, tossing her long chestnut braid over her left shoulder. "It's her, isn't it? She's going to be there?"

"Yes," I answer, trying to cover a smirk. "Yeah...So, there's no way I can put this off." I realize the timing isn't ideal, but it's the perfect chance to work my magic on this girl, whom I can't seem to get out of my head.

Pushing up from my knees, she's again wearing a hole into the floor. "She hates you, Rhett. This is a terrible idea. Not only for your career, but because you're going to end up *disappointed.*"

What she means is depressed. My first Hollywood girlfriend did a number on me, but that was before I knew how industry relationships worked. I keep my heart guarded now—locked up tight in a suit of armor. I just want the chance to play with my sword.

"I'm curious about her," I say with a shrug, my mind wandering to my drummer Nick's birthday party, about three weeks ago. To his cousin, Korie Potter. Her long, wavy blonde ponytail, faded jeans, and Rolling Stones tee. She stood out among the sequins and glitz. Her attempt to fade into the background had the complete opposite effect. Only adding to her appeal was the easy manner with which she carried herself. She had a confidence—an honesty—about her that I don't see much in the circles I run. I can't help but smile, remembering how unimpressed she was with everything Rhett Taylor. What did she call me again? Oh, yeah. *The bad boy of country music.* Someone's been paying a little too much attention to TMZ.

At any rate, life gets rather boring when you can literally have anything you want. Any*one* you want. I hadn't realized how willing I'd become to settle until life dangled temptation, in the form of a sassy-mouthed, blonde-haired, green-eyed, fiery little vixen, right under my nose and shook things up a bit—shook *me* up a bit.

Yeah, Korie is just the challenge I need.

"The label won't like it."

Having had about enough of her negativity, I rise to my feet, towering over her five-foot frame. It's not often I ignore her advice. We've been best friends since elementary school; she's one of the few people in my life I actually trust. "I don't give a damn what they like or don't like, Anika. I'm tired. I need to rest. The boys and I *are* taking this trip."

Her pointed jaw ticks as she stares me down, arms crossed on her chest in a stance that I'm assuming she means to be intimidating. "Does she know you'll be there?"

I snort. "Of course not."

She gives one final resigned shake of her head, blowing out a laugh. "You're gonna regret this."

"Or," I say, thumping her nose because I know how much it pisses her off, "I could enjoy it very, *very* much."

"And Nick is okay with this?"

"Abso-fucking-lutely," the hulking, six-foot-three, tatted oaf himself announces, entering through the back door. "A week of tits, booze, and fun in the sun? *And* I get to watch him follow Korie around like a lovesick puppy while she hands him his balls in a sling? Sign me up for that shit."

OTHER BOOKS BY
HEATHER M. ORGERON

Romantic Comedy

Cajun Girls Series of Standalones
Boomerangers (Single mom/Second chance)
Doppelbanger (Single dad/enemies to lovers)

Pour Judgment (Fake relationship)

Take Two (Vegas wedding/second chance)

Contemporary Romance

Breakaway (Sports romance)
Heartbreak Warfare (Military romance)

Women's Fiction

Vivienne's Guilt

ACKNOWLEDGEMENTS

First and foremost, thank you to my hubby and kids for your many sacrifices so that I could write this novel.

Thank you, Momma, for showing up to clean, to cook, to tend to your grandkids. Being able to count on you still today as an adult, means more than you will ever know.

A huge thank you to my girls, Kate Farlow, Harloe Rae, Lauren Brynolf, Shain Rose, Hollis Wynn, Renee Mccleary, Sammi Hyatt, and Nicole Davis for helping dig me out when I got stuck! For your endless support and coddling. For loving me. Encouraging me. And let's be honest here… tolerating me.

Keri Roth, Katherine Caron, Sara Koelsch, and Marie Saunders; thank you for taking the time to beta read and provide your excellent suggestions and words of encouragement. It takes a village and I'm so lucky to have you in mine!

Thank you, Michelle Lancaster, for shooting the cover shot. I have been obsessed with this image from the moment you shared it on FB and knew it had to be mine!

Mason Kreidt, thank you for giving such a beautiful face to my novel.

Kate Farlow with Y'all That Graphic, I can't thank you enough for creating such a beautiful cover. You believed in my vision and brought it to life. Your talent is endless and your friendship invaluable.

Thank you Kiezha Ferrell for once again polishing my words and cleaning up my manuscript. Even if you did take out half of my ellipses… ;)

Misty Boggs Punch, Abby Thomas, Kathy Webber, and Katiria Rosario, thank you for proof-reading and catching those last-minute misses!

To my girls at Give Me Books… THANK YOU! Thank you for always fitting me in and being so quick to respond and accommodate me!

Candi Kane, thank you for taking me on and all that you've done and are doing to get Mourning Wood into the right hands.

Thanks to Stacey with Champagne Book Design for adding all the little details in formatting.

Thanks to my reader group, Heather's Hunnies. Friends tell me all the time how amazing you ladies are, and I couldn't agree more. You never cease to amaze me with your endless love, support, and well-timed dick jokes. You get me. You really get me!

Thank you to anyone else who helped along the way. It is one of my greatest fears to leave someone out. I'm sure I do every time but know that it is not intentional. I'm so grateful for my tribe.

ABOUT THE AUTHOR

Heather M. Orgeron is a Cajun girl with a big heart and a passion for romance. She married her high school sweetheart two months after graduation and her life has been a fairytale ever since. She's the queen of her castle, reigning over five sons and one bossy little princess who has made it her mission in life to steal her Momma's throne. When she's not writing, you will find her hidden beneath mounds of laundry and piles of dirty dishes or locked in her tower(aka the bathroom) soaking in the tub with a good book. She's always been an avid reader and has recently discovered a love for cultivating romantic stories of her own.

AUTHOR LINKS:

Website: www.heathermorgeron.com

Facebook: www.facebook.com/AuthorHeatherMOrgeron

Facebook Group: www.facebook.com/groups/1738663433047683

Twitter: twitter.com/hmorgeronauthor

Instagram: hwww.instagram.com/heather_m_orgeron_author

Pinterest: www.pinterest.com/HMOrgeronAuthor

Goodreads: www.goodreads.com/HeatherMOrgeron

Newsletter: view.flodesk.com/pages/5ef8117d6d32be0026396571

Tiktok: www.tiktok.com/@heathermorgeron?lang=en